Death Has a List

By
T.J Moran

Copyright © 2023 by – T.J. Moran – All Rights Reserved.

It is not legal to reproduce, duplicate, or transmit any part of this document in either electronic means or printed format. Recording of this publication is strictly prohibited.

Dedications

Dedicated to my take-no-prisoners editor and wonderful wife, Lydia

Acknowledgements

No man is an island, especially an author. Their final product is always the result of the contributions of multiple people, whether it's readers, editors, information sources, or many others. They all help shape the book that is eventually produced. I want to thank everyone that assisted me in the writing of this book, especially my writing group on the Monterey Peninsula – Joyce Kreig, Hugo Gerstl, Paul Karrer, Donna Young, Katharine Bell, and Dan Presser. And a special thanks to Madeline DiMaggio who got me started and kept me going through some dark hours.

About the Author

T.J. Moran is a retired cardiologist, now spending his time writing. His first two books were collections of short stories – *Stories for the Starving Romantic*, *Stories for the Hungry Romantic*. Now, using his medical knowledge and experience, he has written his first full length novel, *Death Has a List*. He lives in Carmel with his wife, Lydia, and five kids.

Table of Contents

Dedications ii

Acknowledgements iii

About the Author iii

Prologue 1

Chapter One 3

Chapter Two 21

Chapter Three 30

Chapter Four 35

Chapter Five 39

Chapter Six 52

Chapter Seven 56

Chapter Eight 65

Chapter Nine 77

Chapter Ten 85

Chapter Eleven 89

Chapter Twelve 104

Chapter Thirteen 110

Chapter Fourteen 117

Chapter Fifteen 121

Chapter Sixteen 128

Chapter Seventeen 136

Chapter Eighteen 142

Chapter Nineteen 151

Chapter Twenty 161

Chapter Twenty-One 166

Chapter Twenty-Two 179

Chapter Twenty-Three 187

Chapter Twenty-Five 203

Chapter Twenty-Six 211

Chapter Twenty-Seven 222

Chapter Twenty-Eight 229

Chapter Twenty-Nine 241

Chapter Thirty 251

Chapter Thirty-One 258

Chapter Thirty-Two 272

Chapter Thirty-Three 279

Epilogue 284

February 16, 202-
Monterey, California

Prologue

Very few people are given the knowledge of when they're going to die. Hans Ludwig was no exception. He had no idea that today would be any different from his past fifty-eight years when he flipped on the light switch and illuminated the dog pens.

There were ten pens in the long room, each separated by a high, stout, chain-link fence, each with its own gate. The cement floor was hosed down frequently, but still the room smelled of urine and furry animals. As Ludwig approached the pens, he got varying responses from the dogs. Several approached their gates and whined, hoping he'd stop and pet them. Others looked up from their sprawled positions, identified who it was, and put their heads back down. Three dogs barked and jumped at their gates, but it was more in the form of a greeting than a warning.

Hans shuffled past them, calling out names, even reaching through the fence to pet two of them. When he arrived at the tenth pen, tagged with the name 'Midnight', he unlocked the gate, and pushed it open. "Come on out, girl", he said, and then continued on down the corridor.

He stepped into the adjoining area and switched on the fluorescent lights. This room was designated "the dog lab," but Ludwig thought it looked more like something out of an old black-and-white Frankenstein movie. A myriad of chemical analyzers, microscopes, and racks of test tubes were spread across large, elongated, steel tables. In the far corner, there was a tall, open shower stall – extending all the way up to the raised ceiling – used to douse an investigator if they were involved in a chemical spill.

Ludwig walked to the nearest table, opened a drawer, and lifted out a large notebook. On the cover, in thick black letters, he'd written "Citadel Pharmaceutical Company: Chem 18." Ludwig pushed aside several pipettes, and set the ledger on the table. He flipped past his daily notations to his monthly summary statements, the last written four weeks earlier.

"After nine weeks of testing, my impression is that the drug is working very well. The dogs have responded superbly to the medication with no apparent side effects. I would agree with our testing of this drug in humans even though the dog study is not complete."

He glanced up and smiled as a large Doberman pinscher quietly entered the room.

"Well, Midnight, you took your time coming to see me." He reached into his pocket and pulled out a dog biscuit. "Here, I've got your favorite snack," he said, holding out his hand.

Midnight rushed toward him, leaped, and sank her teeth into Ludwig's throat, ripping flesh and arteries as Ludwig screamed with surprise and pain. Knocked to the floor, Ludwig tried to call out for help, but the only sound that emerged was the gurgling of air bubbling up through the blood in his lacerated throat.

Curled in a fetal position on the floor, trying in vain to hold off the dog's continued assault, Ludwig's last conscious thought was, *My God! What have we done?*

Four months later
Monterey, California

Chapter One

Dr. Parker McGraw's first conscious thought was to dedicate the remainder of his days to total abstinence. Alcohol wasn't worth it. Not if it meant waking up with unbelievable headaches like this. At least that's what he attributed his headache to -- a severe hangover. Strangely though, he couldn't remember drinking the night before. In fact, as he thought about it, he couldn't even remember the night before.

Cautiously, he opened his eyes, and found his vision a blur, his surroundings vague and indistinct. He blinked several times, trying to clear the haze, but it only intensified his headache so he closed his eyes. He'd seen enough, though, to know he wasn't in his own bed.

Despite the jackhammers working furiously at his temples, he began to identify certain familiar sounds and smells. The sigh and hiss of ventilators, the sporadic alarming of intravenous drip systems and heart rate monitors, a faint but well-remembered odor, that acrid mixture of antiseptic, blood, and unwashed bodies. He was in an Intensive Care Unit.

Yet he had no memory of being brought to a hospital, much less being placed in an ICU bed.

He struggled to sit up, only to fall back amidst waves of nausea and dizziness. He reached up to massage his forehead and found it swathed in bandages. Blindly he groped for the nurse call button, and pressed it as urgently as any first time ICU patient.

He heard a familiar voice from the side of his bed. "I am glad to see you awake, Dr. McGraw. You had us very worried."

Parker turned his head slowly and opened his eyes. After a moment, his vision cleared enough to recognize the shadowy, dim figure standing next to him. It was Janet, one of the ICU nurses who'd worked with him in the past.

She smiled. "Can I get you anything?"

His reply was limited to a harsh croak. Clumsily he sipped the water she offered, and tried again.

"What...?" he coughed and cleared his throat. "What am I doing here?"

"You've had a severe concussion from a head injury."

"What kind of head injury?"

She hesitated slightly before replying. "A gunshot wound."

"How... how did I get a gunshot wound?"

She wrapped a black cuff around his arm to take his blood pressure. Finished, she began to unwrap the cuff, all the time avoiding his eyes. In frustration, he reached toward her with his other hand, but the cold ring of steel brought his arm to an abrupt halt. His left wrist was handcuffed to the bed railing. He looked back at Janet and found her staring at his new bracelet.

"Janet! What's going on?"

"I'm so sorry Dr. McGraw, but we've been told not to discuss the case with you." She turned to go.

"What case? What are you talking about? Why am I handcuffed?"

She stopped in the doorway, hesitated a moment, then quietly said, "You're accused of murder."

Eleven pm, shift change time in the ICU. The noise level had picked up markedly as the evening shift nurses transferred the care of their patients to the oncoming night crew. Groups of blue-clad nurses, standing and sitting, lined the long nursing station counter, pouring over the lab results, doctors' orders, and pertinent vital signs of their respective patients. Behind the nurses, encircling three sides of the nursing station, were the ten patient rooms or cubicles. Each cubicle opened onto the station through a sliding glass door, so that the patients were visible from the nursing counter.

In ICU cubicles 3 and 4, the patients lay motionless, only their chests moving, rising and falling in unison with their ventilators. They could have been twins when viewed from a distance except for the large white bandage on the head of ICU 4.

In ICU 8, an old man, his gray hair disheveled, struggled against his wrist restraints, trying to reach the catheter draining his bladder, hoping to yank it out.

Next door, in ICU 9, a listless young child lay quietly on his back, occasionally moving his extremities, all except his right foot. It was tied down to keep him from dislodging the IV needle inserted two hours earlier.

The overhead fluorescent lighting at the nurses' station gave Janet a pale drawn complexion as she reviewed her two patients with Monica, her night shift replacement. Her short dark curls bounced as she spoke, belying the weariness she felt at having to work a double shift.

"ICU 4 is a post-craniotomy for a leaking aneurysm. Still comatose on a ventilator. Spiked a temp today. Surgeon thinks it's probably due to aspiration pneumonia and has covered him with antibiotics, while awaiting the culture results." Janet paused and waited for Monica to finish her notes. "Any questions?"

"No. Sounds pretty straightforward. It's always hard, though, coming back after a weekend off." Monica sighed. "Who else?"

"ICU 6. Tell me if he sounds familiar. Tall, dark hair, nice looking. Handles the cardiology cases." She smiled. "You had a crush on him."

Monica's pen stopped. "Dr. McGraw's in here?"

"Yes," Janet glanced down at her own shift notes. "He woke up tonight for the first time since his head injury. I notified the police per instruction. They'll be sending someone tomorrow."

"What an absolute shock. You work with side by side with someone for years and then this." Monica shook her head. "I think there has to be a mistake. No one tries as hard as he does to save lives, then murders someone."

##

"Thank you, nurse."

Ray Stone ended his phone call and looked around his small apartment, still dark in the early morning light. Slowly he smiled.

He punched in Gloria Wilhelm's number. Gloria was the district attorney in the Monterey office, and as such, Stone's boss.

"Gloria? It's Ray. Sorry to call so early but I have an urgent favor to ask."

"Let me guess. You want to prosecute the McGraw murder case."

"How'd you know?"

"You're not the only one who's been checking on his condition. Nor the only one who wants to handle that case."

"Come on, Gloria. You owe me for the Albright case."

There was a pause. "Okay, Ray. It's your baby, but don't foul it up 'cause there's going to be a lot of publicity on this one."

Stone set his cell phone down, and slapped the kitchen counter top. He grinned, thinking of the comfortable life waiting for him in a swank law firm, away from the thankless drudgery and endless hours of the D.A.'s office. Already, he had feelers out checking the job market. Several firms had been interested, but none had made an offer, yet.

But with the press and TV coverage I could get on this case that will definitely change.

And he had plans for lots of news coverage, just as he had plans to make sure he won the case.

"Never give a sucker an even break" was Stone's credo. He did whatever was needed to win a case. And for this case, there were no holds barred.

# #

Parker awoke slowly, his ICU room bright in the early morning light. He gingerly moved his head and looked around. His vision had cleared, but the ICU and the handcuffs still remained.

"So it wasn't a dream," he mumbled, trying to hold his panic down. Amnesia, head injury, murder -- there had to be some simple explanation. He had tried desperately to get information from his night nurse. She had been friendly but uncommunicative, reiterating the fact they weren't to speak with him about the case. Finally, he fallen asleep, exhausted by his stress, and head injury. Now that morning had arrived, he'd try to get a phone and find out what in God's name was going on.

"Good to see you awake, Park."

Parker was startled out of his reverie by the appearance of a tall, lean man with cropped white hair set atop a pale, freckled face. Bill Logan, a neurosurgeon, wore his usual three-piece suit. People could set their watches by Bill's attire. His coat was the first to come off at about nine o'clock. The tie was loosened at noon, followed by the shedding of his vest around three. By five the sleeves were rolled up and all semblance of proper dress was gone. Seeing Bill fully clothed was a sight for the early risers only.

Logan halted at the foot of the bed, hooked his thumbs into his vest, and shook his head.

"Thought you were a goner when I first saw you in the emergency room, Park. You're a lucky man. We should be deciding whether to turn your ventilator off, not asking what you want for breakfast."

Parker stared at him, shocked with what he'd inferred. "Exactly what is the extent of my head injury?"

Logan slid around the side of the bed, and half-leaned, half-sat on the bedside console.

"You were shot in the head. The bullet entered the right temporal region of your scalp. Had it gone through the skull, you'd be lying on the autopsy table now. Due to a combination of bullet angle, luck, and your own hard head, it was deflected along the right side of the skull and out the back. Just left a little furrow under the scalp."

He watched Parker assess his explanation and then added, "Probably hurts like hell, but it'll improve rapidly." Logan reached into his coat pocket and brought out a small ophthalmoscope. Bending over, he examined Parker's eyes.

"What's the last recollection you have before waking up here?" he asked.

The light boring into Parker's eyes with the intensity of a searchlight didn't help his concentration or his headache. "What day is today?"

"It's Wednesday, July tenth." Logan pulled out a percussion hammer and began tapping on Parker's knees.

"Wednesday?" Park tried to keep his alarm down. "What happened to Tuesday?"

Logan finished checking Parker's reflexes and looked up. "Tuesday's a blank?"

Parker closed his eyes, trying for any recollection of the last few days. After a minute, he said despondently, "All I remember is sitting in my office doing dictation on Monday. There's nothing after that."

"And now it's Wednesday. Not really that surprising." Logan dropped the percussion hammer back into his pocket, and leaned against the wall. "Amnesia from a concussion is not uncommon as you know."

"Amnesia isn't something I deal with in cardiology," Parker said. "So pretend I'm not in medicine and explain it to me."

"Sure. There are basically two types of amnesia related to trauma. Retrograde amnesia, which is a loss of memory regarding events occurring before the head injury, and ante-grade amnesia, which is the loss of memory concerning things which occurred after the injury. You seem to have a bit of both."

Parker hesitated before asking his next question. "Is it permanent?"

"Not always. It may take days, weeks, even months, but often much of it will return."

"That's encouraging," Parker said, some of his anxiety receding. He then lifted his handcuffed left wrist. "Now I have some questions about this."

"I have some questions about that also, Dr. McGraw."

Logan and Parker both glanced over at the man entering the room. He was middle-aged, medium height, and rounded at all the corners. With thinning silver hair and a grey speckled, trimmed beard, he might have passed for a slimmed down Father Christmas in a sports jacket, until Parker looked closer. The roundness was muscular and his black eyes shone with an almost frightening intensity. He wasn't here to give away toys.

"I'm Detective Hall from the Monterey Police Department," he said, flashing a gold police shield. His voice matched his eyes. Flat and cold.

"You're a welcome sight, Detective." Parker said, realizing he could now get some answers. "Someone seems to have made a terrible mistake."

Hall nodded." Yeah, I'd say someone has, Doctor."

Bill Logan interrupted. "Excuse me, but isn't he entitled to have his lawyer present for any questioning?"

"That's up to the doctor," Hall replied. "If he wants one that can be arranged." He turned to Parker. "Well?"

"I'm just happy you're here so we can get this mess straightened out," Parker said waving the sergeant to a chair.

"I'll check in on you this afternoon," Logan said, moving toward the door.

"Thanks, Bill." Parker turned to Hall. "Detective, I don't know what I'm accused of or why I'm handcuffed."

Hall shook his head. "I'm not here to answer questions. I'm here to ask them."

Parker paused for a moment. "How can I answer any questions when I don't know what I'm accused of or why I am handcuffed?"

"You're in no position to dictate terms."

Parker placed his finger on the nurse call button. "I ring for the nurse, she calls Dr. Logan, and you're out of here."

Hall snorted, and leaned back in his chair. "Okay, ask."

"First off, your attitude."

"White collar or blue collar, I treat lawbreakers all the same," Hall snapped. "Just because you're a physician, it doesn't lessen your criminal actions."

Parker was shocked. *This guy already has me convicted and sentenced.* "Criminal actions? What exactly have I done? Why am I handcuffed?"

Hall settled himself in the chair, unbuttoning his coat. "Let's take things one at a time, doctor. I'll answer your questions, but first I want to inform you of your rights under the Miranda decision." Hall pulled a digital recorder out of his jacket pocket, placed it on the bedside table midway between the two of them.

"I will be recording our conversation. Any problem with that?"

Parker shook his head.

"Please give a verbal response to all questions."

"No problem with recording our conversation."

From an inside pocket, Hall produced an index card and read Parker the list of his rights. When he was finished, he pushed the recorder closer to Parker.

"State your full name for the record, doctor."

"Parker Garrett McGraw."

"Age?"

"Thirty-seven."

"Married, divorced, single?"

"Single."

"Occupation?"

"Physician."

"To answer your previous questions, Dr. McGraw. You're accused of first-degree murder. You're handcuffed with a policeman stationed just outside the ICU because that's departmental policy when a criminal suspect is quartered anywhere other than the county jail."

Parker rose up on his elbow. "Murder? You have to be kidding! Who did I murder?"

"Does the name Michael Beckman ring any bells?"

"No. Should it?"

"He's the man you are accused of shooting and killing."

Parker struggled to a sitting position. "That is absolutely crazy! I've never even fired a gun, much less killed someone." His sudden motion caused the room to spin, making him nauseated. With bile rising in his throat, he reached toward the bedside console, but the emesis basin sitting on it was just beyond his grasp. Stretching as far as his handcuffs would allow, he tried again but still the basin remained out of reach. Realizing it was too late to call for a nurse, Parker bent over the side of the bed and vomited.

Hall switched off the recorder, passively watching the entire scene, never offering to help. As Parker wiped the vomitus from around his mouth, Hall finally spoke: "If you have to throw up again, make sure you keep it on that side of the bed."

His nurse, responding to the call light, entered and saw the vomit on the floor.

"I'm sorry, Janet," Parker said, wiping his mouth with some tissue paper. "I couldn't reach the emesis basin."

"My fault," she said, moving next to the bed and putting her hand on his shoulder. "Are you okay now?"

"Yeah, it was just a quick flash of nausea."

She smiled and then quickly cleaned the floor. When she finished, she moved the emesis basin within Parker's reach.

"Call me if you have any more symptoms," she said.

After she'd gone, Hall leaned forward in his chair and switched the recorder back on. "What do you remember about last Friday night?"

Parker stared at Hall. *Protesting my innocence to this cold-hearted bastard isn't going to help me one bit. I'll need facts before I can argue anything with him.*

"Did the shooting happen on Monday night?" Parker asked.

"Yes, it did." Hall replied. "Tell me what you were doing that day, beginning with the morning hours."

Parker closed his eyes and tried to return to Monday. Although only thirty-six hours ago, it seemed like a lifetime. "I vaguely recall seeing patients in the office during the morning, and then doing exercise stress tests in the hospital that afternoon. I think I returned to the office to clear up paper work and do some dictation. After that, everything is a blur until I woke up here."

"That's all you remember? Nothing more?" His tone implied there was much more.

"No. Nothing else. It's the result of the head injury. Dr. Logan can..."

Hall cut him off with an abrupt wave of his hand. "Yeah, I heard his spiel about amnesia while I was waiting outside your room." His black eyes riveted Parker like the twin barrels of a shotgun. "He also said that the memory often returns, sometimes within a few days." He paused. "I'm sure you'll inform me the moment it does."

For the first time Parker began to worry. *What if the missing pieces of my memory hurt my case? If that happens, this cop would be the last person I'd call.*

Parker nodded. "You'll be the first to know, officer."

The lie seemed to hang in the air for a long moment. Hall eyed him narrowly then leaned back in his chair.

"Where did you receive your training, doctor?"

"I graduated from UCLA, did my internship and residency at Wadsworth V. A. Hospital in West Los Angeles. After that, I did a two year cardiology fellowship at St. Mary's Hospital in Long Beach."

"Please speak louder, doctor." Hall adjusted the cell phone. "You moved to this area when you finished your training?"

"No. I was on staff for three years at UCLA-Harbor General Hospital in Los Angeles, overseeing their Coronary Care Unit prior to moving here."

"Why did you move here?"

"Five years ago, I made two decisions. To go into private practice, and to escape the craziness that was becoming L.A. The Carmel area allowed me to do both."

"So you weren't forced to leave because of loss of hospital privileges, complaints about incompetence, or just plain fired?" Hall's voice was accusatory.

"No. None of those things."

With an insinuating, derogatory tone, Hall went on to ask about malpractice suits, experiences with illicit drugs, access to prescription medications, and arrests for drunk driving.

Parker had had enough. "I'm done with your questions and attitude, Detective."

Hall's face hardened. Leaning over, he switched the recorder off. "Listen, and listen well, doctor. We've got you dead to rights. If we took this case to court right now, without any further investigation or evidence, a first-year law student could convict you and get a minimum of twenty years, no problem."

He pointed a thick index finger at Parker. "All you rich guys think your money and position places you above the law. Well, not in my town."

Any retort by Parker was interrupted by the entry of Nancy, the head ICU nurse. She planted herself between Hall and Parker, folding her arms firmly across her ample bosom. "Detective Hall,

I'm to inform you that your time is up for today. Dr. Logan left strict orders that your visit shouldn't exceed twenty minutes. It's now been twenty-five."

Nancy's size and her imposing, no-nonsense visage had the desired effect.

Hall rose from his chair. "I'm not sure I believe your amnesia game, but for now I'll give you more time to recuperate." He dropped the recorder in his pocket and, as if an afterthought, said, "You ever been involved with cocaine, doctor?"

"No. It's not something we use in cardiology."

"I'm not talking about your medical experiences with it," he said. When Parker didn't reply, he continued, "Ever have your medical license suspended or put on probation for drug related problems?"

"No, never."

Hall slowly nodded. "I guess there is always a first time," he said as he left the room.

Between his headache and his run-in with Hall, Parker was drained. He made a phone call to his lawyer's office and then spent the rest of the afternoon dozing off and on. That evening, when his dinner arrived, he found his appetite was returning. With his one free hand, he was clumsily finishing his meal when he heard a voice from the doorway.

"Hello, Park."

Parker looked up and found Jeff Gilman, his lawyer, leaning on the doorjamb.

"Thank God, you're here," Parker said. "I don't know what's going on, but I need your help."

Jeff dropped his briefcase on the floor, removed his coat, and settled himself into the lone chair in the small room. Loosening his tie, his usual boyish smiling face was furrowed with concern.

Parker had first meet Jeff Gilman four years ago when the attorney came to his office for evaluation of chest pain. At the time,

Jeff was thirty-two, overweight, smoking one pack a day, a stranger to exercise, and had the cholesterol level of an egg. His chest pain was not cardiac in origin, but soon would be, Parker knew, if his risk factors for heart disease weren't modified.

Parker spoke with Jeff's wife, a gourmet cook, who Jeff assured him could never make a low cholesterol meal, and explained the facts to her. She put him on a tight Mediterranean diet two days later. When he balked at her attempts and started sneaking greasy burgers, she kicked him out of the marriage bed. After a while, his appetite gave in to his libido and he fervently embraced his new diet. Parker had no such favors to withhold, but with a bit of pushing and pulling, he got him exercising. Jeff dropped forty pounds, quit smoking, ran two marathons, and became Parker's best success story. Along the way, Parker discovered that Jeff was a Harvard Law School graduate, had a great sense of humor, a compassionate nature, and was an excellent companion for an occasional late-night drink. He'd originally done criminal law for the D.A.'s office, but after five years had switched to criminal law in the private sector. Through the years, they'd become good friends.

"Sorry I couldn't get here sooner, but I was stuck in court all day." Jeff reached into his briefcase and pulled out a newspaper. "I had my investigator, Dave Vicker, check on what the police had that wasn't in the paper. He's an ex-cop and has a few friends with the Monterey police." He handed the newspaper to Parker. "Start with this and then I'll fill in the rest."

Parker had made page one in the local newspaper, *The Herald*, with the headline, `Physician Accused of Murder in Drug Deal.' They'd even unearthed his driver's license picture which filled part of the upper page. Maybe he was overly sensitive, but it seemed that he had a very furtive look in the picture. The average reader would have no trouble envisioning that face committing all types of heinous crimes. He hoped the story would be less convicting than the picture. It wasn't.

"Monday night in Monterey, one man was killed and another critically wounded in what police sources feel was a drug-related shooting.

"Michael Beckman, 57, of Carmel, was pronounced dead at the scene with a gunshot wound to the chest. Dr. Parker McGraw, 37, also of Carmel, was taken to Community Hospital with a gunshot wound to the head.

"Beckman, previously convicted of embezzlement, had been released recently from Soledad State Prison after serving twenty months of a three-year sentence. McGraw, a local cardiologist, has practiced on the Monterey Peninsula for the past four years.

"Responding to a call from Beckman's daughter, Susan Beckman, 34, of San Francisco, police went to the office of Maxwell Pollock located on Holman Highway in Monterey. They found both victims, an undisclosed amount of cocaine, and an undetermined amount of cash at the scene. Pollock, a private investigator, was out of town at the time and unavailable for comment.

"Susan Beckman told police investigators she'd just arrived at Pollock's reception area to pick up her father when she heard gunshots from an inner office. She forced her way into that office where she discovered the injured victims."

The rest of the story just reiterated more of the same. Parker laid the paper down and turned to Jeff.

"I'm not really clear on what happened."

Jeff unfolded his five-eleven frame from the chair and began pacing the limited confines of the room.

"I swung by the D.A.'s office on the way over here. As your lawyer, and an ex-prosecutor myself, I wangled a peek at Susan Beckman's account of what happened. She'd just entered Pollock's office reception area to pick up her father when two shots were fired from within Pollock's inner office. She tried to get in, but the door was locked. She managed to force the door and enter the office.

There she found her father dead and you unconscious with a head wound. Each of you had a gun."

"Holy shit!" Parker whispered.

"Yeah, and it gets worse. My sources say the ballistic tests confirm that the gun in your hand was the weapon that killed Beckman, and that the only fingerprints on the weapon were yours. If that's not enough, the only way in and out of the murder room was the office door which, according to Beckman's daughter, was locked from the inside."

Parker slapped the bed with the flat of his hand. "This is ridiculous! None of this makes sense. That woman has to be lying."

Jeff shrugged. "I had my P.I. check her out. She lives up the coast in San Francisco where she has her own interior decorating business. A quick credit check showed that financially she's doing very well. She has no black marks on the police blotter. No driving violations with the D.M.V. She had apparently come down here to visit her father. In short, there is no reason to suspect her of lying."

"Then she's mistaken. There must have been someone else in that room."

"According to her statement, there were only the two of you when she forced her way in."

"Then the other person got out a different way. Maybe through a window."

"I've been told all the windows were locked from inside, but I've yet to visit the crime scene." Jeff picked up the newspaper and dropped it into his briefcase.

Neither spoke for a while.

"Can you remember what you were doing in Max Pollock's office that night, especially since he was out of town?" Jeff asked.

"Well, Max and I are good friends, but I don't remember a thing about that night. I barely remember that day. In fact, that's what I told Detective Hall."

"When did you speak with Hall?"

"Earlier today."

Jeff bowed his head, running his hands over his face and into his razor cut brown hair. Looking up, he said, "As of this moment, you will speak to no one about this case without first consulting me. Especially not the police. Is that clear?"

"Yes, but..."

"Is that clear?" Jeff said decisively.

"Hey, I got the message, but I didn't give him anything."

"Believe me, you have no idea what you may or may not have given him." Jeff shook his head. "Doctors. They think they know it all."

Still upset, Jeff stood up and strode over to the cardiac monitor mounted on the wall. A good thirty heart beats flashed by on the screen before he spoke again.

"Park, I've got a question to ask, and all I want is a simple yes or no. No matter what the answer is, I'll help you all I can."

After reading the newspaper and hearing Jeff's previous comments, Parker had been expecting this. "Jeff, the answer is no! I didn't kill him!"

"But you said yourself that Monday night is a blank. Maybe some strange set of circumstances resulted in you shooting Beckman... say, in self-defense. After all, the gun he was holding was apparently the one that shot you."

"What happened to innocent until proved guilty?" Parker said, rising up in bed. The sudden movement increased his headache, adding to his vehemence. "You've already assumed I'm guilty, and now you're trying to figure how to make me look less guilty. Is that your plan?"

"I'm here to help, Park," Jeff snapped back. "As your lawyer, I have to take every possible scenario into consideration. Right now, the weight of the evidence is overwhelmingly against you. Until we can prove something different, our best defense is going to be self-defense."

"So we ignore the fact that I'm one of the most anti-drug people you know. That I've never even used marijuana, much less cocaine. That I don't own a gun. That I've never heard of Michael Beckman. And that there is no way I would have been involved in a cocaine buy."

Jeff plopped down into the chair and rested his head against the back edge. "Yeah, for now, we have to ignore those things and assume the worst."

"Which is?"

"Which is, for some inexplicable reason, you met with Beckman and were forced to kill him."

##

Detective Hall threw his coat on the metal rack, and dropped into his office chair. It had been a long, hard day. Setting his digital recorder down on his desk reminded him of his interview that morning with McGraw.

"Lying bastard!" he said off-handedly.

Hall turned on his computer to check his emails. He'd made his way through half of them when his vision strayed to the picture on the corner of his desk. Mesmerized by the photograph, he picked it up and stared at it for several minutes. His features hardened, as he carefully set the picture down, picked up the phone and tapped in a number.

"Captain? It's Ivan Hall."

"Working late, aren't you?" the Captain asked.

"Got a lot of paperwork to get through. You know how it is."

"I sure do, Ivan."

"I've seen the doctor involved in the Beckman killing."

"And?"

"He's going to play it cute... memory loss, never knew Beckman...that kind of crap." Hall glanced again at the picture. "I'm going to need some more help on this one."

"Seems like an open-and-shut case to me, Ivan. Why the extra manpower?"

"I want to make sure it stays open-and-shut, Captain."

There was a pause. "Okay. I'll look over the duty roster in the morning, and see who's available."

"Thanks."

"Oh yeah, Ray Stone in the D.A.'s office wants you to give him a call."

Hall hung up, and went back to his paper work. He stopped only once to gaze at the picture on his desk corner. Three girls stood around a frail young boy. The children were of varying ages. All had similar facial features. It was a happy, warm scene except for one discordant note. The young boy sat in a wheelchair.

Chapter Two

Parker had a miserable night's sleep. He blamed this partially on his conversation with Jeff, but more on the patient who'd been admitted to the cubicle next to his during the night. He was a drug overdose who screamed obscenities at anyone who came near him.

At three a.m., Parker was roused from his fitful sleep by the overhead page. "Dr. Strong. Dr. Strong. ICU stat!" "Dr. Strong" was the hospital code for help in dealing with an unruly person. Every able-bodied male on the night shift charged past Parker's glass sliding door into the cubicle next to his. From snatches of conversation, it was evident his new neighbor, not content with verbal abuses, had physically assaulted one of the nurses. They'd summoned help to place him in hard restraints.

Morning arrived, all too soon for Parker. His eyes were burned from lack of sleep. Rubbing them offered no relief.

A uniformed officer arrived drinking coffee with one hand, jingling keys in the other.

"We're moving you to one of the floor beds," he said as he unlocked Parker's handcuff from the bed railing.

Rubbing his wrist, Parker asked, "And then what?"

"Don't quote me, but probably tomorrow we'll move you to the county hospital. That's where we like to house prisoners that need medical care. It's too expensive to keep them in a private hospital like this." He then cuffed Parker's wrists together. "Once the doc there feels you're medically fit, you'll be shifted to the county jail and an arraignment will be set up."

"I thought arraignments had to occur within 48-72 hours of arrest," Parkers said.

"With your head injury, the D.A. wanted to make sure you were medically fit to give a plea," the guard replied as he helped the nurse transfer Parker into a wheelchair.

The floor room was much larger than the ICU cubicle, allowing space for two chairs, a TV mounted on the wall, and a private bathroom. The bathroom would get little use since Parker was again handcuffed to the bed railing, limiting him to the bedside commode.

Like most others, Parker's room had a sliding glass door opening onto a common balcony shared by the two neighboring rooms. Best of all, though, no more raucous noise at shift change. No more phones ringing or alarms buzzing. No more feeling like a fish in a glass bowl when patients' families walked by.

Parker had hoped daybreak might bring some return of his memory, but it only brought the morning paper. On the front page was a grainy picture of Michael Beckman, clear enough to substantiate Parker's impression that he'd never meet the man.

Why would I kill a stranger? Even in self-defense, he'd never contemplated killing someone, so why would he have shot Beckman? For that matter, where would he have obtained a gun? In truth, he didn't even know how to use one except from what he'd learned watching TV.

"Hello, Dr. McGraw."

Parker glanced up at the older nurse entering his room. "Boy, it's nice to see a friendly face. How are you, Francie?"

"I'm fine, thank you." She spread her hands out, looking down at him on the bed. "I am so sorry to see you like this. I'm sure there is some kind of a mistake."

"That's what my lawyer is trying to figure out." He lifted his cuffed hand. "This is driving me crazy."

"Well, if it was up to me, there'd be no cuffs." She cleared her throat. "No one has asked my opinion, but I know they're wrong. There is no way you would murder someone."

Parker was touched. It was nice to know that some people still believed in him. "That means a lot, Francie. Thank you."

She checked his urinal and measured its contents. "How's your head today?"

"Gettin' better." He glanced out the open door. "Haven't seen any of my fair-weather friends about, have you?"

She walked over to the edge of his bed. "There's a large policeman sitting outside your door with orders to keep out all visitors, except your lawyer. And as you've noticed, there's no phone in the room." Patting his hand, she smiled. "Your friends haven't forgotten you. They're just not allowed to visit."

The next few hours were sheer boredom until Parker ventured to use the bedside commode. That's when he discovered hospital pajama bottoms were never meant to be untied or tied with just one hand. He was still struggling to get them back up when he heard the sliding glass door on the balcony slide open behind him.

Pulling the hospital bottoms up as best he could, Parker twisted around to see who was there. This wasn't the position he wanted to be in when Detective Hall returned.

"I always wondered if doctors could handle those gowns any better than the rest of the public," Maxwell Pollock said *sotto voce* as he gently slid the door closed.

"Still sneaking into peoples' bedrooms, eh, Max?"

If the ideal private investigator is a nondescript neuter who melts into his surroundings, then Maxwell Pollock was the exact antithesis. He stood out in any crowd. A big bear of a man, he was in his mid-fifties with the slightest hint of a German accent. His easy laugh, perpetual tan, expensive clothes, and wavy brown hair completed what was a very distinguished and handsome man. He was definitely not the typical gumshoe, unless the typical gumshoe wore Gucci loafers, hobnobbed with the well-to-do, and spent much of his time at the Beach and Tennis Club in Pebble Beach. Parker had met Max at the Rotary Club, and they'd struck up a friendship which had grown over the years.

"If you're here to offer your services, Max, I can definitely use them. First to get my ass into these pajamas, and then to get it out of this murder charge."

Pollock lent a helping hand, and then settled himself in the bathroom doorway. Catching Parker's questioning look, he replied in a low voice, "This way we can talk, and yet I'm hidden if the guard suddenly opens the door to check on you." Pollock leaned against the doorjamb. "Park, we're on a short fuse here, so let me ask the questions." He paused. "And don't be put off by them. Okay?"

"Okay," Parker replied as he slid as far across the bed as his handcuffs would allow to hear Pollock's whispered comments.

"Did you know Michael Beckman or have any connection with him in the past?"

"I saw his picture in the paper this morning. I'm certain I've never met him."

"What were you doing in my office that night?"

Parker sighed. "I'd hoped you'd be able to answer that one. I have no idea. From Monday afternoon on everything is a blank."

Pollock frowned. "That doesn't help matters." He gazed up at the ceiling for a moment, and then his eyes burrowed into Parker's. "Do you use cocaine or have any involvement with it? Don't lie. Your life may depend on the answer."

"I've never had any connection with cocaine."

Pollock visibly relaxed and said, "That's what I thought, but I had to know before I told you my suspicions."

A knock on the door, and then a gray-haired, matronly nurse's assistant entered.

"How are we doing, Dr. McGraw?" she asked mechanically, oblivious to Pollock slipping behind the bathroom door.

Parker rattled his handcuffs. "I've had better days."

"I need to get your vital signs."

They made small talk while she proceeded to take his blood pressure, pulse, and temperature. When she was finished, Parker hurried her out as fast as diplomatically possible.

No sooner had the door closed, than Pollock reappeared at the bathroom doorway. "About two weeks ago Michael Beckman came to my office. He felt someone was trying to kill him. He didn't know who or why, and he had no hard evidence. Merely a feeling that someone wanted him dead. Several times he thought someone was following him. Twice, he had near fatal accidents. At least, the first one he attributed to an accident. With the second near miss, he started having doubts. That's when he came to see me."

Parker was silent for a moment, then slowly nodded. "If someone was trying to kill Beckman, my alleged shooting of him came at a convenient time." He paused. "Coincidence?"

Pollock sighed. "With two ex's, the only coincidence I believe in is marriage and divorce."

"You said my life depended on my answers," Parker said.

"Well, if this whole thing is some kind of elaborate frame, I would think from your wound that you weren't supposed to survive." Pollock pushed away from the doorjamb and brushed off his jacket sleeve. "Yet, somehow you did. Now person or persons unknown may be very concerned about what you might tell the police if your memory returns."

"What do you mean?"

"I mean they're going to want you dead!"

Shot. Handcuffed. Accused of murder and drug dealing. A possible prison term ahead of me. And now this. Parker shook his head. "I keep waiting for this nightmare to end. Instead, it just gets worse."

Pollock crossed the room and patted him on the shoulder. "It always looks darkest before the dawn, my friend." He flashed a smile of confidence at Parker. "Let's see what I can dig up."

#

"Call for you on line two, Detective."

Detective Hall turned from the autopsy report on the computer and reached across his desk for the phone.

The caller said, "This is Jeff Gilman. Dr. McGraw's lawyer."

"I'm busy as hell right now, counselor. What do you want?"

"I want to lighten your work load a bit."

"What? Has the good doctor decided to confess?"

"No, Detective. The good doctor has, as per my instructions, decided he will be making no more statements to anyone, especially the police, without me present." A pause. "So you can cancel any plans you had for further interviews unless you want to sit through a litany of 'no comments'."

"Your client waived his right to have an attorney present when I interviewed him."

"Rights? You've got a lot of nerve talking about rights after forcing an interrogation on my client while he was still in the hospital, not even recovered from his injuries, his memory in shambles."

"Save it for the jury, Gilman. It's wasted on me."

"Just wanted you to know what our response would be if you tried to use anything my client told you in court."

"And a good day to you too, counselor." Hall banged the phone down.

#

"Max Pollock told you this today?" Jeff Gilman's voice seemed to echo in the small confines of the hospital room that evening.

Parker nodded. "Yeah. He snuck in through the balcony."

"I like it," Jeff considered. "Dave Vicker's mother in New York has taken ill so he'll be gone for the next few days. When he gets back I'll put him on it."

"Why wait? Hire Max to investigate. If he finds something, maybe that will convince the police I'm innocent and they'll let me go."

Jeff shook his head. "It doesn't work that way, Park. Short of a signed confession by the murderer, anything we find that helps establish your innocence or suggests someone else might have killed Blackman stays with us to use at trial."

"But if Max goes to the police with what he knows?"

Jeff put up in hands in a stop gesture. "And tells them what?" He paused. "Tells them that someone was trying to kill Beckman? He has no proof, just Beckman's suspicions. And how does that explain you in a locked room with Beckman's corpse and a couple of kilos of cocaine? Not to mention the smoking gun in your hand." He sighed. "If nothing else, Hall might figure you, Pollock, and Beckman were involved a three-way business deal, and two of the partners had a falling out."

Jeff stared at his tasseled loafers. "I will call Max and officially hire him. There are a number of things I want him to check out while Vicker is out of town."

Parker said, "What about this guy, Hall? He's already biased against me."

"Having Hall as the investigating officer has its pros and cons," Jeff said.

Parker grunted. "I don't see any pros."

"The pro is that he has a reputation as a sharp detective which could work to our benefit." He sighed. "The con is that he has an obsession with wealthy people and drug-related crime. I just hope that won't prejudice his investigation."

"But why me? I'm not wealthy."

"You're a doctor, right?"

"Right."

"Then as far as Hall's concerned, you're wealthy."

"Where does he get this fixation?"

Jeff loosened his tie. "I was curious myself so I asked around. No one knows the exact story but it seems that Hall used to be a cop in some university town back east. His son was hit by a car driven by a rich college kid, high on cocaine. The college kid's parents hired a heavy hitter lawyer who managed to get the case thrown out. Some problem with the evidence collection. Hall's son was left a paraplegic."

"That's really sad," Parker said shaking his head. "But it does sound like our judicial system."

"Well, Hall looked the college kid up and found him in a bar with a couple of his buddies. The kid, by the way, played linebacker for the college team, and his two buddies weren't much smaller. Hall beat the crap out of all three of them, especially the kid."

"I could learn to like Detective Hall."

"The whole thing created quite a stir. The end result was a compromise. No charges were filed against Hall. In turn, he resigned from the force, packed up, and left town. He showed up here five years ago. Word is he's the best in the department." Jeff paused. "That's why when Hall runs into the combination of drugs and wealthy people, he's more rabid then a born-again Christian talking religion."

They sat in silent for a moment.

"Look on the bright side," Jeff said, "Hopefully, he'll examine this case more thoroughly than some other detective might. Maybe he'll even come up with something helpful for our side. Who knows?"

"What if he does? With his built-in bias, he might suppress it."

Jeff shook his head. "No, Hall has a reputation as an honest cop. I don't see him sitting on evidence."

Parker wasn't so sure.

#

"Cordoba!"

Detective Hall's voice cut through the noisy flak of the police station at shift change. On the other side of the room a thin Mexican-American male, dressed in an expensive tailored suit, talking with a group of blue uniforms, glanced up.

Hall waved him over.

Cordoba sauntered up to Hall's desk. "What do you want, Ivan?"

Hall gestured at Cordoba's clothes. "You're dressing awfully snazzy these days. Where'd you get the money for a suit like that?"

Cordoba put his arms out and half turned to either side. "Looks good, doesn't it." He flashed his gleaming white teeth. "The chicks love it."

"That wasn't what I asked?"

Cordoba looked around then dropped his voice. "I've got a connection at the Goodwill Store. Calls me whenever something smooth comes in." He pointed a finger at Hall. "If this gets out, I'll know who's to blame."

Hall smiled and shook his head. "Captain says whatever you're working on, drop it. I need you on the Beckman case."

"What for? That doctor's as good as convicted."

Hall jabbed at him with his finger. "That's exactly the attitude that allows these assholes to walk. I want this guy to do hard time. No plea bargaining bullshit! No release on a technicality. That means a good tight case with no loose ends." Hall shook his head. "So far, everyone who knows him paints a picture of a competent doctor who is well-liked and respected in the community. We need to break that image."

"What do you want me to do?" Cordoba ran his fingers through his wavy black hair.

Hall sat down in a swivel chair and leaned back. "He claims he never knew the victim nor had any dealings with him."

"So?"

"So if we can show he's lying, that there was prior contact with Beckman, then we've got him by the 'nads, and his image is toast."

Cordoba smiled. "Where do I start?

Chapter Three

Parker just wanted a shower. His meetings with Max and Jeff had left him emotionally and physically drained. The thought of standing under a hot stream of water, washing two and a half days of accumulated sweat, grime, and dried blood off, sounded like the key to physical and mental rejuvenation. But of course, his room shower didn't work.

So the policeman assigned to Parker, along with one of the hospital security guards, loaded him into a wheelchair and pushed him down the hall toward an empty room with a functioning shower. We must be a strange procession, Parker decided, as they passed the nursing station. His bandaged head, three-day beard growth, and bloodshot eyes gave him an appearance that easily matched the charges against him: a drug dealing murderer. The policeman and security guard beside him just furthered that impression.

A hush fell over the nursing station as he rolled by. He saw several nurses that he knew, but they were 'preoccupied' as he passed and didn't look up. He had become the proverbial pariah. Don't acknowledge him or associate with him; his ill-fortune might be contagious. *Thank God for nurses like Francie.*

The shower cleaned the surface grim away, but the bleak feeling of ostracism remained.

#

"Can I help you, sir?"

The dark-skinned man with a pony tail, casually removed his hand from the wine glass on the food tray, turned and stared at the nurse standing in the doorway. She felt a sudden urge to close her sweater under his gaze.

"Maybe you can," he replied. The softness in his tone contrasted sharply with the hardness in his eyes. "I'm looking for Bill MacDonald. I thought this was his room."

The nurse forced a smile. "I'm sorry. This is Dr. McGraw's room. If you'll step out in the hallway, I'll check with the front desk and find out what room your friend is in."

At almost the same time the nurse returned to tell the man there was no Bill MacDonald registered in the hospital, he was climbing into the passenger side of a black Trans Am. He'd no sooner closed the door when the hulking blond driver hit the gas pedal. They roared off, nearly clipping an elderly volunteer coming out of the hospital entrance.

#

The policeman tucked Parker back into bed, handcuffs and all. Parker's dinner tray had arrived while he was showering, but he had no appetite. After a few bites, he pushed the food tray away and lay back in bed.

His eyes had just closed when he heard the balcony glass door slide open. Glancing up, he saw a somewhat emaciated, bearded young man in patient garb slip into the room.

"Hi," the youth said. "I'm Jackson Rivers, your next-door neighbor. Not much on TV, so I thought I might come over and talk." He looked around, and then eased himself into a chair.

"Recognized you in the hall from your picture in the paper." Rivers shook his head slowly, "Man, you're in deep shit. Like I've had disagreements with my supplier, but never anything as heavy as that."

Parker rolled his eyes. His ostracism apparently wasn't total, and in fact, in certain circles these same crimes made him rather admirable.

"Like I'm in here 'cause of a bum trip," Rivers continued. "Smoked something that had more dust in it than I thought. I guess I got a little crazy, even for me. Manhandled some young thing in the ICU after I was admitted. Now all the nurses are afraid of me. Treat me like polite shit. Hell, I didn't even know what I was doing."

Suddenly, it clicked and Parker placed River's voice. The last time he'd heard it, the volume had been much louder. He was the overdose that had ruined his sleep the other night in the ICU.

"Well, it looks like you've recovered well enough," Parker replied.

"I guess I beat up my girlfriend pretty bad before the police got there. Hell, I don't remember a thing... Old lady says any more of that shit and I'm out on the street."

He looked over Parker's dinner tray. "You gonna' drink that."

Parker glanced at his tray and saw a glass of wine. He didn't remember ordering it. "Wasn't planning on it."

"I'm still a little shaky coming off the drugs, and that sure would help." He reached over and grabbed it before Parker could reply.

"I'll tell you what," Parker said. "The wine's yours, but take it next door so I can get some sleep. Deal?"

"Sure, man." His greedy eyes had already finished it several times over by the time he grabbed the glass. "See you later and... ah, thanks."

"Anytime."

#

Parker came awake with a start. He glanced quickly around his room but couldn't figure what had caused his sudden arousal. Hearing a noise in the hallway, he leaned forward and peered through his partially opened door. Two of the nurses were pushing the cardiac arrest cart rapidly by his door.

Old habits die hard. His subconscious must have picked up on the overhead page of "Code 111" and told his conscious to get its act in gear. Now here he was with his heart racing and his hands shaking from the adrenaline rush.

"Code 111" was the hospital shorthand for cardiac arrest, and it meant that the in-house doctors should rush to the scene to help resuscitate the victim. In the old days, everyone used "Code Blue" as the signal for an arrest, but as the public became aware of what that meant through TV and other medical dramas, hospitals had shifted to new phrases so as not to alarm the other patients or their relatives.

A "full code" was not a pretty thing to watch, and often, the activities which accompany it, were grossly misunderstood by the public. Parker remembered an old tale about a patient admitted to an ICU. After the nurses had settled him into bed and attached his monitor leads, he began making conversation with the elderly man in the next bed. He started asking questions about all the machinery around him, and the routines in the unit. The elderly gentleman cut off his questions and, instead, told him what had happened to the previous occupant of his bed.

"I was talking to him and he was doing fine. I turned to get myself some water, when suddenly the bell above his bed started to ring. Looking over, I saw several nurses and doctors run up to his bedside and start to pound on his chest. Next thing I knew, they were sticking needles all over him, jamming a tube down his throat, and continually electrocuting him. When they finally finished and left the bedside, he was dead. They'd killed him." He paused to let his description sink in. "So the only thing you have to know about being in here is if that bell above your bed starts to ring, get the hell out of that bed!"

In the morning, the code 111 was long forgotten, for Parker's attention was occupied with his impending transfer. The powers-that-be had determined he was stable enough to be moved to the county hospital, to finish his hospitalization. At nine o'clock, two large sheriff's deputies arrived with an ambulance crew to transport him. They'd brought an orange jumpsuit with COUNTY JAIL stenciled on the back. He felt a little wobbly as he changed from his hospital gown into the jumpsuit, but decided it was due more to his prolonged bed rest than the result of his head wound which now felt better. Catching sight of himself in the mirror, he felt overwhelmed by embarrassment and shame at how far he'd fallen.

The ambulance crew strapped him onto their gurney and maneuvered it out of the room. He hadn't realized he was a celebrity of sorts until they exited the hospital. He went from the relative peace and serenity of the hospital setting to the unbelievably chaotic, cacophonous, outside world of a frenzied news media. Photographers and reporters surrounded him. It became obvious there were more than just local newspapers and TV stations covering the story. Microphones were pushed in his face, accompanied by a multitude of shouted questions. The continual camera flashes distorted his vision and caused his headache to flare.

Now he understood why they had sent two large deputies. They cut a wide swath through the crowd and then, miraculously, he was in the relative silence of the ambulance. The quiet, though, was more like being in the eye of a hurricane, for the media circus continued to swirl around the outside of the vehicle.

One of the officers remained with him in the back of the ambulance, while the other followed by car. As they pulled out of the parking lot, no one noticed the black Trans Am following behind.

Chapter Four

The county hospital lay in the town of Salinas, twenty miles inland from the Monterey peninsula. The two areas were connected by a meandering highway which ran through rolling hills, horse farms, a golf course, and alongside the Laguna Seca raceway. Emerging from the foothills, Salinas lay sprawled out in a long valley, with U.S. Highway 101 running north to south through its center.

Salinas had begun as a farming community. And even with the passing of time and the arrival of industry, agriculture still played a dominant role. Despite its burgeoning housing sprawl, which hometown-boy John Steinbeck described as "crab grass spreading toward the foothills", Salinas remained surrounded by large areas of fertile farmland extending up and down its valley.

The reporters had given up the chase long before the ambulance pulled up to the county hospital emergency entrance. They off-loaded Parker and wheeled him through the automatic doors.

One of the ambulance attendants checked with the admitting desk and obtained a room number. They pushed Parker into an elevator, rode up a floor, and then moved him down several colorless corridors before finally stopping at one of the doorways.

His new accommodation was a small, drab room with two beds and a large window through which, one of the deputies cheerfully pointed out, was a view of Parker's future residence, the county jail.

After climbing off the stretcher, Parker walked to the window and stared across the open field at the county jail -- delicately known as the Adult Detention Center. He saw a squat, two story, gray structure with narrow, oblong, recessed windows, crisscrossed with horizontal and vertical bands of rusting iron. A barricade ran along the top of the building, capped with barbed wire. A twelve-foot-high fence circled the grounds.

Apprehensive, even fearful, of what that building might hold for him, Parker turned away. The deputies helped him onto the hospital bed, and then locked a thick leather strap around his left wrist.

"What happens if there's an emergency and I've got to be released?" Parker asked.

The larger of the two deputies, a husky Black man, smiled back. "Doc, you're gonna have your own policeman sitting right outside the door. He'll have the key if it's needed."

Parker's new roommate, a wizened elderly Latino with unwashed, disheveled black hair, watched disinterestedly as the ambulance attendants loaded their equipment on the stretcher and started for the door.

A white-coated, young man with a beard, long hair, and a stethoscope around his neck, squeezed around the departing ambulance crew and strolled over to the deputies.

"Hi. Who's got the paperwork?"

The Black deputy stepped forward, "Right here, doc." He handed him a sheaf of papers. The young man glanced through them, nodding his head as he did.

He looked up. "Well, for once everything's here. How about you guys step outside while I examine the prisoner."

Both deputies left the room as the young physician pulled a chair over and sat down next to Parker's bed.

"I'm Dr. Crow. I'll be your doctor while your here, Dr. McGraw."

Parker leaned forward and shook hands with him. "Glad to meet you." *Thank God he's a stranger. It lessens my humiliation.*

Crow pulled out a paper and pen, and launched into a comprehensive history and physical exam. His stiffness at the start slowly lessened. By the end of the exam, he was more relaxed in his questions and his motions. Finally finished, he rose to leave then stopped.

"I've heard you lecture here several times in the past, Dr. McGraw."

"I hope I kept you awake."

Crow smiled slightly. "I enjoyed the talks very much. In fact, I wish you'd spoken here more often."

I wish I wasn't secured by handcuffs and accused of murder so I could enjoy your compliment.

#

Max Pollock spit into his swimming goggles, and rubbed the spittle across the lens to keep them from fogging. He rinsed the goggles in the pool water before putting them over his head and adjusting them to his face. With a deft and practiced motion, he dove under the water and surfaced five yards down the swimming lane, breaking into a smooth freestyle stroke.

It was a beautiful day at the Beach and Tennis Club, and Pollock shared the pool with only one other swimmer. He swam slowly but strongly, conserving his energy for the many laps to come. Today he was going to try for a mile and a half.

Pollock loved to swim, enjoying the forced solitude. There were no conversations to distract him, no noise or commotion to pull him away from his endeavor, just the continuous churning motion of moving from one end of the pool to the other. Where some people couldn't stand the monotony, Pollock thrived on it, for it allowed him to put his limbs on autopilot while he concentrated on other things. Today all his concentration was on the Beckman murder.

He had been dismally unsuccessful investigating Beckman's claim that someone was trying to kill him. Despite hours of interviews and record searching, he'd found no reason why someone would want him dead. True, there had been a few who would have gladly smiled if misfortune struck the man, but still he'd found no one with enough motive or hate to commit murder.

Pollock's concentration shifted to swimming as he neared the end of the pool. Rolling smoothly into a flip turn, he pushed off strongly toward the other end and resumed his steady rhythm. He loved doing flip turns for they made him feel young and agile, assuaging his concerns about encroaching old age.

Back to reality, you old fart. You missed something somewhere. And now your client is dead.

What galled Pollock most was that he had been ready to tell Beckman that his fears were groundless, and that the accidents had been just that and nothing more. Now he could tell it to Beckman's corpse. Someone had wanted Beckman dead. That was very clear. What was not clear was Parker McGraw's involvement. *It was my office. How would someone know that Parker would be showing up there?*

Max swam another thirty laps before a frightening possibility surfaced.

Maybe it was supposed to have been me in that room with Beckman. A double murder with me as the second body. That scenario makes a lot more sense than McGraw being involved since he has no connection with Beckman. But what do I know that is so important someone would want me dead?

He spent the rest of the swim trying to answer that question.

Chapter Five

The scream in the alley was not loud, but it had a quality of sheer terror. It ended as it had started, suddenly. It was followed by a shuffling sound, a low laugh, and then footsteps which faded quickly into the distance.

Rubbing the sleep from his eyes with his filthy, tattered jacket sleeve, Mason Seger rose quietly from inside a dumpster and peered back down the alley.

"What the hell?" he whispered. He'd heard a lot of strange noises in the alleyways of San Francisco, but never anything like that.

A car door slammed at the mouth of the alley, and he turned in time to see the tail end of a black Trans Am pull away.

He cautiously climbed out of the dumpster and walked farther back into the alley, toward the direction of the scream. He was drawn to the sound of a dripping faucet. Only there were no faucets in this alley.

Moving toward the sound, he quickly discovered a slow trickle of bright, red blood dribbling out of a pile of flattened cardboard boxes. He lifted the edge of one of them, stared for a while, and then dropped it.

"Ain't nothing old Mason can do for that boy," he said.

Mason didn't waste time wondering why the man under the boxes had his throat cut. Instead, he cleared the cardboard off the body and went through the man's pockets. Nothing. Not even loose change.

Slipping off the man's wristwatch and gold pinkie ring, Mason headed back out of the alley. He'd only gone a few feet when he found a wallet. As he expected, there was no money, just a driver's license for a Harry Winn and a business card with the name of a parole officer. *Probably would have been safer if he'd stayed in prison.* He wiped his fingerprints off the wallet, tossed it into a nearby trash can, and left to find a quieter place to finish the night.

##

The next day, a Friday, the doctors concluded that Parker could be moved. He was subsequently transferred via sheriff's cruiser from the county hospital to the Adult Detention Center. The squad car pulled under an arched entryway at the center and stopped. Both sheriff's deputies accompanied Parker through a reinforced concrete doorway into the booking area where a clerk checked him in. His belongings were registered, and then he was fingerprinted, photographed, and given an identification wrist band.

The clerk offered him the proverbial phone call, pointing to a bank of pay phones on the far wall. Alongside the phones, someone had tacked up various ads for bail bondsmen.

Parker declined the use of the phone. He'd spoken to his lawyer, Jeff Gilman, the day before who'd explained that once the county doctor certified Parker's head wound had no residual effect on his mental status, he'd be transferred to the county jail and a preliminary arraignment would be set up. That was when the charges would be read against him, and bail determined. Since it was already mid-day Friday, the arraignment wouldn't happen until Monday.

A leather-faced deputy, smelling of cigarette smoke, escorted him down a drab, cheerless hallway to a large bathroom. There, under the eyes of another officer, he underwent a not very pleasant strip-search procedure, followed by a shower. The deputy then handed him a red jumpsuit.

"These outfits are color coded to match the crime," he explained. "Red's for felons or those accused of a felony."

The deputy led him through a maze of interconnecting corridors, each separated by heavy metal doors. Hearing the doors slam shut and lock behind him, Parker found himself losing the clinical detachment he'd been trying to maintain. All the horror stories of prison, the abuses by both guards and prisoners that he'd heard and read about, flooded his mind, filling him with fear and dread. He tried to ignore these images, telling himself not to panic, but with each step into the bowels of this sterile, impersonal burrow, he came closer to losing it.

They went around a corner and the deputy pulled him to a halt.

"Your new home," he said, pointing to the left.

Parker looked through thick steel bars, and saw beyond a large dormitory-like room.

"We call these cells, pods," the deputy said.

The room existed in the shape of a triangle. The base of the triangle sat against the steel bars, and was partially occupied by metal tables with attached chairs. Bunk beds ran along the slanting walls on either side, filling most of the space. There was bed capacity for about thirty people and, at a glance, the room appeared full.

Another guard approached and unlocked the cell door as the deputy unfastened Parker's handcuffs. Parker stepped into the cell and stopped. For the moment, he had become the object of everyone's attention.

Be cool. Don't let'em know you're scared shitless. The sudden loud noise behind him, as the door slid shut, caused him to jump.

He heard several snickers and tried to ignore them as he looked around. The pod held a mixed bag of humanity with the only common feature being that they all wore red. The inmates reminded Parker of the crowd he use to see in the county emergency room on a Saturday night. In the far corner, several Latinos - their jumpsuits pulled down around their waist -had elaborate tattoos on their backs and arms. On the other side of the cell, a small group of Blacks, with shaved heads or elaborate hairdos. Between these two groups, there were beer-bellied bikers, emaciated druggies, and God knew what else.

Parker opted to search for a bunk among the center group, hoping to avoid any turf wars. As he walked toward the beds, he could feel the tension in the prisoners, like animals who had staked out their territory only to have a stranger arrive and start prowling about. He tried to ignore their deadly stares as he passed amongst the beds, keeping his eyes down, never fastening on any one person's face for long. Finally, he found an empty upper bunk, climbed in, and lay down.

After a few minutes, he rose up on one elbow and casually glanced around. A few people still continued to stare, inviting confrontation, but most were now ignoring him, continuing their card games, their whispered conversations, or their snoozing.

Parker lay back down and closed his eyes. Despite his head injury, all feelings of fatigue were gone. His senses quivered on high alert, wary of any noise or movement that might signal danger coming in his direction.

He heard the continual swearing, the taunts, the veiled threats that the inmates tossed back and forth at each other. He took in the fetid smell of sweat and urine... and something else - the odor of fear. It permeated the pod. It was in the way the inmates looked, with pinched faces and darting eyes. In the way they walked, always glancing around them. And in the way they smelled.

Yeah. You definitely can smell fear. And it's on me as strong as anyone.

A few hours later, a loud bell clanged. A meal wagon arrived at the cell door, and the prisoners started lining up for their fare. Parker decide hospital food seemed like gourmet cuisine compared to this swill. Choosing a table, he sat down. The man sitting across looked a cut above the rest, and must have sensed a kindred spirit in Parker.

"First time?" he asked.

"First time," Parker replied.

"Third for me," he said between mouthfuls. "I'm serving time for repeat DUIs."

Using a piece of bread, the man wiped up some of the sauce on his plate, then popped it into his mouth. Leaning across the table, he quietly intoned, "Let me give you a few hints for surviving in here." He cast a brief look around. "Keep your mouth shut and your eyes down. Don't antagonize anyone. There are animals in here that would maim or kill you just for the exercise, much less for a reason."

Parker nodded.

"What are you in for?" he asked.

"A misunderstanding," Parker replied.

Before his new companion could probe further, a loud commotion erupted behind Parker. He turned to see a fat bull of a man, with a full beard and shaved head, throw someone to the floor and start kicking them. The screams of pain brought the guards running, and they broke up the confrontation.

Parker's tablemate quietly advised him to shift his attention elsewhere.

"Remember the rules for survival," he added.

Parker swiveled around to his plate. "Who was that big guy?"

"No one you ever want to cross. He's called the Fat Man." He paused for a moment, and then said, "Without being too obvious, check out the man sitting next to him."

Parker glanced back. "You mean the guy with the Manson-like eyes?"

"Yeah. His name is Rupert. He and the Fat Man run this pod. They're awaiting trial for robbery and assault."

"Don't the guards keep things in order?" Parker asked.

His new friend's laugh was short and harsh. "Yeah, like the police prevent crime." He took another mouthful of food. "Some big farm boy told Rupert off when he first arrived, and even shoved the Fat Man around a little before the guards broke it up. That night, while he was sleeping, the hayseed got a knife in his back and was rushed off to the hospital. No one has hassled them since."

They finished eating and Parker returned to his bunk. He'd just closed his eyes when someone gave him a violent shove. Opening his eyes, he found himself looking directly into the pig-eyed stare of the Fat Man.

"You're in my bunk, asshole." His voice had a harsh grating sound that shook the particles of food clinging to his beard.

Parker sat up and glanced around. Everyone seemed busy looking in other directions, except a stocky Black man in the corner who was watching with an amused expression. Parker swung his legs over the side of the bed and hopped down.

"Sorry, I thought this bed was empty."

He walked over to a lower bunk and lay down.

The Fat Man followed him over.

"You don't get it, do you dipshit?"

"Get what," Parker asked, his stomach beginning to knot up.

"These beds are all my beds," he said with a grin, exposing his few remaining teeth, all dark yellow. "So you'll have to pay me to use one of them."

This was it, Parker knew. The beginning of the harassment, the torment, the cruelty. Either he made a stand now or he'd end up as someone's sweetheart down the line.

He closed his eyes, took some slow deep breaths, and thought about his sensei, Yoki. *What was it he said about fear? 'One must convert the energy of your fright into the power of your attack.'*

Parker felt a shoe nudge him in the side. "Hey, shithead. You pass out on me or something"

Opening his eyes, Parker looked up at the hulking figure towering over his bedside. Slowly his perception of this mountainous blob of terror changed. Instead of an object of threat and alarm, he now saw the Fat Man as the embodiment of all the frustration and humiliation he'd been forced to suffer over the last few days. His fatigue and fear faded, replaced by an overpowering, energizing anger.

Convert the energy of your fright,

Parker smiled slowly.

"I guess this is one bed you won't be charging for, fatso," he said, sitting up and swinging his legs over the side.

The Fat Man colored slightly, amazed that someone would dispute his authority. Slowly he grinned, like a hungry wolf viewing an innocent lamb. He reached down for Parker and as he did, Parker hooked his left foot behind the Fat Man's right foot, and kicked the Fat Man's right knee with his other foot. The Fat Man toppled backwards like a felled tree, hitting the floor with a resounding crash.

Into the power of your attack.

Dazed, it took the Fat Man a moment to realize what had happened. Fixing his eyes on Parker, his bloated face changed into a thing of pure evil as he laboriously climbed to his feet. All other sound and movement in the pod had ceased.

"Get the fuck up!" he hissed. "I'm going to kill you slowly."

"You and who else?"

The Fat Man lunged forward, but Parker leaned back forcing the Fat Man to come under the upper bunk to reach him. As he grabbed Parker's shirt, Parker straight armed his chin, snapping the Fat Man's head into the iron frame of the upper bunk. At almost the same time, Parker smashed the Fat Man's exposed throat with his other hand, setting his larynx into spasm and cutting off his air flow.

Gasping for breath, the Fat Man released Parker's shirt and pulled back. When he did, Parker drew his knees up to his chest and lashed out, catching the Fat Man full in the stomach with the force of his kick. The Fat Man flew across the room onto the floor and lay there stunned, his breath coming with a loud rasping sound each time he inhaled.

Parker stood up, his adrenaline pumping, looking to release more of his frustration, and glared around. "Anyone else think this is their bunk?"

He got no replies.

He was twisting back toward the bed when someone yelled, "Watch out!" He realized his mistake instantly.

Rupert!

Spinning around, he found Rupert lunging toward him with a makeshift knife. Parker jumped sideways, but Rupert's blade still pierced his shirt and grazed his chest. Quickly Rupert pulled back to try again, but this time Parker was ready. With Rupert's next thrust, Parker dodged to his left and kicked Rupert hard against the side of his right knee. The knee buckled and Rupert started to fall. As he went down, Parker stepped in and punched him viciously on the side of the neck. Rupert hit the ground with a grunt and lay still.

Wheeling about, Parker checked for the Fat Man, but he was still on the ground, holding his throat, trying to breathe.

Parker picked up Rupert's knife and tossed it through the bars onto the hallway floor. Returning to his bunk, he paused to nod his appreciation to the Black man in the corner who'd given him the warning yell.

##

The buzz of the cell phone shattered the stillness of the small apartment. It hadn't completed its first ring when the blond man rolled out of bed and picked it up. He moved amazingly fast for someone his size.

"Yeah?" Any remnant of sleep disappeared when he heard the voice on the other end.

"It would seem that your incompetence has produced a complication. I don't want it growing into a larger complication."

The room had a chill the blond man hadn't noticed before. "I have a solution, sir. Just a few more days."

"We don't have a few more days. Certain corrections are required now."

The blond man listened in silence for the next few minutes, and then spoke. "I'll need help."

"That I'll leave up to you. Don't fuck this one up."

"He's as good as..." He realized he was talking to a dead line.

##

In the dim, artificial light of the pod, Parker spent a long sleepless night, every moment expecting Rupert or the Fat Man to descend upon him. He knew their conflict wasn't over. Far from it, for he'd shamed them both in front of the entire pod population. If they hoped to regain their control position, Parker had to be punished. The more brutal, the better. Only this time, there'd be no warning. Just a sudden, unannounced onslaught.

At breakfast, Parker positioned himself next to the man whose warning yell had prevented Rupert from skewering him. He introduced himself and thanked him for his help.

"No big thing, bro."

The man's name was Sparks, Parker learned, and he was in for assault or "barroom brawling" as he termed it. That was where his nickname had originated, for whenever he was in a bar and had a few drinks, the "sparks" would fly.

"Where'd you learn to fight," Sparks asked.

Parker took a sip of juice and replied, "I spent years taking martial arts classes in L.A. Yesterday was the first time I've ever used it outside the dojo."

"Was a prime time to use it, man." Sparks took a bite. "Ever come across a karate instructor in L.A. named George Yokohama?"

Parker paused from cutting his food. "You mean Yoki Yokohama?"

Sparks smiled. "The same."

"He was my sensei. How do you know him?"

"We go way back, even before he opened his studio."

"That studio is a place I'll never forget," Parker said. "I was running errands and my car stalled. I didn't have my cell phone. The only open building was this karate place. I went inside to see if I could use their phone and came out two hours later, sore from my first martial arts lesson, and signed up for a whole course." Parker laughed. "Yoki was a very persuasive man."

They traded Yoki stories for a while, and then Sparks told his favorite.

Business had been very slow when Yoki initially opened his karate studio, and it looked like he might go under. He'd gone to the bank and drawn out the last of his savings to buy groceries for his family (or so Yoki told it). While he was unlocking his car, three toughs from a local youth gang accosted him, demanding his money. Yoki was short and slim, with a very aesthetic appearance, heightened by wire rim glasses. When he refused, the gang never thought twice about jumping him. The ensuing fight was, as Yoki described it, "too short, but most satisfying". Yoki came away unscathed, while all three of the thugs required medical care before going to jail.

The episode would have probably have died in the police annals except that the three gang members tried to sue Yoki for assault, claiming he'd attacked them. When it came to trial, the judge dismissed the suit when he learned that these same youths had similar histories of assault and robbery. The ensuing publicity made Yoki a local hero. The thought that this Japanese Woody Allen could easily vanquish three of the town's local bad guys, and barely get his hands dirty, was a great story. The TV newscasts played it for all it was worth, and the result was that Yoki's karate studio became an overnight success.

When breakfast finished, Parker wandered back to his bunk and lay down. As much as he fought it, his eyes kept drifting shut. During one of these dozing spells, he sensed someone leaning down toward him. Throwing up his arms, he started to strike out when he realized it was Sparks.

"Hey, man. You're a little jumpy," Sparks said, backing away.

Parker rubbed his face. "You'd be too with no sleep, just waiting for those two assholes to sneak up on you."

Sparks glanced over at Rupert and the Fat Man, both of whom were watching their interaction. "Never did like those two," he murmured. He looked back at Parker and grinned wickedly.

"Climb out of that bed for a few minutes and I'll guarantee you a good night's sleep."

Parker stood up and followed Sparks out to an open area near the bunks. Sparks spun around, facing him.

"So you think you got all the moves, huh, white boy," he said loudly. "Well, let's see you handle some of these."

Immediately, he started throwing kicks and punches at Parker. It caught Parker by surprise, but as he dodged and parried, he quickly recognized the moves as a collection of Yoki's warm-up routines. The two of them easily fell into it, moving back and forth, exchanging thrusts and blocks. To the average onlooker, it appeared to be a real fight but in reality it was as staged and practiced as a dance routine. The rest of the inmates stopped their activity and watched the two of them spar. Even Rupert and the Fat Man joined the half-circle of observers.

Spotting them both out of the corner of his eye, Sparks smirked and said aggressively to Parker, "You lookin' pretty good, whitey. So try this." He faked to his right, took two steps forward, and leaped into the air, beginning a sweeping round house kick. His foot flew past Parker's face, grossly off mark, and went on to connect with the Fat Man's unprotected chest. The sound of ribs cracking blended with the Fat Man's cry of pain as he dropped to the floor.

Sparks, his face filled with shock and concern, rushed toward the Fat Man. He moved so quickly that he 'inadvertently' knocked Rupert down who was turned, looking at his injured friend.

"Jeez, I'm sorry," Sparks said to both of them. He put his hand out to Rupert, "Let me help you up." He grabbed Rupert's right hand before he had a chance to decline, and begin to pull him up. As Rupert was rising, Sparks suddenly slipped forward, apparently pulled off balance by Rupert's weight, He fell on top of Rupert, all the while maintaining a firm grip on Rupert's right hand. Rupert screamed in agony, "Mother fucker! You've broken my wrist!"

Sparks stood up and glanced down at Rupert, who held his wrist and rocked back and forth on the floor. "Man, I'm really sorry about that."

As if on cue, the guards arrived and separated everyone. Two of the guards helped the Fat Man and Rupert up, while another asked what had happened.

Head down, Sparks stepped forward. "It was my fault, sir. I was goofin' around with this friend of mine here, showing' him a few moves. I missed with a real powerhouse kick and the fat guy, there, was just too close and caught it in the chest. The other guy got knocked down in the excitement and when I tried to help him up, he pulled me down on top of him and snapped his wrist. Two tragic accidents." Sparks gestured around him. "Hey! You can ask anyone."

The guard looked Sparks straight in the eye for ten seconds then snickered and looked around the pod. "Anybody see it different."

The few responses he got were all negative.

The guard moved next to Sparks and spoke so quietly that Parker, who was nearby, could barely hear it. "Bullshit and you know it, Sparks. If it was anyone other than these two scumbags, I'd have your ass." He turned and followed the other two guards out of the cell as they led Rupert and the Fat Man to the infirmary.

Parker watched them leave, the Fat Man clutching his chest, groaning with each breath, and Rupert holding his deformed wrist, pale, sweat dripping from his forehead. He knew that neither of them would be a threat for quite some time.

When they'd stepped out of sight, Sparks put his hand out and Parker slapped it.

"Sleep tight tonight, my man," Sparks said, grinning.

Parker only wished it were that simple.

##

Max Pollock tossed his digital recorder onto the passenger seat of his BMW and climbed into the car. Dusk was his favorite time of the day and he felt good. He was on to something. Something big. Something unbelievably shocking if he was right. He wanted to attribute it to his astute deductive powers, but he knew his discovery had been a fluke. How it all came together he wasn't entirely sure, but he'd find out. That he was sure.

He backed his car out of his garage, and drove to Highway 1. His appointment was in sixty minutes which gave him ample driving time. Turning right, he headed south toward Big Sur.

Despite his outward calm, he had trouble reining in his impatience. This interview could be a real turning point in the case, and he was anxious to get it started. So anxious in fact, that he failed to notice the black Trans Am that turned right on to Highway 1 and dropped in far behind him.

Chapter Six

Saturday afternoon, Parker's memory of the fateful night that the shooting occurred returned.

It happened while he was being led down a long corridor, similar to the one in his and Max's office building. When the guard opened the door at the end, Parker suddenly had a flash of *deja vu*, and it was as if he were opening Pollock's office door. The memories came flooding back.

He remembered working late in his own office after his nurse had gone home. He'd finally closed up for the night and was walking toward the exit, when he decided to see if Max Pollock was in. His office was only a few doors from the exit.

He found Max's office door unlocked and the reception area light on. Stepping into the reception room, he noticed a light under Max's inner office door and knocked. A voice within mumbled a reply so he opened the door and entered the room. And this is where his memory ended. His next recollection was Janet in the ICU.

Parker spent the evening lying on his bunk, trying to decide what to do with his new-found but limited memory. For what it was worth, he'd let Gilman know in the morning.

For now, he rationalized, it was enough to know that he'd gone to Max's office for purely innocent reasons and he hadn't been carrying a gun.

##

On Sunday, Rupert and the Fat Man were back, but both stayed far away from Sparks and Parker. By the time they mended, Parker hoped he'd be out on bail. The rest of the pod, having seen what Sparks and Parker were capable of, treated them with respect and distance.

After breakfast, Parker and Sparks spent the morning reading the paper, talking sports, and politics. Parker scanned the obituary notices, hoping he wouldn't find any names from his practice. One name caught his attention, but he couldn't place it: Jackson Rivers. It wasn't until he started reading that he remembered: the overdose patient who had wandered into his hospital room. The notice mentioned that he'd died in the hospital of an unknown cause. Parker wondered if he had been the Code 111 that had awakened him the morning of his transfer. Briefly, he pondered the different causes of death in someone that young, and then moved on to another page.

#

Monday arrived, and with it came another transfer. Parker was moved to a holding area in the sheriff's station next to the county court house for his arraignment. He had a brief meeting with Jeff Gilman who explained what would happen at the arraignment.

"What about me getting out of here?" Parker asked.

"I'm hoping they will release you on bail," Jeff said. "If so, will you be able to cover it?"

"I will pull whatever I need out of my home equity account," Parker replied. "I'm not spending another night here."

"Good. If the judge sets bail, I've got a bail bondsman lined up."

At nine o'clock, the sheriff's deputies took him and a number of other inmates over to the courthouse. Handcuffed in his red felon outfit, shuffling along with the rest them, Parker couldn't help wondering again how he had ever gotten into this mess. And if he'd ever get out.

His only salvation was Max Pollock. The police were content with Parker as the culprit and were unlikely to look any farther. So it all rested on Max's detective abilities. He hoped Max was up to the challenge. In fact, he more than hoped, he prayed.

When Parker's time arrived, the courtroom had a number of media personnel obviously following his story. One of the officers escorted him to the defendant's table next to Jeff Gilman.

The bailiff stood and announced, "Case of McGraw vs State of California" then sat down.

The judge focused on the prosecutor's table where the assistant DA, Ray Stone, now rose. "The charge against Dr. McGraw is felony murder," he said, emphasizing the last two words. "He is accused of murdering a man while involved in a drug deal with him." With a malignant glance at Parker, he resumed his seat.

The judge turned back to Parker. "How do you plea, Dr. McGraw?"

"Not guilty, your Honor," Parker stated with as much conviction as his voice could hold.

Taking a step forward, Jeff added, "We'd like to discuss bail, your Honor."

Stone popped up. "The state would strongly advise against that, your Honor. The seriousness of his crimes make him a real flight risk, not to mention the danger to the public of releasing an accused drug-dealing murderer."

The judge swung back to Gilman. "Counselor?"

"My client has ties to this community, owning a home and successful medical practice. He has been an upstanding citizen with an excellent medical reputation for the five years he has lived here. He has never been arrested or accused of a crime, and has no prior history of violence. I do not consider him a flight risk or danger to the community. If anything he's saved a number of lives in the community while he's been here."

The judge looked over at the prosecution table then at Parker, staring at him for at least thirty seconds. "Bail is set a one million dollars." This was punctuated by the thud of his gavel and then his monotone cry, "Next case."

It took until late afternoon before bail could be arranged and Parker finally released. Jeff had brought some clean clothes, and after a quick change Parker met him in the lobby. They walked out together.

"So how does it feel to be out of there?" Jeff asked as he opened the door for him.

Parker stepped outside into the warm sunlight, closed his eyes and took a deep breath. He stood for a moment. "I was only in there for three days. I can't imagine spending years in there."

"Let's hope it doesn't come to that."

"Let's plan on it."

Jeff patted him on the shoulder. "With a bit of luck, Max will come up with something soon. And once my PI is back, will have him on the case also."

"Before I forget, there's a guy I met in there I'd like you to help." He handed Jeff a piece of paper with Sparks' full name on it.

Jeff stared at the paper for a bit, then shrugged. "What's your connection?"

"He helped me in a big way and I want to do the same for him."

They started down the steps of the building and noticed several reporters with camera crews waiting at the bottom.

"Look confident, keep your back straight, and no comment to any questions they ask. I'll do all the talking," Jeff said out of the corner of his mouth.

The questions came, loud and fast.

"Will you be practicing medicine while you are waiting for your trial?"

"If you didn't kill him, do you have any idea who did?"

The verbal barrage continued as they made their way to Jeff's car. Occasionally, Jeff would give a short two or three word response. Some of the questions, Parker thought, deserved a four letter response, but as ordered he kept his mouth shut. He was climbing into the car when a reporter managed to shout out one last question.

"Do you think there is any connection between your case and Max Pollock's death?"

Chapter Seven

This is a nightmare! Parker reflected on his drive back with Jeff Gilman to the Monterey Peninsula. *A rollercoaster ride straight into hell. Now my best chance of getting off is gone.* Parker squeezed his eyes shut, trying to erase his frightening visions of prison, but to no avail. Even opening his eyes and watching the passing fields with their patches of purple wildflowers didn't help. Thoughts of prison continued to dance about in the periphery of his mind, casting a cloak of depression over everything he saw and felt.

Before leaving Salinas, Jeff had cornered the reporter who'd asked about Pollock's death. The detective's car had gone off Highway 1 south of Carmel, and continued five hundred feet straight down into the ocean. The highway patrol had pulled the car out at low tide, but they found no body in or around the wreck. They assumed Max's body must have been carried out to sea with the tide and, if not taken by the sharks, would turn up later somewhere down the coast. There were no witnesses to the accident, so they were examining the car for some explanation. At present, the highway patrol believed the crash had occurred late on Saturday, and that Max had been alone.

Parker fought with alternating emotions; saddened and tearful about the loss of a very good friend, and depressed and angry about the departure of his possible savior. He found himself caught up in this flood of conflicting emotions, not the least of which was guilt. Guilt that he'd allowed Max to get involved. Guilt that his sorrow about Max's death was overshadowed by his own selfish concern about his future.

Jeff turned into the parking lot of Parker's office building, and pulled up next to Parker's car. Pine needles and tree sap had been accumulating on it since that fateful Monday, one week ago.

"Park, again I'm really sorry about Max. I know you two were close."

Parker nodded slowly. "Thanks."

"Don't worry about the case. My investigator will be back next week, and I'll get him right on it. It'll be months before we go to trial. A lot can happen before then."

"This case wasn't worth losing Max."

Jeff's brow furrowed. "You think his death was related to this case?"

"Max had a mistrust in coincidences. I find his accident a little too coincidental for me."

Jeff placed his hands on the steering wheel. "A car crash on that dangerous stretch of highway doesn't make it murder. People have accidents along that road all the time. But I agree with you. It is suspicious."

Parker told him about his memory return. "At least it confirms that I didn't go there to make a drug buy, and that I wasn't carrying a gun," Parker said. "So either Beckman had two guns on him, which seems unlikely, or someone else was there."

They sat in silence until Jeff spoke. "There are definite inconsistencies in your case which I can't explain. I'll have my investigator speak with you as soon as he's back and we'll see what we can come up with."

Parker brushed the pine needles off his windshield, and then stuck his key in the car door lock. He didn't turn it. There was something he had to face before he could go home. His office.

He'd been trying to ignore the repercussions that his criminal charges would have on his medical practice, but he could no longer avoid it. He left his car and walked down to the building complex.

His office was nine hundred and fifteen square feet in the middle of an office complex. Parker had designed his own layout, and liked to think he ran the business himself. In reality, he knew the office could go for some time without him, but couldn't last a day without Doreen Danforth. Receptionist, typist, nurse, accountant, and office manager, she was not only the backbone of the organization, she was the entire organization. As such, she'd been forced to cope with this whole mess while Parker was in jail.

Parker eased the office door open and stepped into the waiting room. Through the glass partition at the counter, he glimpsed Doreen on the phone, sitting in front of the office computer. Edging closer, he noticed she was deleting a patient appointment. She hung up as he reached the partition. She didn't look happy.

"Good to see the hired help looking so content," Parker said.

Startled, she glanced up and seeing Parker, smiled softly. "Well, it's about time you showed up for work. I hope you have a good excuse for missing last week."

Parker grinned and walked around the partition.

"It's nice to be home," he said, then gave her a long hug. When they parted, he noticed tears in her eyes. "Hey! Come on! Things aren't that bad... I hope"

She turned away, drying her eyes. "I'm sorry. I don't know why I'm crying. I guess I've kept up a business-as-usual pretense for so long, it felt good to let go." She dabbed her eyes once more. "I really am glad to see you. And no, things haven't been that bad."

Doreen's husband had been a helicopter pilot in Afghanistan, a dangerous assignment. Yet she had coped with that stress amazingly well, or so her husband Wendell claimed. Her tearful reaction now made Parker that much more aware of his present predicament and how other people viewed the inevitability of his conviction. He slumped back against the wall. "Do I have any patients left or have they all been scared off?"

Doreen sighed. "The newspaper article appeared Tuesday. On Wednesday, I began receiving the phone calls. Some were inquiries as to whether we would be open, but the majority were cancellations. So rather than wait and let the practice slide down the drain, I took the initiative and made arrangements for Dr. Cohn to see the patients that had to be seen. The rest I called and rescheduled for two months hence."

Parker pushed away from the wall. "I'm surprised anyone would want an appointment with me after that news article."

Doreen suddenly got busy moving papers around and straightening things that didn't need straightening.

"Okay! The whole story this time," Parker said.

Doreen continued her busy work while she spoke, "Well, the first three people I tried to reschedule begged off for various reasons, and said they would call me instead. I could see the writing on the wall." She looked up, defiant yet a little embarrassed. "I wasn't going to see this practice go under without a fight. Not after the work we've spent building it up over the last five years."

"And so?"

Her reply was slow in coming. "So I lied a little."

Parker stepped closer toward her. "What do you mean, 'lied a little'?"

She stared off over his shoulder. "I kind of hinted that... that you occasionally worked with Mr. Pollock on some of his cases, specifically the ones involving drugs. I intimated this was one of those cases, and that what had occurred had been involved with the investigation and would be cleared up shortly."

Parker groaned and sank into a chair. "What did you think would happen when I came to trial, and the patients discovered the truth?"

"I hoped you'd never come to trial. That you would be cleared of the charges before then." She walked over to the copying machine. "Well, I had to do something! I couldn't just watch us go under." She pointed a finger at Parker. "I don't remember you calling with any bright ideas on how to keep this place together." She turned, placed a piece of paper in the copying machine, and jabbed the copy button.

Parker stood up, went and patted her shoulder. "I'm sorry. The reason I didn't call was because I knew I could count on you." Her angry countenance softened and he stepped back. "Actually, your idea is fine. It keeps some life in the practice, at least until the trial. And if I do end up going to trial, it probably won't matter then anyway."

They spent the next two hours discussing the adjustments needed for running the office. Neither of them felt he could see patients until the case was resolved, for even with Doreen's story, very few patients would want to see a physician accused of murder and drug dealing. They made arrangements for various doctors to help cover the practice. Fortunately, Parker had a small savings account that would help see them through the next few months.

When Parker stepped out of the office into the building corridor, it was late afternoon. With the practice covered, there was one less headache to worry about and some of his depression lifted. He'd just reached his car when his cell phone rang.

It was Jeff. "Park, I previously filed a discovery order to allow us to visit and photograph the crime scene. It's been approved and Hall will meet us at Pollock's office in thirty minutes to let us in."

Forty minutes later, Jeff pulled up in his Lexus with Detective Hall right behind in a police cruiser. As the trio walked today the building, Hall explained, "You have thirty minutes to look around and photograph whatever you want, but don't touch anything."

Jeff leaned into Parker. "Maybe seeing the scene might shake loose a few more memories."

They moved down the building's corridor to Max's office. Parker cupped his hands against the tinted windows and peered in while Hall unlocked the door. Only the reception area was visible, since the connecting door into Max's inner office was closed. He wondered which chair Beckman's daughter had been sitting in when she heard the shots that had killed her father.

Hall told them to wait until he turned on the lights.

"One of the first things I do on any case," Jeff said, "is examine the crime scene. It takes the case from two dimensional to three dimensional, allowing me to visualize what actually happened."

Hall called them in. The reception room was basic without frills. Several chairs, a receptionist desk, and a couple of pictures on the wall. In contrast, Max's inner office had hard-wood paneling, Berber carpet, and two dark red leather chairs grouped in front of a massive rosewood desk. Several towering palms in large brass holders scattered around the room completed a feeling of quiet elegance. This was a calm room, safe from the ravages and pains of the real world. Parker decided a client sitting in one of those deep chairs, with the light filtering through the mini-blinds, would know he'd reached a safe harbor. His problems would soon be solved. No need to worry.

Max had wanted his office to be inviting yet impersonal, feeling that a display of his own triumphs or pictures of his loved ones might increase his clients' feelings of despair and rejection. Despite the absence of these personal touches, Max was still overwhelmingly present. The class, the taste, the regard for fine detail, the warmth and comfort of the room, these were all a part of Max's personality.

Hall interrupted his thoughts. "Pollock had a part-time secretary, only here when clients were coming that he wanted to impress, or when he needed typing done." He stared first at Jeff, then at Parker. "She wasn't working that Monday. The office was closed since Pollock was supposed to be out of town."

Hall strolled over to the large bay windows, turned, and pointed to the entry door. "As you can see, there's only one door in or out of the office. After Beckman's daughter heard the gun shots, no one used that door until she forced it open." He swung back to the windows and opened the mini-blinds. "The only other access out of this room is through these small windows beneath the bay windows. They were locked from the inside when we arrived. In addition, they had outside screens which hadn't been disturbed for quite some time." He moved away from the windows, and settled into one of the red leather chairs.

While Jeff took some still shots, Parker's gaze slowly swept the room. It no longer seemed like a safe harbor. By its very physical structure, it was going to convict him. The calm soothing sensation of earlier had been replaced by a dark threatening awareness. Hall, poised like a vulture waiting to pounce, solidified the feeling.

"Does any of this jar your memory, doctor?" he asked.

"I really haven't any recollection of being in this room that night."

"I can assure you that you were since I watched the ambulance crew carry you out," Hall replied.

"There were no other witnesses except Beckman's daughter?" Jeff asked.

Hall rose from his chair. "At this point, counselor, the tour is over. I'll have to ask you to leave while I lock up."

Jeff and Parker ambled toward the door. "Thank you, Detective," Parker said.

"See you in court, doctor."

# #

A few blocks north of downtown Carmel is a hilly, wooded area referred to as the "tree section" with numerous small cottages and rustic homes scattered amongst stands of oak and pine. Parker's house sat in the midst of this, on a canyon hillside between two streets, and was accessible from either.

His home was what realtors call a Carmel charmer, about eight hundred square feet with a faded wood exterior and a large deck that extended out over the canyon. The inside featured worn oak floors and an aged stone fireplace. Parker tossed his car keys on the mantel and walked out on the deck.

Parker loved the peaceful feeling of sitting on his deck in this quiet neighborhood and listening to the forest sounds. Today was no different. He wanted to settle into his Adirondack chair and, at least for a while, put all of this out of his mind.

But first he had to rid himself of the smell and feel of jail. A long hot shower took care of that. After toweling off and changing into clean clothes, he ventured into the kitchen for a cold soda. Against his better judgment, he plugged his cell phone into a wall circuit, and after a few moments, checked it for messages and voice mails. Forty-two voice mails.

He was torn between listening to the messages versus the urge to erase them. He felt sure many of them would only remind him of what he had hoped to escape for the rest of the day. Duty won out. He settled into his Adirondack chair and one-by-one began to go through the voice mails.

With the late afternoon sun warming his face, and cold soda trickling down his throat, the trauma and stresses of the last week gradually ebbed away. He listened to the recordings, most of which were hang-ups or reporters with questions. How they got his unlisted number he had no idea. One call reminded him he was supposed to arrange for a speaker for the next Diogenes Club meeting, a local Sherlock Holmes society of which he was a member. They hoped it was all set up. Parker shook his head at the irony of the situation. Now he remembered why he'd gone down to see Max Pollock that fateful night. He'd hoped to enlist him as the guest speaker.

For a moment, Parker felt exhilarated with this latest bit of returned memory, but that quickly faded with the realization it wasn't going to change his situation.

At around at around call thirty-eight, his concentration was fading when a voice brought him bolt upright. Max Pollock. He'd missed most of the message so he replayed it. The message had been left Saturday, the day Max had died.

"Park, I'm just going out the door. I've stumbled onto a series of strange coincidences. I can't put it all together but it's very suggestive that Beckman's life was in danger. I'm going to follow up on a lead in Big Sur that might clear some of this up. I'll talk to you and Jeff later."

Son of a bitch. Max lost his life trying to help me, and it's all for nothing.

Frustrated, he slapped the chair's arm. *Got to be some way to find out what Max discovered or who he was going to see in Big Sur. It might lead to other suspects besides myself.*

Parker stood up and paced around the deck. *Max must have kept a file on the Beckman case. Find that and maybe I'll find some answers.*

He called Jeff, catching him just leaving his office. Parker told him about Max's voice mail and the importance of finding his investigative file.

"I don't remember seeing that in the evidence collection list the prosecution turned over, but let me check."

Jeff called back twenty minutes later. "I've gone over all the all the evidence provided, including the list of materials taken from Pollock's office."

"And?"

"There's no mention of any files being removed from his office or home."

Parker thought for a moment. "That doesn't mean that the file doesn't exist. It only means it hasn't been found."

"Interestingly, that's not the only thing that's missing," Jeff replied. "When I interviewed Pollock's secretary, she mentioned a private appointment book he kept. The police never found that either."

"Sounds like someone wants to erase all connection between Beckman and Pollock."

Chapter Eight

"Yes, sir. It went smoothly, and there were no witnesses on the road. A quick bump and the P.I.'s car went over the edge and straight down," the blond said. He'd been having difficulty hearing over the noise of the gym so he'd moved into the locker room for privacy and quiet.

"Very satisfactory. There will be a bonus in your next payment." The man on the line coughed softly. "Now about the other... loose end, our doctor friend. You've made the proper arrangements, I hope."

The blond man switched the burner phone to his other ear. "Yes, sir. We're in position, and waiting for the right timing."

"Remember. It needs to look like an accident."

The blond hung up the phone and returned to the weight room.

A brown, slender yet muscular male with a short pony tail looked up from his supine position on the weight bench. "Was he happy?"

"For him, ecstatic. Even tossed in a bonus."

"All right." The dark male lay back and grasped the barbell poised on the rack above him. "Spot me. Okay?"

#

'I was very sorry to hear about your situation," said Bill Lehrman, the building janitor, glancing over at Parker. "If there is anything I can do, let me know."

Several years ago, Bill had been a recent graduate from an alcoholic rehabilitation program, with a wife and two kids to support, and a past work record filled with his drinking problems. No one would hire him. His wife had called Parker, frantic that he'd go back to the bottle if he couldn't find work.

Parker had met Bill and his wife while caring for their oldest son who'd had a heart condition called mitral stenosis, a scarring of one of his heart valves due to rheumatic fever. Even with Bill's drinking back then, they'd been a close family.

Parker had pushed hard with his building manager and, despite a number of more qualified applicants, had managed to get Bill into the post of janitor on a trial basis.

Three years later, Bill's janitorial service was booming and his family was tighter than ever.

"Bill, I need a favor. I have to get into Max Pollock's office." Parker said, seeing concern appear on Bill's face. "All I need is to look around for a few minutes. You can come and watch if you want."

Bill rubbed his jaw slowly. "You know the police had that whole area marked off."

"They're finished with it."

"Dr. McGraw, I could lose my job if someone found out."

Stepping closer, Parker said, "Bill, I'm about to go to prison for something I didn't do. I need your help."

Bill toed the rug with his work boot. "Well, there's no question that I owe you." Slowly he unhooked his ring of keys from his belt and laid it on the desk with one key separated from the others.

"Sometimes when I'm working, I accidentally leave keys lying around..." He left the sentence dangling as he walked out of the room.

Max's office door swung open easily with Bill's key. Parker closed all the blinds before switching on the lights. He doubted he'd find anything but he'd always wonder if he didn't try. His search began with Pollock's desk, then the filing cabinet and finally the bookshelves. He went over every scrap of paper and looked in every conceivable hiding place, including the books. Nothing.

Parker dropped down into Max's desk chair. *One more dead end.*

Staring at Max's deck, he realized there might be another way to connect Max with Beckman. Parker checked his watch and decided it wasn't that late. Using his cell phone, he called Max's secretary at home. He'd come across her number while combing Max's desk.

When she answered, Parker identified himself, then said, "I'm sorry to call so late but several questions have come up I need to get answered."

"I really don't want to get involved," she said flatly.

He was not surprised by her reluctance, but he had a possible solution. "Let me play you a voice message Max left me just before his trip down to Big Sur."

After hearing it, she remained silent for so long Parker thought she'd hung up. When she did talk, her voice had lost its coolness. "I'm sorry if I sounded rude, Dr. McGraw. Max's death has greatly upset me."

"No need to apologize. I fully understand."

"I do not remember a Michael Beckman as one of Max's clients. I've never seen him in the office."

"Maybe you met him under a different name?"

"Dr. McGraw," she said, in the tone of a teacher explaining something to a slow student. "I followed the newspaper and television accounts. Mr. Beckman's picture was featured prominently and he was a complete stranger to me."

Parker thanked her and hung up. Nothing existed to prove that Beckman and Pollock had ever been in contact with each other. Nothing except Max's message voice message and what Max had previously told Parker. Someone had done an excellent job of eradicating all traces of a relationship between Max and Beckman.

Parker returned key ring to Bill, thanked him profusely, and left for home.

On the drive to his house, Parker reviewed the facts. Beckman claimed someone was trying to kill him. Finding out who wanted Beckman dead was the question and the answer was in his past. But how to explore his past, that was the puzzle. By the time Parker reached home, he knew who might have the key to unlocking that past and how he was going to approach them.

##

Ken Lewis was drunk. Gloriously inebriated and he loved it. It had been a long time since his last drunk. *Too long,* he thought to himself. Capping the empty Jack Daniels bottle, he leaned back in his kitchen chair, and launched the bottle toward the distant wastebasket.

"Two points," he yelled as it bounced off the wall and into the basket.

Laboriously, he climbed to his feet and staggered into the living room. "Damn! I feel good," he slurred loudly to the worn furniture.

With his hands on the walls to support him, he made it to the bedroom before collapsing. It took him almost a minute to realize that he'd fallen not onto the floor but into the bed.

"God watches over fools and drunks," he pronounced in his most commanding voice. He closed his eyes and waited for the effects of the liquor to pull him down into sleep. That deep, dreamless sleep he loved so well.

The next morning, Melvin Cottam, the building manager knocked on Ken Lewis' apartment door. Getting no answer, he pounded on the door, releasing some of the anger he'd built up while having to listen to multiple tenants complaining of Lewis' recurrent late night noise.

Still no answer. Now he was really pissed. His plans for the day hadn't included waking up a hung over ex-con.

He tried the door but it was locked. Using his pass key, he let himself in. "Hey, Lewis! It's the manager. Wake up," he shouted.

No response. He shook his head at the empty beverage cans strewn across the living room carpet, and wrinkled his nose at the smell of flat beer, old cigarettes, and stale food that permeated the place. He walked to the bedroom. Empty.

"Lewis! Where are you?" he yelled. Moving down the hall, he pushed open the bathroom door and got his answer. Lewis was there. And he wouldn't be disturbing anyone again. Not when he was dangling from a cross beam by a rope around his neck, his eyes bulging out like a squashed toad, his tongue black as new-laid asphalt.

Cottam turned and spewed his breakfast into the toilet bowl. Trying not to look at the grisly thing hanging from the ceiling, Cottam grabbed a towel and wiped his mouth. It was then that he discovered the crudely-lettered suicide note.

#

Parker spent the morning calling all the mortuaries in town, trying to determine who was handling Beckman's burial arrangements. Of course, it had to be Zachary's at the end of the alphabetical listings. They were very accommodating when Parker explained he was a distant relative of the deceased and was trying to reach Mr. Beckman's daughter to convey his condolences. Mr. Zachary gave him her hotel phone number and, along with it, his own condolences on losing a loved one.

Parker called the hotel number and was connected to her room. A female voice answered.

"Ms. Beckman?" he asked.

"Yes."

"You don't know me, but I have some information regarding your father's death which you might find very important."

There was a quick intake of breath. "Who are you?"

"My name wouldn't be familiar to you." *Yeah,* he thought, *no more than the President's.* "I'd like to meet with you tonight, and discuss it."

There was a pause. "If you have information pertaining to my father's death, I think the police are the ones to discuss it with, not me."

"You might not want the information I have exposed to the police. Or at least, you might want to hear it before I turn it over to them."

"Is this a blackmail attempt? Because if it is, I have no money and wouldn't pay even if I did. My father's reputation is long past salvaging."

He was losing her.

"No, this isn't blackmail," he said with as much indignation as he could muster. "I was a close friend of your father's and I wanted to see justice done to his reputation." He paused for effect and then continued. "But if you care so little that you can't spare an hour of your time..." Parker held his breath. This was it. She either took the bait and he had a chance, or she hung up and it was back to square one.

An eternity passed before she spoke. "It has to be in a very public place."

Parker wasted no time. "Sorrento's on Ocean Ave in Carmel, at eight pm. Wear something distinctive."

Again the pause. "How about a long black coat?"

"Fine. See you at eight."

Parker sat sipping his beer in Sorrento's, a small, cozy bar restaurant on the lower part of Ocean Avenue, the town's main street. He loved the homey atmosphere - the low ceiling, dim lighting, and large fireplace. He'd spent a lot of nights in the place and it felt like a second home.

Even more than the surroundings, he enjoyed the clientele. They were mostly locals who'd long since become jaded to the dress and antics of the occasional drop-in tourists. Very little seemed to affect the general background din of the place. Lady Gaga could walk in and not much would change. Parker, therefore, was understandably surprised when the noise level dropped. He looked up from his beer, and the reason became obvious.

A number of women had walked through Sorrento's Dutch doors over the years, but none that Parker could remember as beautiful as this one. Long, blonde, permed tresses, an hourglass figure, and a face that would be a photographer's dream.

She stopped a few feet inside the door, gave the room the once over, then walked to an empty table and sat down.

Taking another sip of his beer, Parker reminded himself that he was here on business. Gradually, the conversational noise resumed its previous level.

Parker checked his watch for the hundredth time. Eight-twenty five and still no girl with a long black coat. It looked like a no-show. He decided to wait ten more minutes and leave. But where to go now for help, he had no idea. *Probably to the church down the street. It's getting to be desperation time.*

Parker was now drinking plain tonic. His attention wandered back to the gorgeous blonde. During the last twenty minutes, several men had approached her and been turned away. She shifted position and pushed the empty chair at her table around. He choked on his tonic and nearly spit it out. A long black coat lay draped over the back of the chair.

How could I have missed that?

Parker knew he wasn't the shy type, but considering the situation combined with her looks, he found himself hesitant to approach her. Trying to swallow his heart back down into his chest, he rose from his seat. Carrying his drink over to her table, he sat down in the empty chair next to her.

She turned toward him. "I'm sorry, but that seat is taken. My husband is due any minute."

Parker was confused. "You are Susan Beckman, aren't you?"

She half-smiled. "No, I'm not."

Very embarrassed, Parker retreated back toward his table, only to find it occupied. He glanced around. The only available seat in the house appeared to be a lone bar stool. Parker went over and plopped onto it.

"Sorry, but that seat's taken," the woman on the next stool said. "I'm expecting someone."

"Do you mind if I sit here until they show?"

The voice became cold. "They might not show at all with you sitting there on my coat."

As he clued in on her last words, Parker glanced down on the floor between their two stools and there lay a long black coat. It must have slipped off the bar stool before he came over.

Remind me never to use a long black coat for recognition. Everyone has one, and I never notice them anyway.

"Excuse me. Are you Susan Beckman?"

Slowly she pivoted toward him and for the first time he got a good look at her. Long, dark hair framed a beautiful face: prominent cheek bones, a clear tanned complexion, and large dark eyes. She wore a plain black knit dress that accentuated her slender figure. Probably in her late twenties or early thirties.

She stared at Parker while he was taking his inventory, and slowly her features changed.

"You! You're the one that got me here?" she exclaimed, her voice a mixture of surprise and disgust. She moved to get up. "I want nothing to do with you," she hissed.

Parker put up his hands in a stop gesture. "Please, I didn't kill your father. Just hear me out!"

"There's nothing you can say that I want to hear," she said.

"Look," he pleaded as she partially stood and asked for her bar bill, "I didn't murder your father. If you just give me five minutes, I can prove it." He saw her hesitate. "You owe it to him, if no one else."

Susan stared straight ahead, all the while half out of her seat, then finally sat back down. "Don't ask me why, but I'm going to give you your five minutes, then I'm gone."

"I really appreciate this. You won't be sorry," Parker said.

She closed her eyes, and took a deep breath. "Get on with your explanation." Her tone icy.

Parker tried to keep desperation out of his voice. "First, I never knew your father. He was a complete stranger to me when I saw his picture. Second, I have never used or been involved with illicit drugs. Anyone in town who knows me will back that up. Third, I've never owned a gun which the police can confirm. Fourth, your father hired a private detective several weeks ago because he felt someone was trying to kill him. He'd had several near misses…"

She cut him off. "Who was this detective? I'd like to speak with him before I'd believe any of this!"

Parker knew this was coming, but there'd been no way to avoid it. "The detective was Max Pollock. It was his office reception area that you were waiting in when this all happened."

"There was nothing on his office door about him being a detective."

"Max liked to keep a low profile regarding his business, so the door is just marked Max Pollock, Inc." He paused. "Unfortunately, you won't be able to speak with him."

"Why not?"

"He was killed in a car crash two days ago."

She shook her head. "How convenient. Your supporting witness is dead."

"He was enroute to meet with someone concerning your father's death when he was killed."

"Killed? You mean it wasn't an accident?"

Parker shrugged his shoulders. "The official version is an accident, but it seems too coincidental to me."

She reached out for her purse and started to rise. Parker put his hand on her purse. "Please, just give me a few more minutes."

She glared coldly at him and then through him. "Your time is up and I haven't heard anything to change my opinion."

A frantic call interrupted their confrontation. "Help, someone! My husband can't breathe!"

An anxious, white haired lady stood behind an elderly gentleman who had his hands at his throat, choking on something. *Probably his dinner,* Parker thought, seeing a half-empty plate in front of him. While Parker watched, the color drained from the man's face as he struggled to breathe.

For the second time, the noise level in Sorrento's dropped as everyone turned to look at the desperate scene before them. Several men rushed to the choking man, including John the bartender. Parker half-rose, ready to assist, but hoped John was capable. He knew if he went to help, he'd lose his chance with Susan Beckman.

A good Heimlich maneuver should be enough, he rationalized.

John had no problem lifting the victim into the proper position. Standing behind him, John put his arms around the man, locked his hands together just below the man's rib cage, and jerked them up suddenly into the man's stomach, trying to force the air out of the man's lungs to dislodge the food caught in his throat. A perfectly executed Heimlich, yet nothing happened. John tried once more without luck.

Parker hurried to help, pushing his way through the crowd.

The choking victim lay flat on the floor in a stupor. John started mouth-to-mouth resuscitation. Parker told the onlookers to clear back and grabbed a ballpoint pen from one of the nearby waitresses. Kneeling next to the man, he clicked the pen so the tip was out, and then told John to back off. He palpated the man's neck, locating the cricothyroid membrane. He placed the pen at that point and started to push it through the skin into the throat.

As Parker began to push, the man's wife cried, "My God! You're killing him!" She grabbed Parker from behind and began to pull.

"John! Get her off me or this guy is dead!" Parker yelled.

John pulled her off just as the pen punctured through the man's neck into his trachea. Parker unscrewed the top of the pen, removed the metal ink filler, and began blowing into the pen casing which now served as an airway, below the obstruction, into the man's lungs.

After a few minutes of Parker breathing into the pen, a sickly white replaced the blue. The man's pulse, which had been weak and slow, became stronger and faster. His limp extremities began to move. In the distance, Parker heard a siren. Next thing he knew, the paramedics were beside him.

Between breaths into the pen, Parker identified himself as a physician and told them what had happened. He asked for a laryngoscope and a set of long forceps. With one of the paramedics breathing through the pen, Parker used the laryngoscope to look into the patient's mouth and down his throat. He found a piece of meat tightly wedged in his pharynx, at the level of the vocal cords, causing the obstruction to his breathing. Even with the forceps, it proved difficult to remove. No wonder the Heimlich maneuver had been unsuccessful.

With the obstruction now gone, the victim's color became pink and he was able to breath on his own. As the paramedics prepared him for transportation, he opened his eyes. Since it was no longer needed, Parker pulled the pen casing out of the man's neck

The man's wife dropped down on her knees next to her husband and rubbed his forehead. "Jack. I'm right here. You're going to be all right."

Jack slowly looked around, finally focusing on her face. He mumbled a few unintelligible words as the paramedics loaded him onto a stretcher. The wife, tears streaming down her face, stood up and threw her arms around Parker. "Thank you. Oh, thank you so much!" She followed the paramedics as they wheeled her husband out to the ambulance.

The background noise picked up its tempo and the onlookers slowly drifted away. Several of them gave Parker slaps on the back and words of congratulations as he made his way through the crowd.

He couldn't find Susan Beckman at the bar, and all the stools were occupied. Finding an open slot between two stools, Parker leaned up against the bar. Before he could order, John set a drink down in front of him.

"Vodka tonic tall, as you like it. Nice job."

"Thanks, John. I can use this right now."

He smiled. "I bet you can. But don't thank me; thank the lady who bought it for you."

Parker turned in the direction John was pointing and saw Susan Beckman sitting at a small table near the fireplace.

Chapter Nine

"You may wonder why I stayed," Susan said, as Parker sat down at her table with his drink.

"The thought crossed my mind."

"I actually did start to leave, but my morbid curiosity got the better of me." She glanced up at Parker.

He nodded for her to continue.

"When it was over, I wanted to congratulate you like everyone else. Then I remembered who you were and why I was here." She paused. "I was torn with what to do, then decided at least I could wait and hear you out."

"Thank you for this second chance."

"My staying doesn't mean I believe you." Her voice had become a bit more intense. "It only means I've decided to listen to your side of things." She lifted her wine glass and took a long swallow.

"Let me tell it from the beginning," Parker said, "and hold your questions until I'm finished. Okay?"

She agreed, and Parker launched into his tale of death and confusion. He included enough background material about himself, hoping to improve his credibility. By the time he had completed his recital and answered her questions, a good half-hour had passed. Slumping back into his chair, he watched her expectantly.

For several minutes, Susan remained immobile, her gaze fixed at the bottom of her empty glass. Finally, she broke the silence. "The problem with your claim of innocence is that you seem to have forgotten that I'm the one that heard the shots and found you alone in the room with my father. How can you explain that?"

"I can't explain it except to say that I didn't kill him." He lifted his hands. "I know it looks bad, but haven't you heard of 'locked room murders' where the initial obvious solution is later proven to be false."

Susan shook her head. "Unfortunately, this is real life not pulp fiction. And in real life, the obvious solution is usually the right solution."

She pushed back her chair and stood. "I'm not sure why you want to convince me of your innocence. You should save your energy for the jury." She lifted her coat from the back of her chair and began to put it on.

Parker rose and tried to help her, but she eased away.

Edging closer, he said, "I've tried to convince you because I need some questions answered about your father."

"Then you have wasted your evening. I haven't been involved with my father's life for years." She shook her long hair free from the confines of the coat.

"You still know a lot more about him than I do."

She grimaced. "I know that basically he was a nice man and you killed him. Nothing changes that. Now if you'll excuse me."

She started for the door but Parker crossed in front of her, blocking her path. "Please. Just answer two quick questions about your father and I won't bother you again."

She looked up at him. "Just two questions?"

Parker nodded.

"Okay, ask them."

Parker glanced around. "Why don't we either sit back down or step outside. I feel a little awkward with everyone staring at us."

Susan gestured toward the entrance. As they left, Parker nodded a goodbye to John.

They stepped from the warm confines of Sorrento's into the cool of the evening. The stars were out in magnificent array, acting as a backdrop for a full moon that lit up the empty streets. The only sound in the night was the wind whistling gently through the pine trees.

"Go on, ask your questions," Susan said.

"I know your father spent time in jail for embezzlement, but was he ever involved with drugs? Either using or selling them?"

Susan took her time before answering. "As far as I know, he was never mixed up with drugs on any level. He was even against the use of marijuana."

"So didn't it seem strange that he was killed over a drug deal?"

"Yes, but I assumed that prison changed him."

Parker nodded. "Okay. Next question. Did your father ever own or use a gun in the past?"

"No, he didn't. And again, I felt it was the effects of prison." She tossed her hair back and started to turn away. Parker reached out and lightly touched her arm.

"One more question, please?" Parker asked. She shrugged her shoulders and turned back toward him.

"How was your father supporting himself after being released from prison?"

Susan lifted her coat collar up around her neck against the night air.

"He had some bonds which he cashed and I lent him some money. He told me that he wanted to relax for a few months and then he would start searching for work." She looked up at Parker. "And with that, our question-and-answer period is over."

"While you're lying in bed tonight, ask yourself if it all makes sense. Would your anti-drug, anti-gun father, recently out of jail, apparently with adequate funds, suddenly be involved with a cocaine deal and have a gun with him? Do you think he could have changed that much?"

For almost a minute, Susan stared down at the ground. Then abruptly, she turned and walked away, heading up the sidewalk.

Parker's car was a block down on the other side of the street. He stepped off the curb and started angling in that direction. He'd gone about fifteen yards when he heard his name screamed from behind him. He spun around to look for Susan. Not twenty feet away, a car with its lights off raced toward him. He lunged toward the curb, diving over the front hood of an automobile parked there, but he didn't quite make it. The speeding car smacked his feet and sent him spinning into space.

##

"Shit. I had the son of a bitch." The blond man struck the steering wheel with his palm. "Who the hell screamed?"

His dark-haired companion took a long sip of his beer before replying, "That chick he was with." He tossed the empty bottle into the back seat, picked another bottle out of the six-pack at his feet, and twisted the cap off.

"Pass me one of those, Carlos," the blond said.

Carlos handed him the opened bottle, and grabbed another for himself. They drank in silence. The blond was the first to speak.

"What'd you think?" he asked.

"I don't think you killed him."

The blond nodded. "Remind me not to steal one of these pissant foreign cars next time. No pick up and no hitting power."

##

When Parker opened his eyes, all he saw was an intense white light, so bright that it made his head hurt. He raised his hand to push it away and the light vanished, but the headache remained. He rubbed his eyes to clear his vision. When it did, he found himself looking up into the face of the neurosurgeon, Bill Logan.

Logan set the flashlight down. "Seems like deja-vooo to me, Park," he said, exaggerating his southern accent.

Parker realized he was in one of the emergency department exam rooms. "How did I end up here?"

"Ambulance brought you in." Bill smiled. "You were playin' bumper cars, only you didn't have a car. Got a nice whack on the head when you hit the ground."

Parker put his hand up to his throbbing head and felt a huge lump of bandage.

"Don't worry. You have a large scalp hematoma, but only a small laceration over it. Couple of stitches should close it." Logan rolled up his sleeves. "There's no indication of anything more serious, but I'm going to get a CAT scan of your head to be safe and keep you overnight for observation. You should be out in the morning."

Parker felt too much pain to argue. "One request, Bill."

Logan looked up from the suture set he was opening. "What's that?"

"No handcuffs this time."

While suturing, Logan relayed what he knew about the accident. Susan had seen the careening car and yelled when she realized the danger. Her scream had attracted a couple leaving Sorrento's, and they'd run back in and called for an ambulance. Susan had stayed with Parker until the paramedics arrived and then followed them up to the hospital.

Logan chuckled. "Hell, it'd be worth getting hit by a car just to have that little filly hovering by my bedside when I awoke."

"I'd like to agree with you, Bill, but all I see hovering by my bedside is a tired old surgeon," Parker replied.

Logan laughed. "Just gimme a minute and I'll get her in here."

It was more like ten minutes before he was done and Susan arrived. Hesitantly, she looked around the room, then came over to the X-ray table where Parker was lying.

"How are you feeling?" she asked.

"Alive, thanks to you," he answered.

"Oh, yeah. Like I did so much."

"Well, you did save my life, and according to an old Chinese custom I am now your responsibility."

"Since I'm not Chinese, I'll pass on that one." Her expression became somber. "It seemed so deliberate. I really can't believe it. The car had its lights off. After it struck you and scraped a parked car, it just kept going. The driver must have known he'd hit something."

Parker groaned as he sat up and put his legs over the side of the table. "Max, the detective I mentioned earlier, warned me this might happen."

"That what might happen?"

"Someone might try to kill me. He thought it was a mistake that I'd survived the shooting, so now it was even more important that I didn't continue to survive."

Susan stared wide-eyed at him. Turning away, Parker gingerly felt the right side of his chest where he'd landed.

"I think Max made only one mistake," he said.

"What was that?"

"He thought I was the only one they wanted dead."

The CAT scan showed no evidence of cerebral trauma, just a small collection of blood under the scalp. The X-rays revealed no evidence of rib fractures.

"All in all, a pretty boring case of trauma," Logan said.

"I'll be happy to trade," Parker replied. "You can feel like you've been worked over by a professional boxer and I'll be bored."

Logan grinned. "No thanks, my friend." He admitted Parker for overnight observation, and went home.

Susan left soon after. She'd been both silent and pensive at Parker's bedside. He wasn't certain whether she'd been more shaken by the deliberate murder attempt she'd witnessed, or the fact that his claim of innocence might actually be true.

They'd decided this was too much to contemplate at this time of night, especially since Parker was starting to feel the aftershock of his trauma and could barely keep his eyes open. They agreed to meet in the morning and discuss the whole thing.

##

"Hi. Detective Hall? Ray Stone from the D.A.'s office."

"What can I do for you, Mr. Stone?" Hall looked at his wife and rolled his eyes. She reached across the table and picked up his dinner plate. "I'll keep it warm for you," she whispered as she walked toward the kitchen.

"The McGraw-Beckman case has been dropped in my lap. I've reviewed all the reports. Seen all the evidence. Now I want an update on your investigation. What directions you're taking? That kind of stuff."

"We're pursing three lines of investigation, Mr. Stone. First. Trying to establish prior contact between Beckman and McGraw. Second. Demonstrate some previous connection between drugs and either Beckman or McGraw. Lastly. Search for a motive for the killing, other than the obvious."

Stone was silent for a moment. "What's wrong with the obvious? A drug dealer and his buyer got into an argument and killed each other. Happens every day."

"But why these two? Beckman has no past history of violent crimes and neither does McGraw. And yet they both show up armed to the teeth, ready to use their weapons."

The line was silent for a moment, and then Stone spoke.

"My philosophy is keep it simple. As you know, the prosecution doesn't have to supply a motive. So trying to find some esoteric reason for what happened will just confuse the issue, and more importantly, the jury."

Hall's grip on the phone tightened as he tried to keep his voice loose. "Stone, since we're talking philosophies here, I'll give you mine: No one tells me how to run a case." He paused. "And I do keep it simple. I let the D.A.'s office do the prosecuting while I do the investigating." He paused again. "Any questions?"

"Look, Hall. I don't give a goddamn what you do as long as you don't screw up this case. I'm just offering advice. Take it or leave it."

They hung up and Hall went back to finishing his dinner.

"You don't look happy, Ivan. What's the matter?" his wife asked.

"Usually I enjoy working with the D.A.'s office. But that's one guy who always rubs me wrong." He took a bite and chewed. "What's worse, I don't trust him."

Chapter Ten

After being transferred from the E.R. to a regular hospital bed, Parker had just fallen asleep when the nurse came in to do a neuro check - a quick exam to make sure that he was neurologically stable and that his sleeping was exactly that, not him slipping into coma.

At first the checks were every hour and then later, every two hours. She would wake him, ask a few questions and have him perform several simple motor tasks. He'd just fall back to sleep and it would be time for the next check.

In the morning, Detective Hall paid him a visit. Hall explained that the Carmel police had been contacted last night about the "accident" since it occurred in their jurisdiction. Parker had been spared from questioning then because Logan had claimed he was in no condition to be interviewed until he'd had some rest.

"When I saw your name on our accident report this morning, I offered to do the interview for them," Hall said, after he settled into a chair.

"You mean `interrogation', don't you?" Parker answered.

"Feeling a little paranoid this morning, doctor?" Hall said. "Look, I saw your name on the report and was... concerned. That's all."

"Yeah, concerned that your shoe-in murder conviction was almost killed before his trial." Parker said. "And if there's no trial, there's no conviction credit to put on your record. Right?"

Hall stared back, his face expressionless.

"I'm not pressing charges," Parker said. "I was in the middle of the street and some poor bastard didn't see me. Let's leave it at that."

##

"Dammit! Can't you do anything right?" The man stood up, walked around from behind his desk, and glared down at the blond man seated before him. "McGraw's survival jeopardizes us all."

"But he knows nothing!" the blond man responded defensively.

"Are you willing to stake your life on it?"

The blond man hung his head. "No, I guess not."

"Do you have some reluctance in removing him?"

The blond snickered. "Did you notice any reluctance with the others?"

"No, in fact you have been most ingenious." The man lifted a long white lab jacket off the oak coat rack and put it on. He paused in the middle of buttoning the coat and looked up. "My sources tell me that the case against McGraw is iron clad." He smiled to himself." Maybe we should let the state finish the job for us." He laughed. "How poetic."

"So what do I do, sir?" the blond asked.

The man finished buttoning his jacket, and then moved to a wall mirror to check his appearance. "For now, just keep an eye on him." He straightened his tie. "But have no hesitation in terminating him if the need arises."

##

Parker caught an Uber home from the hospital, unlocked the front door, and plopped into his deeply cushioned Morris chair. It was only 10 a.m.. He looked around his small domicile and sighed. Nothing had changed - his dirty laundry still lay on the bedroom floor, the dishes were still waiting in the sink, and his unopened bills sat on his desk.

He closed his eyes, trying to decide what to do. With his head injuries and various bruises, exercise was out of the question. He did the next best thing. He lay down and slept. When he awoke several hours later, he was ready to go out and slay some dragons. Small ones, of course.

The first item on his agenda was Susan. Last night she'd begun to have doubts about his guilt. Parker wanted to encourage these doubts to the point she might help him explore her father's past and maybe find a reason why Beckman's life might have been in danger.

He knew Jeff would tell him to leave this to his own investigator. But he wouldn't be back in town for several days to even a week, and Parker couldn't sit passively waiting for his return.

Parker punched in Susan's hotel number.

The desk clerk answered. "I'm sorry. Ms. Beckman has checked out."

"What? Are you sure?" Parker asked.

"Quite sure," he replied.

Parker was dumbfounded. "Ah... did she leave a message for a Dr. McGraw, or give another local contact?"

The clerk was silent for a moment. "Apparently not, sir."

The sand felt squeaky smooth under Parker's feet as he strolled along Carmel Beach. He doubted that the beach had changed much from when Vizcaino had first seen it in 1602 from the surrounding hills or when Portola, the next to find it in 1769, viewing it from the sea. The sight remained a glorious one, Parker knew, from whatever vantage point.

The beach is a long strip of fine white sand bound on either end by rocky headlands. The northern point is topped by the lush green of the Pebble Beach golf course, while the southern headland is covered with homes and pine trees. Expensive homes are spaced along a cliff rising above the sand strip, and set back far enough to minimally intrude on the serenity of the beach.

Today, a large fog bank obscured the offshore horizon, but the beach and its prominences were bathed in bright sunlight. The rhythmic sound of his feet slapping the wet sand and the waves pounding the shoreline began to clear his head and he let his mind drift over the events of the last few days.

No matter which tact he'd tried, he'd run into a dead end. The police had shown no interest in investigating anyone else. Max's findings had gone to the grave with him. Beckman's past remained a closed book. And now Susan had deserted him.

An attractive redhead, walking her golden retriever along the sand, passed Parker, and he noticed she wore a Big Sur River Run T-shirt. It made him think of Max Pollock. Year after year, Max had tried to convince him to join the River Run, a 10K race through the redwoods of Big Sur. A Dixieland band played at the finish, along with enough beer to make one forget they'd even broken a sweat. Max hadn't been a runner, but he had been a true bon vivant, and had rarely missed such events.

If only Max given more details when he phoned, Parker thought. And then, he realized Max had dropped a clue during the phone call after all.

Chapter Eleven

Parker called Max's office as soon as he returned from the beach, and luck had been with him. Max's secretary was there attending to last minute details regarding the business. He asked her for a record of Max's phone calls made during the week prior to his death.

"I'm afraid I can't help you, Dr. McGraw. Our office phone bill won't be here for another two weeks." She was apologetic but her tone conveyed a lack of interest.

"Look, I don't think Max's death was an accident." Parker explained. "I think it's tied in with whatever Max was investigating for Beckman."

"But Dr. McGraw, there is no evidence that Mr. Beckman was ever seen by Mr. Pollock. No bills. No files. Nothing to connect the two," she responded.

"What about the recording I played for you the other night? Wasn't that Max's voice."

She remained silent. "Yes. Yes, it was." She paused again. "But why a list of his phone calls?"

"Max had been on his way to meet with someone in Big Sur. He must have made an appointment, and to do that, he probably used the office phone. That phone bill should list any calls he made to Big Sur. If we find out who he called, maybe then we can find out why two people have died."

"I'm afraid I still can't help, but I know someone who can. Her name is Mary Getty. She's been Max's inside source at the phone company."

Parker immediately dialed the new number.

"AT&T Headquarters."

"Mary Getty, please."

"One moment." The elevator music seemed to last forever.

"Hi. This is Mary." The voice completely impersonal.

"I need your help to catch Max Pollock's killer." Parker had decided on the direct approach.

"Who is this?"

"My name is Parker McGraw and I was a close friend of Max's."

A sharp intake of breath. "Dr. McGraw? The one accused of murder?" she asked.

Parker knew she was about to hang up. "Wait!" he yelled into the phone. "Max was trying to prove my innocence when he died. He was killed in a car crash, but it was no accident."

Several seconds passed. "Go on," she said tersely.

He explained the background behind Max's investigation and the series of events that had lead up to his supposed accident. At first, Mary Getty's tone was hostile and suspicious, but gradually she began to loosen up.

Hoping to add the finishing touch, Parker offered to pay her at whatever rate Max had used.

The silence was deafening, lasting almost a full minute before she replied in a hoarse, strained voice. "You couldn't afford it."

Parker waited for more and finally it came.

"My husband was killed in Afghanistan. Max and I dated for a bit, during which time he became the surrogate father my young son so desperately needed. He turned my son's life around." I heard a catch in her voice. "So don't talk to me about money!"

"I'm sorry. I didn't know," Parker answered.

When she did speak again, her voice was hesitant. "I'm not sure about you, McGraw. But if there is a chance Max was murdered, and this might help find that person, I'm all in. What do you need?"

"A list of all calls made from Max's office or home to the Big Sur area during the four days prior to his death. Since cell phone reception is so poor down there, most people have land lines."

Parker sat out on his deck waiting for Mary's call. The day continued to be beautiful, and in Carmel one made the most of them since the weather was so variable.

His cell phone rang.

"I've just been notified by Ray Stone of the D. A.'s office that they're going to try and step the trial date up," Jeff Gilman said.

"Is that a good thing?"

"Not really. We need more time to establish our case. I figure Stone is hoping to make a reputation, and doesn't want this trial too long out of the public eye." Jeff paused. "But hang loose. I'll get us more time."

Parker made an appointment to meet with Jeff the next day and hung up. He'd just finishing some stretching exercises when Mary called back.

"I've found a total of six calls Max made to Big Sur during that specific time period," she said.

"Excellent."

"To save you time, I checked our records for the names and addresses associated with those phone numbers. That's what took me so long." She then went on and listed each of them.

Thanking her profusely, Parker hung up and went over the list. Four of the calls had been to restaurants in the area, while the other two had been to a William Harris. The restaurants had street addresses, but Harris only had a post office box. Parker tried phoning him but got no answer. On a hunch, he phoned each of the restaurants and asked for Bill Harris. With the third attempt, he got lucky. Harris worked there as a waiter but wasn't expected in until the following evening.

Parker had no intention of waiting until then to meet with Harris, so he gave them a song and dance routine about Harris having left some tools on his porch for Parker to pick up. Unfortunately, he'd lost the directions to Harris' house after driving all the way down from Monterey. Yes, he tried the phone but there was no answer. No, he couldn't wait for Harris to come into work. He needed the tools for a job today.

With a little more of this, he eventually wrangled directions to Harris' home.

Driving down the coast on Highway 1, Parker thought it a perfect afternoon to be heading to Big Sur. Minimal breeze, not a cloud in the sky, and a weekday so the traffic remained light. He turned up the radio volume as the highway dropped down to Monastery Beach.

The location is named for the Carmelite Monastery that sits on the hillside on the opposite side of the roadway. The beach is a long expanse of curving white sand nestled amongst aqua blue waters and craggy rock formations. A favorite picnic site for out of town visitors.

Parker slowed as the roadway curved past the entrance to Point Lobos, the state park just south of Monastery Beach. The inlets and bays of the park used to be filled with sea lions which the Spanish called sea wolves (lobos), hence the name.

Entering a sharp curve, he downshifted and then accelerated out of the turn. He was driving his restored 1964 Porsche 356C. The inside was about as glamorous as a stripped down VW bug, and the engine merely a souped up VW four cylinder. The handling, though, was definitely not VW. Even back in the early 60's, the Germans knew how to make a car that would hold the road.

Before leaving town, Parker had stopped at Jeff's office. They had discussed the case, possible avenues to explore, and varying defense options. Jeff's investigator, Dave Vicker, was due back in several days, and Jeff assured Parker that his only priority would be his case.

"I know that you want action now, and the thought of waiting is driving you crazy, but that's what you have to do," Jeff had said. "Dave is excellent. He was a detective in LA for 20 years before retiring and opening his own investigative business. If there is anything to find, he's the man to do it."

Parker had no intention of waiting for some unknown investigator to chase down the lead he had discovered.

Bill Harris lived in The Coastlands. This was a small conclave of homes, thinly scattered over the hills that extended from Highway 1 down to the ocean, and inter-connected by a labyrinth of one lane dirt roads.

After driving into the Coastlands entrance, Parker promptly got lost in the network of unmarked lanes. Forty minutes, three wrong turns, several discussions with various neighbors, and he found Harris' residence.

It was a small one story, faded redwood house on the side of a canyon, with a limited view of the ocean. *All in all, not bad on a waiter's salary. I wonder about his other sources of income?*

He pulled into the driveway, next to an old Jeep pickup, and climbed out. No one answered the door after several minutes of knocking and yelling. Circling around the house, he still couldn't find anyone. He did discover a small marijuana garden in the back, but having that in Big Sur was like having a pool in suburbia.

Returning to the front porch, Parker pondered his next move and in the process noticed the absence of any near neighbors. He tried the front door, and found it unlocked.

With a last look around, he turned the door knob and stepped into a small, tidy living room. Immediately, he heard voices in the back of the house. He wondered how they'd missed his pounding at the door, and then stopped wondering when he got closer and heard the conversation. Although the voices were muffled, the words were distinct enough.

"You can't hope to get away with it. They'll find out you murdered him and then they'll be after me," said a husky female voice.

A cocky baritone voice answered back. "Not the way I set it up. It's the all-time great frame job. That poor schmuck will take the fall and I'll be long gone."

"You mean we'll be long gone, don't you," the girl asked.

Baritone voice gave a snide laugh. "Sorry, baby. There's been a change of plans. You're the only one who can connect me with the murder and that won't do."

Parker now stood just outside the room where the conversation was taking place. The door was partially closed, blocking any view of the interior.

With no stretch of the imagination, Parker knew he was the 'schmuck' they were talking about, and whomever 'baby' was, he would need her to prove his innocence. Although their voices sounded strange, he stopped thinking about it when he heard 'baby' scream. Adrenaline surging, he kicked open the door and charged into the room. Just as he entered, a shot rang out. He did a rolling dive onto the floor and came up on his feet ready for action, only to find the source of the voices -- a television.

He snapped it off in disgust.

The smell and the flies told him he wasn't alone. A man lay sprawled on the bed in the corner. If he was Bill Harris, he was done waiting tables.

Parker walked over and stared down at the body. As the initial shock gradually dissipated and he became accustomed to the odor, Parker's clinical interest returned. What had caused Harris' death? There was no sign of violence. No blood stained sheets. He'd almost convinced himself that it might be natural causes, when he noticed the empty pill bottle on the floor next to the bed.

Overdose? He moved the vial gingerly with his shoe so he could see the label. Secobarbital 100mg. Take as directed. Number 100. Refill 5. *My God, who the hell is giving out barbs in quantities like that?*

At the bottom of the label was the prescribing doctor's name. Parker felt a chill clear through as he read the name: Parker McGraw, MD.

The sheriff's office said it would take over an hour to respond to Parker's call in this remote area.

Parker had debated about slipping away, but there were too many loose threads that could incriminate him: Mary Getty giving him the phone number, the neighbors supplying him with directions, and of course, any fingerprints that he'd inadvertently left in the house.

But before calling the sheriff's department, he'd removed the label from the pill bottle and flushed it down the toilet. Then after wiping the pill vial clean of fingerprints, he'd tossed it down the canyon.

How his name had gotten on that prescription, Parker had no idea. Why his name was on it was a different matter. Until he'd seen his name on the prescription, Parker had assumed that Harris' death was a run-of-the-mill overdose -- Harris had just been too careless with the number of pills he'd ingested. Finding the vial made Parker reevaluate the whole scene.

Overdose or calculated murder, he wondered, standing over Harris' corpse. He tried to recall all the nuances of a barbiturate overdose. 'Barb blisters' were the first physical finding to come to mind. When the normal person lies down to sleep, he is continually tossing and turning throughout the night, never lying in one position for any length of time. As a result, no one part of the anatomy has to bear the body's weight for a prolonged period. With a drug overdose, all is changed. The person, heavily sedated from the drug, will lay in the same position, immobile, for many hours. This unrelenting pressure to the supporting areas of the body impairs the blood flow to the skin in those regions, resulting in tissue damage which takes the form of a blister. With barbiturate ingestions, these have been referred to as "barb blisters".

Harris appeared to have died from a barbiturate overdose, of which the natural course is somnolence, followed by a prolonged period of deepening coma and respiratory depression, eventually resulting in death if no one intervenes. Enough time for blisters to develop.

Wearing only boxer shorts, Harris was stretched out flat on his back. Parker knelt next to him, and gently lifted his shoulder while at the same time pushing down on the mattress, trying to observe the skin on his back without really moving the body.

He found no evidence of blister formation in any of the expected locations, but that could have several explanations. One, the bed was so soft that the pressure was minimal and therefore the stimulus for blister formation was absent. Two, Harris had died so quickly that blister formation never had a chance to occur. But why would he die quickly from what Parker had assumed to be a recreational use of barbiturates? A chronic user might make an error in judgment, but usually not so great that he would immediately succumb... unless it was a suicide. Yet Parker found no note to suggest that possibility.

With careful examination, he found a vein in the right lower leg with a small hematoma, a collection of blood which may leak out of a blood vessel into the surrounding tissues if the vessel has been injured, such as stuck with a needle.

Harris may have ingested some pills, knowingly or unknowingly, but what'd killed him was whatever someone had injected into his vein while he was out.

That someone, Parker decided, had gone to a lot of trouble to eliminate Max's potential informant and, in the process, to incriminate him. He could imagine the police's reaction to his claims of innocence regarding Beckman's drug related murder after it appeared he was handing out barbs like candy and someone had died as a result.

Parker was sitting on Harris' front porch steps when the sheriff's cruiser pulled up. Two officers climbed out of the green and white and briskly approached him.

"Good afternoon, sir," said the older of the two, removing his reflecting lenses. "Are you the one that called in the report?"

"Yes, I did officer," Parker replied.

Brushing his thinning gray hair back into place with his hand, the older officer spoke over his shoulder to his short, dark-haired partner. "Carl, why don't you get his story while I look around?"

The junior officer pulled out a small notebook. "I just need to ask a few questions, if you don't mind. Let's start with your name."

"Parker McGraw."

"What's the purpose of your visit here, Mr. McGraw.?"

"I wanted to ask Mr. Harris a few questions."

"Is Harris the person you found inside?"

"I think so. I've never meet him, but this is supposed to be his home."

"What's your relationship with Mr. Harris?" Suddenly, the officer's eyes got bigger and he straightened up. "Wait a minute. Are you the Dr. McGraw who was recently arrested?"

"Yes, the same."

The officer nodded his head slowly several times. "Explain again what you're doing here."

Trying to keep his story short and without frills, Parker said, "I came down to see Harris because there's a possibility he might have information that would be helpful in the case that is pending against me."

"I'm aware of that case, doctor." The officer looked up from his note book. "There were drugs involved in that situation, weren't there?"

Parker could see where this was going and decided to head it off. "I was with friends in a busy Carmel restaurant from seven until ten pm last night, then under observation for a head injury in

Community Hospital from ten until this morning. If you check the time of death, I think you'll find I'm covered."

"I wasn't insinuating anything, doctor. Merely making an observation." His look of disappointment, though, spoke a different story.

After that exchange, the remaining questions became more routine, ending with the usual warning to keep himself available for any further inquiries.

Inside the house, the senior officer's voice could be heard on the phone asking for the crime unit to come down and bring an ambulance. "No. No rush on the ambulance."

##

Across the canyon from Harris' house, two men stood in the shade of a large pine tree.

"Son of a bitch! They're lettin' the asshole go," the blond said as he handed the binoculars to Carlos.

"Bernie, the guy's not dumb. He must have found the pill bottle and ditched it before the sheriff arrived."

"Shit! I told the boss if we're not going to kill this jerk, we should at least put him out of commission. Now he goes and screws up a beautiful frame." The blond climbed into the black Trans Am and angrily slammed the door. "Come on or we're going to lose him," he shouted at his companion.

Carlos settled into the passenger seat as the car accelerated down the narrow dirt road and slid around the corner, sending up a rooster tail of dirt and gravel.

##

Parker had no difficulty finding his way back to the main highway. Twenty yards before he reached the blacktop, he noticed a group of mailboxes on the opposite side of the dirt road. Drawing closer, he saw one with Harris' name on it. He stopped his car, walked over to the box, and checked its contents. Two business flyers, a letter, and a postcard. He heard a car coming up the road behind him. Since the road was only wide enough for one vehicle at this spot, Parker grabbed the mail, returned to his car, and drove off.

Half a mile later, he pulled off into the parking lot of the Pfeiffer Big Sur State Park. He briefly thumbed through the mail. Finding nothing of importance, he dropped it on the seat next to him, and climbed out, in search of a cold soda at the camp store.

When he strolled out of the store, cold drink in hand, he noticed a black Trans Am parked near his car. The door on the driver's side of Parker's vehicle was open and a dark-haired, wiry man with a pony tail leaned inside. His companion, a huge muscular blond, sat perched against the Porsche's rear-end.

Parker descended the store steps and walked toward his car. The blond saw him and rapped on the Porsche window. The dark-haired man looked up, closed the car door, and moved over next to the blond.

As Parker drew closer, the blond pulled his right hand out of his jacket, and tucked it behind his back. He did it so casually that Parker wouldn't have noticed if the sun hadn't glinted off something metallic in his hand.

This is definitely not a couple of old car buffs. Not with brass knuckles.

Parker glanced around. Not another person in sight. Everyone else seemed to be in the store. Continuing his approach, Parker put his unopened soda behind his back and began to shake it.

"You guys interested in buying my Porsche?" he asked. "I'd be happy to sell it at a bargain rate."

The blond giant smiled, and Parker saw him nod slightly to the other man. "Yeah," the blond replied, sarcastically, "we're real interested in the car. How much you want for it?" While the blond spoke, the dark-haired man nonchalantly moved away from him.

Parker was now within ten feet of them. He focused on the blond, who appeared to be the more dangerous of the two.

"Well, let me open my soda and we can dicker about it," Parker said as he brought the can from behind him and thrust it out to the blond. "Here, have a sip."

The blond looked down at the soda as Parker popped the tab open. The soda exploded, showering the blond's face. Crying out in surprise, he threw his hands up to his eyes, at which point, Parker kicked him hard in the stomach, doubling him over with pain. Grabbing the blond's head, he pulled it down to meet his swiftly rising knee. The impact was brutal, crumpling the blond amidst the sound of splintering cartilage and a metallic bang as the brass knuckles hit the ground.

Parker dropped into a fighting stance and spun to the right, where he had last seen the dark-haired man. He was no longer there. A powerful kick smashed into Parker's left flank, throwing him up against the Porsche.

Ignoring the pain, Parker quickly turned to face his attacker. The dark-haired man attempted another kick but Parker blocked it and made a straight finger thrust into the man's face, hoping to stab his eyes. The man brushed the thrust aside and kicked out at Parker's stomach. He managed to turn and lessen the impact, but even so, it rocked him, leaving him breathless and nauseated.

Slowly they circled, each weighing the other, searching for an opening. The dark-haired stranger feigned a straight kick which Parker moved to counter. This changed to a roundhouse kick, catching Parker on the side of the head, staggering him. Quickly, the dark-haired man stepped in and delivered two vicious punches to Parker's left side. Backing away, Parker tried to shake off the effects of the head and body blows.

The attacker tried another kick which Parker blocked. Using his momentum, Parker continued with a spinning motion into a three-hundred-and-sixty degree turn, aiming his foot with all its power at the dark-haired assailant's head. The man effortlessly dodged it and kicked Parker full in the back, tossing him up against the Porsche.

Parker slid to his knees, the wind knocked out of him. He knew he couldn't take another hit like that and hope to walk away. In fact, he didn't think he could take another hit.

Groaning, Parker pulled himself up, leaning heavily against the car. It was now or never. As Yoki, his old instructor, would say, "It is the time of the possum. One must feign weakness in order to gain strength."

Parker remained against the car, his back to the dark-haired assailant, trying to appear beaten and defenseless. With what felt like broken ribs and several crushed vertebrae, it wasn't hard.

Closing his eyes, Parker blocked out all other sounds, intent on listening for just one thing. The silence seemed to go on forever before he heard it. The assailant's sudden intake of breath. The sound that starts the move. Parker twisted toward the sound, bringing up his left hand in anticipation of the kick he prayed was coming. And it was.

With his left arm, he partially deflected the incoming kick without lessening its force. The man's foot continued its slightly altered course, scraping Parker's side, and crashing through the Porsche's back side window. The safety glass broke and telescoped inward but didn't break away as his foot went through. When the dark-haired man tried to pull his foot out of the hole, the window glass closed back around the foot and held it tight.

Parker, now facing his assailant, wrapped his left arm around the man's imprisoned leg and brought his knee up into the man's exposed groin with all the force he had. And then did it again.

The dark-haired man collapsed with a soft groan.

What's this guy made of? I'd be screaming.

Parker managed to pull his attacker's foot out of the Porsche window, then opened the car door and started to climb inside. He never made it.

A huge pair of hands clamped around his neck and began to squeeze. *The blond! How'd I forget him?!* Parker struggled to pry the fingers apart, but it was like trying to open a locked safe with bare hands. He attempted to stomp on the blond's instep, then kick his shins, but the blond easily dodged the attempts. Parker's vision began to gray over as his strength rapidly ebbed. In desperation, he pushed back against the blond, forcing him up against the Trans Am but the vice-like hold on Parker's neck never slackened.

His vision now began to go black. With a last feeble attempt to survive, Parker reached back with his right hand, grabbed the blond's testicles, and squeezed them with all he had left. Through a fog, he imagined a high pitched noise and then the pressure on his neck suddenly lessened.

Parker mind was now a blur. He couldn't remember why he was squeezing whatever was in his right hand, but he knew he had to continue. *If I let off, I'm dead.* Then he blacked out.

"Hey, fella, you okay?"

The voice was so distant that Parker didn't think it could be addressing him. Besides, he wanted to keep sleeping. He felt exhausted.

"I think he's dead. Should I do CPR on him?" That distant voice again.

"Okay. I'll give him mouth to mouth and you pump on his chest." There was a pause, then a loud voice, "Hell, I don't know what the ratio of pumps to breaths is, just do it!"

Parker felt something clamped over his mouth and then someone tried to inflate his lungs to twice their normal size. About the same time, he experienced a crushing pain on the center of his chest.

Coughing, choking, spitting, Parker came fully awake and tried to push himself up. His vision, at first hazy, slowly cleared. He found himself the center of attention with people standing around him and two kneeling next to him. Confused, he stared at them for several seconds before he remembered why he was stretched out in the Pfeiffer State Park parking lot.

Two people helped him up and guided him to the front porch of the store, where they settled him into a chair. He tried to speak, but the words barely squeaked out. He remained quiet, letting his strength return, while his rescuers told their story.

One of the store patrons had come out and saw the blond strangling Parker. He quickly notified the store clerk who phoned the ranger. By the time the two of them came out of the store, a small crowd had formed around Parker, who lay unconscious. His two assailants were gingerly piling into a black Trans Am.

"They was both walkin' kind of carefully, if you know what I mean," the clerk added. He gestured to a man standing next to him.

"Frank, here, took some video on his phone," the owner said. "But all he got was the backside of those two guys, and their mud smeared license plate as they drove off."

Parker could only mumble a thank you, his voice still hoarse from his throat trauma. By the time the park ranger arrived to interview him, Parker could speak with slightly more clarity.

The ranger made it clear that filling out a lot of government forms, which was necessary if Parker elected to make an official complaint, was not a job he relished. Croaking out a long description of what had happened and knowing that nothing would come of it, was not Parker's idea of fun either. Even if the law did find his assailants, they would rightfully claim that he had struck the first blow and they were merely protecting themselves.

In the end, the ranger took Parker's explanation that it was a friendly argument that had gotten a little out of hand. He didn't believe it, but he was happy to avoid the paper work.

The ranger started to walk away then turned back. "You'd better walk wide around those boys. Next time, you might not be so lucky."

Chapter Twelve

On his drive back from Big Sur, Parker decided he'd spend the night in bed, covered with ice packs, and zonked out on pain meds. He wondered why the two men had assaulted him. He felt sure they had followed him from the Coastlands because he remembered their car coming up behind him at the mailboxes.

The only thing that makes sense is they wanted to limit further investigation. The type of limitation one gets from a professional beating... and those guys were professionals if nothing else.

He was still trying to put the pieces together when he pulled into his driveway. A hot shower, bottle of water, and several ibuprofens later, he felt more comfortable, or at least less like he was dying. He curled up in the softness of his Morris chair and reviewed his options. They were damn few. In fact, he could only think of one.

With little hope, he called telephone information. Surprisingly, Michael Beckman had a land line and an address in Carmel. Parker tried the phone, but got no answer suggesting the house might be empty. Over the next few hours, he tried several more times with the same results.

Near midnight, Parker parked his car down the street from Beckman's house, and switched off his lights.

The street, one block long, with trees arching over much of its length, resembled more a country lane than a city avenue. The closest street lamp stood near the end of the block, so enshrouded by trees that little of its illumination extended to Beckman's single story home.

A natural fence of Japanese boxwood, standing shoulder height, stretched across the front yard and then angled in, lining the edge of the driveway up to the garage. The hedge was interrupted by a small wooden gate near the garage, and another larger more ornate gate fronting on the street. The house was classic Carmel with board and batten construction, and a Carmel stone fireplace. Flower boxes hung under the windows. Not the type of residence Parker would have associated with a man like Beckman, but then he'd never known the man.

The smaller gate opened without a sound. Once inside the front yard, Parker used a pencil flashlight to find his way around toward the back.

Moving along the side of the building, Parker tested the windows but they were all locked. A set of French doors opened onto a brick patio in the back, but were also locked.

"Probably the only house that's locked in Carmel, and it's owned by a crook," he swore as he pulled out a roll of masking tape.

He bent over the French doors and, using his tape, crisscrossed a window pane set at the level of the door handle. With a sharp tap, he hit the window with the butt of his flashlight. The sound of glass breaking shattered the stillness of the evening. Parker crouched back in the shadows waiting for the inevitable dog to bark, lights to flicker on, or sirens to start.

Nothing.

The masking tape had kept the broken window pane in place. Parker removed several of the larger pieces, reached in, and unlocked the door.

With his flashlight on, he went in search of Michael Beckman. Or at least what this house could tell him.

He entered a small dining room. Off to his right lay a tiny kitchen, while in front of him, the living room. He walked forward, flashing his light around. The house was sparsely decorated with several pieces of worn furniture, two bookcases, and a small throw rug. No personal items.

A doorway at the right of the room appeared in the beam of his flashlight. Crossing the living room, his foot struck a small brass spittoon and set it spinning and clanging across the floor. He waited for his hands to stop shaking before he ventured further.

Once through the doorway, he found himself in a long hallway with several rooms opening off to his left. The first three, a bathroom and two bedrooms, were basically empty. At the end of the hall where the master bedroom should be, was a closed door.

The door knob felt cold in his hand as he turned it and stepped into the darkened room. He sensed a sudden movement to his left. Immediately, he twisted to his right, but not fast enough. Something struck his left shoulder with such tremendous force that his arm went numb and he dropped the flashlight. The pain was excruciating, but it didn't prevent him from viciously kicking out in the direction of his attacker. His foot struck something soft and yielding, bringing an exclamation of pain followed by the sound of a crash. After that, all went quiet.

Parker sank to his knees, his right hand clutching his throbbing shoulder, trying to fend off waves of agony. Fumbling around in the dark with his right hand, he managed to locate his flashlight.

He shone it about, and discovered his assailant lying against the far wall, unconscious. The crash he'd heard had been their head striking the wall. Crawling over to the wall, he directed his light onto the attacker's face. His heart skipped a beat. It was a face he knew.

"You didn't have to kick me!" Susan Beckman said when she regained consciousness.

"You didn't have to clobber me with that brass candleholder," Parker replied. "If you'd hit my head, it could have killed me."

"Well, what would you have done?" she said defensively. "I awoke to a noise in the living room. Next thing I know, there's a suspected murderer sneaking into my bedroom." She paused and looked accusingly at Parker. "Since I'm the only witness against you, I figured you were here to kill me."

Susan was still lying on the floor, only now she was propped up against the wall with two pillows and an ice pack on her head.

Parker also sat on the floor, with his back against the opposite wall, alternating between rubbing his shoulder and sipping a bottle of water.

"Why are you here?" Susan demanded.

Parker looked at her. "I know you find this hard to believe, but I didn't kill your father. I'm here trying to prove my innocence."

"If breaking into my home and assaulting me proves your innocence, you've got strange ideas, McGraw."

"My intention was to look through your dad's personal belongings, not beat up his daughter."

She stared at him for a while, then shook her head. "Could you actually be innocent?"

"Would you still be alive if I wasn't?"

It didn't take long for Parker to examine Michael Beckman's belongings. Susan had packed his possessions into three small cardboard boxes. The only helpful material he obtained came from Susan. Whether it reflected a new-found belief in his innocence or just too tired to argue, she opened up about her father.

Michael Gilbert Beckman had been a struggling investment counselor in San Francisco when Susan was born. With hard work, a forceful personality, and a lot of luck, he started to rise. He made a few investment recommendations to an influential client that hit big. The grateful client referred his rich friends, and dad was on his way. Her parents were in the well-to-do class by the time she hit her teen years.

Unfortunately, with success came some of its less desirable trappings. One of those was alcohol. What started as a weekend social indulgence gradually developed into three martini lunches, followed by a couple of drinks before dinner to relieve the tensions of work. Finally, libations were consumed even in the morning to prepare for the ordeal of the upcoming day.

As the intake increased, her father's ability to function coherently decreased. Investments fell through, and clients began to withdraw as word got out. He was arrested several times for drunk driving, the last involving an accident with a mother of four who fortunately was not injured. That incident, though, was the final straw. Susan's mother, who had put up with his excesses for years, kicked him out of the house. Soon after, his business folded and so did he.

In order to support Susan and her brother Tyler, their mother started working as a real estate agent. While trying to learn the business, she was forced to sell everything they had just to keep food on the table. Her initial clients were mainly old friends who employed her out of pity, but her style and taste, along with her innate business sense, quickly dispelled their concerns and rapidly brought her new referrals. The real estate boom hit about this time causing housing prices to soar along with real estate commissions. With this sudden influx of money, Susan's mother eventually opened her own agency.

Presently her mother lived in Sausalito, and according to Susan was "attractive, socially active, and financially independent".

And her father? With the failure of his business, he drank his way down the ladder of small brokerage houses until finally there was no one who'd touch him. He was living on the street and taking handouts from care centers when he finally went to an Alcoholics Anonymous meeting. The effect was drastic to the point that he eventually became a counselor for AA. Later he moved to Fresno and started a pool cleaning business. He must have had some phobia about success because as soon as the business started to thrive, he began drinking again. The same downward spiral developed, only this time, he passed some large, bad checks to cover his debts and ended up in jail.

"And that brings us to the present," Susan said.

"What about enemies or long-standing grudges?" Parker asked.

"Everyone who met my dad liked him, even the ones that lost money on him." Susan gave a derisive laugh. "Yeah, he was never short of drinking companions."

The mantle clock showed 2 a.m. as Parker rose stiffly to his feet.

"Thank you for your help," he said.

Susan stood up. "I don't see what help I've been."

"You've made me wonder if your dad's murder was related to his time in prison. He had enemies before that, but no one it seems who wanted to kill him. "

"So what do you do now?" she asked.

"Find out more about his stay in prison."

"And how will you do that?"

"Well, we talk to the warden. Maybe we can even speak with some of the inmates who knew him," Parker replied.

"What do you mean 'we'?" Her voice had risen an octave and all semblance of fatigue gone.

Parker spread his hands out. "We, as in you and me."

"Don't be including me in any 'we' related to you!" she stated firmly.

Parker drew himself up. "Great! You think I'm innocent, but you can't be bothered to help me prove it." He hesitated for a moment. "And how about your father's murder? Do you just walk away from that?" He shook his head. "Aren't you the loving daughter? Grab the inheritance and run. Damn the circumstances."

"Look it's late and I don't know what I want," she said. "Why don't you call me in the morning when my head's a little clearer?"

"Will you still be living here tomorrow or moved to some other hidden location?" he said with a half-smile.

Susan expression was unreadable. "I'll be here in the morning. Call me then."

Chapter Thirteen

Susan was civil but not enthusiastic when Parker called the next morning. Initially, she was resistant to the idea of accompanying Parker to the prison but gradually she relented.

"One question before I accept," she said. "How were you able to get an appointment to speak with the warden about my father when you're accused of his murder?"

"The warden didn't make an appointment with Parker McGraw."

"He didn't?" she'd asked.

"No. He made an appointment with Susan Beckman."

"Pretty sure of yourself, weren't you?"

Parker continued,"... and Tyler Beckman."

She was silent for a moment. "I wouldn't happen to be speaking to that same Tyler Beckman?"

"The very same," Parker replied. "You told me you had a brother named Tyler. Since I wasn't sure you'd go, I covered my bets."

The drive from Monterey to Soledad State Prison, euphemistically called the Correctional Training Facility, meant driving over to Salinas, and then heading south on Highway 101 through the heart of Salinas Valley. With mile after mile of farm fields on either side of the highway, it could be a long and boring trip. Susan's companionship made the usually dull drive actually pleasant. They were riding in Parker's 1964 Porsche C. He'd duck taped his broken side window.

Parker's Porsche turned off the highway and drove up to a multi-story, nondescript building with bars on all the windows, surrounded by a high fence topped with barb wire, combined with guard towers and armed sentries.

Parker checked his watch. "Since we are a few minutes early, I need to call my lawyer." He searched his pockets. "Damn, I left my cell phone at home." He turned to Susan. "Can I borrow yours?"

She pulled her's out of her purse and handed it over. Parker started to punch in numbers, and then looked back at her. "Do you ever charge this thing. The battery is essentially dead."

She grabbed the phone. "I swear there is something wrong with this battery. I just charged it last night."

They walked over to a small, single story building located just outside the entrance gate, termed the Visitors' Center.

Parker glanced over at Susan. "You're going to need I.D. Where's your purse?"

"I've got my driver's license in my pocket. Left my purse in the car."

Parker opened the Center's door and followed Susan inside. They entered a large rectangular room divided in half by a heavy wooden counter. On their side of the counter, a number of people milled around or where seated. On the other side were several prison employees, each wearing army khaki-colored uniforms with law enforcement insignia. The only access to their side of the counter was through a metal detector.

Parker and Susan eased their way up to the check-in area where a black woman, dressed in a guard uniform, took their names and compared them to a list on her clipboard. Satisfied, she handed them two numbered passes and told them to be seated.

Parker figured that was a subtle joke since there were three people for every seat. He took Susan's arm and they angled over to a glass display counter along one side of the room. It was filled with a bizarre collection of crafts which a sign explained had been made by the prisoners and were on sale.

Gazing down at the display, Parker said, "Only six more months till Christmas. Maybe you can find something for that person on your list who has everything."

Susan jabbed him with her elbow. "Be serious!" She nodded toward the wooden counter. "I've been watching them screen the visitors. Everyone has to show identification before the guard lets them pass through the metal detector."

"So?"

"So how do you expect to get in as Tyler Beckman?"

Parker pulled his wallet out and held it open for her. "With a driver's license in the name of Tyler Beckman."

"Where the hell did you get that?"

"Sssh. Not so loud." Parker put the wallet away. "Called a friend of mine late last night in Santa Cruz. Picked it up this morning. It's an old hobby of his."

"A hobby! Who has that kind of hobby?"

Parker's retort was drowned out by a loud voice, "Numbers seventeen and eighteen!"

They walked over to a different section of the counter, manned by a young red-haired guard who had paged their numbers. He asked them to produce proof of their identity.

Parker nodded toward Susan. "How about if my sister vouches for me?" he said smiling.

"Sorry, sir, but I'll have to see some I.D." The guard's interest in Susan had piqued, though, with the realization that they were brother and sister.

Parker placed his open wallet on the counter and smiled again, as the guard gave it only a cursory inspection before turning to Susan. He spent several minutes reviewing her license and jokingly comparing her picture with her face. Little notice was given to Parker.

The identification complete, they emptied their pockets into a small basket, passed through the metal detector, and retrieved their belongings on the other side. The same red-haired guard escorted them through two locked gates and into the administrative building which was sealed off from the prison itself.

The guard left them at the warden's waiting room and Susan thanked him with a bewitching smile. The warden's plump, bespectacled secretary looked up from her computer.

"Warden Morris will see you in a few minutes. Please wait here and have a seat," she said, returning to her keyboard.

Where else would we wait with several thousand hardened criminals just outside the door.

They sat down on a narrow couch.

"Finish the story about the I.D.," Susan whispered.

"The warden's office is not the place to talk," Parker whispered back.

"But it was okay in front of the prison guards?"

"It was so noisy back there that no one could hear anything."

"Well, she's too far away to hear us, so finish it."

Parker shook his head. "Are the terms forego or abandon in your vocabulary."

"No, they're not." She stared at him. "But the words strike and damage are."

Parker nodded, and lowered his voice. "There's a guy I knew in high school who just loved to sneak into shows, amusement parks, bars, whatever. Yet he was always getting nabbed. By the time he reached college, he was sneaking into rock concerts, professional sporting events, you name it, only now he wasn't getting caught." Parker twisted slightly to get more comfortable. "He discovered a flare for reproducing tickets, gate passes, press passes, and," he paused, "driver's licenses. By the time he graduated from college, there were very few major entertainment events that Jack couldn't get us into."

"So he made your I.D.?"

"Yeah, he did. Set a new personal record in speed." Parker shook his head. "He must pull down four hundred thousand a year as a litigation lawyer, but he still loves sneaking into big events. It's more than a hobby now; it's a point of pride. Making this driver's license was ho-hum with his talents."

The secretary coughed politely. "Warden Morris will see you now."

Warden Morris rose from behind his desk as they were ushered into his office. He was of medium height, trim, and had his silver hair in a crew cut. There was a starched freshness about him, an ex-military air. His handshake was firm and his eyes lingered on Susan no longer than appropriate.

Waving Parker to a chair, he positioned another one for Susan. Settling back behind his desk, he picked up a pen and slowly twisted it in his hands.

"I was sorry to hear about your father," he said. "I didn't know him well, but my few interactions with him were very positive. He was not the usual type we see here. Basically, he seemed like a good man."

"Thank you, Warden. We appreciate that," Susan replied.

"So how can I be of help?" He put the pen down and leaned back in his swivel chair.

Parker cleared his throat and tried to assume the look of concerned son, yet practical man of the world. "We were shocked by the death of our father. Through the years, we hadn't been very close but since his recent release from prison, he seemed to have changed. It was like we had a father again. He called us frequently. Invited us on outings with him. In general, he showed a real concern about us and our lives."

Parker paused to give the warden time to assimilate this new fatherly image he was ascribing to Beckman.

"His death, allegedly the result of a drug deal that went bad, didn't make sense to us in light of what we knew about him. We were assured by the police, though, that the case was open and shut. Although unhappy with the implications, we felt nothing was to be gained by pursuing the case so we let it drop."

Morris nodded.

"Two days ago, the question of why he died took on a whole new perspective. We were notified by an insurance company that our father had a million dollar life insurance policy with a double indemnity clause attached."

"Which means?" Morris inquired.

"Which means if he died in any other manner than a natural death, the value of the policy doubled."

Morris smiled. "It looks like you and your sister will have some money coming."

"We thought so too, but unfortunately there is an unusual stipulation in the policy. A stipulation I'm sure my father never even considered applicable when he purchased the insurance." Parker shook his head in mock despair. "The stipulation is that if death occurs during or as the consequence of a criminal act performed by the policy holder, the entire policy is null and void."

The room was quiet except for the creak of Morris' chair as he leaned back.

"I see your problem," he said, "but I'm not sure how I can be of help."

Susan took over. "My father had a very strong aversion to any use of drugs. Somehow he could rationalize his use of alcohol, but he was fervently against any other type of drug use. My brother and I find it hard to believe that with his strong dislike of drugs and his attempts to re-establish a relationship with us, he would ever condone dealing in drugs."

"People change in here, and often it's for the worst," Morris remarked sadly.

"We know that, warden," Parker said. "And if we can find indications of that type of change, we will stop our queries. But, if we can't, then we plan on obtaining professional investigative help to try to prove his death was not related to any criminal activity."

The warden leaned forward in his chair, supporting his chin with his hands.

This is it. Either he goes for the explanation or we're up the proverbial creek.

"I think you're wasting your time. From the little I've heard about the case, it seems a fairly straightforward drug-related killing."

Parker' slumped back into his chair.

Morris, noting his dejected appearance, said, "Don't get me wrong, son. I'm not saying you can't speak to your father's cellmate, but I'm just telling you not to get your hopes up." He smiled. "Hell, if I had two million dollars hanging in the balance, I'd give it a run myself."

Chapter Fourteen

The designated visitor area consisted of a cheerless, brightly-lit room with faded bile green walls, worn linoleum flooring, and opaque wire windows. Visitors were scattered around at tables in the hall-like room, mostly in groups of threes and fours.

Parker and Susan were at one end, sitting at a Formica topped table, looking across its scarred and worn surface at the empty, metal folding chair on the other side.

Parker thought about the warden's advice and decided he was right. *This is a fool's errand, but what else is left?*

The entry door for the inmates opened, and a short, round-shouldered man in a blue work shirt and Levis entered. The guard with him glanced around and pointed in their direction. The prisoner hesitated briefly before sauntering over.

"I'm Monroe St. Jude. The warden says you're relatives of Mike's."

He was in his mid-fifties with a full head of salt and pepper hair, and a well-manicured, gray mustache. His face was open, friendly, and a little fleshy. He resembled a prosperous bank president except for his prison pallor and uniform.

"That's right," Parker replied. "I'm his son, Tyler. And this is my sister..."

St. Jude anticipated him. "Susan." He searched her face. "I spent a year with Mike staring at your picture," he said with a soft smile.

Susan tensed and pulled back slightly. "My picture?"

The smile widened. "Yes, he always kept a picture of you above his bunk. You were much younger in the photo... in fact, I'd hardly recognize you now."

Susan relaxed as St. Jude went on. "You looked familiar when I walked in, but I couldn't place it until your brother introduced himself, and then it clicked."

He regarded both of them. "After a year of listening to Mike's tales about you two, I feel like I already know you."

Parker and Susan glanced at each other, more in embarrassment than anything else. Parker decided to change the drift of the conversation since he was in no position to reminisce about Tyler Beckman. Fortunately, St. Jude changed it for them.

"I was sorry to hear about Mike. He was a kind, intelligent man. I'd had better hopes for him when he left."

"So did we, Mr. St. Jude," Susan replied. "But thank you for your sentiments."

"You were my father's cellmate?" Parker asked.

"Yes."

"How long were you together?" Parker inquired.

"I was with your dad during his entire stay here."

Parker was formulating his next question, when St. Jude threw one at him. "May I ask what this is all about? Mike's here for a year and a half, and no one comes to visit him. Now that he's dead, suddenly you both rush down here."

Parker had no idea why Beckman's family had stayed away either. He glanced over at Susan, expecting her to answer, but instead she was concentrating on one of the opaque windows. He coughed slightly, trying to get her attention, but she remained absorbed in the window. If there was to be an answer, Parker realized, it would have to come from him.

He stood up and walked over to a nearby window trying to buy some time. *Who knows. Maybe I'll find an answer on the window glass. Susan seems to be finding something there.*

"What's the matter?" St. Jude asked. "The question too tough or is the answer too embarrassing?"

"It's not a tough question, we're just not proud of the answer," Parker replied. He saw Susan look over at him in apparent wonder. He was wondering too. Wondering what he would say next.

"You know that we wrote him a number of times?" Parker said. *God, I hoped they'd at least written to him.*

St. Jude stared at him for the longest time, and then said, "Yes, he did receive a few letters."

"And you know he wrote several letters to us?"

"Yes, I was aware of that."

"Did he ever read you our letters or tell you what was in his?"

"No, he wasn't that talkative about his correspondence."

Parker smiled. "Well, if he had, you wouldn't have asked the question you did." Parker walked back to his chair and sat down.

"My father forbade us to visit him in this place. He didn't want his children to see him or remember him in the role of a prisoner. Coming here, seeing this place, visiting him in rooms like this, he felt would leave an indelible impression on us. He preferred that we act like he was away on a trip. He'd write and we'd write back."

"Sounds like something Mike would do," St. Jude said. "He never mentioned it to me, though."

"He probably never mentioned my one attempted visit here either, did he?" Parker said.

"No, he didn't."

"He refused to see me, and sent word that he wouldn't see any of us, as long as he was confined in prison."

St. Jude bowed his head once in acknowledgement.

"Now for the second part of your question. Shortly preceding my father's death, he hired a private investigator. He felt someone was trying to kill him. But before any thorough investigation could be made, he was dead and soon after, the investigator was also dead. Neither my sister nor I are satisfied with the police explanation of how or why our father died. I personally think his death may have been related to his prison stay. I... err... we were hoping your knowledge of his time in prison might help clarify our concerns."

St. Jude took his time, digesting Parker's comments. "I'll be happy to assist but I doubt that his death could be a result of his time in here."

"Why is that, Mr. St. Jude?" Susan asked.

He turned toward her. "Your father had one goal in mind while he was here: to get out as quickly as possible. He knew that any problems or complaints about him could interfere with that goal. Therefore, he kept a very low profile. No arguments. No fights. No bad vibes with anyone. Any person he couldn't get along with, he avoided. He wanted no trouble."

"But even with the best intentions, in nearly two years' time, he must have made some enemies in this type of place," Parker said.

Shaking his head, St. Jude turned toward Parker. "Guess you didn't know your dad that well, Tyler. I think he could get along with the devil himself if he had to, and probably sell him something to boot. He was a hell of a salesman, and to be that, you've got to have a hell of a personality... and he was personality plus. No, offhand, I just can't think of anyone who had a grudge against Mike."

"Does the name Bill Harris sound familiar? He was a waiter in Big Sur," Parker asked.

St. Jude ran his finger along the groove of a carved initial on the table top then shook his head. "No, it doesn't."

The interview complete, they stood and thanked St. Jude for his time. Parker watched him walk away and wondered what kind of existence he must be going back to. And then he wondered if he might find out someday. Shuddering involuntarily, he turned to Susan but she had gone.

Chapter Fifteen

The walk back to the car was a silent one with Susan keeping one step ahead of him. Nothing was said as they pulled out of the parking lot and Parker knew it was going to be a long, quiet, ride home. The kind of quiet that screams at you with unsaid thoughts. To make matters worse, as they pulled onto the Highway 101, the tule fog closed in on them.

The tule fog is a dense ground fog, often in patches, that is usually confined to the Central Valley region of California, but on occasion may wander westward over into the Salinas Valley. It closed over them as rapidly and tightly as a drunk's hand over a free drink. One minute it was a balmy July afternoon and the next, it was as if night had fallen. Speeding in tule fog could be treacherous, and had resulted in thirty and forty car pile-ups. Parker slowed down to twenty-five mph and tried to relax.

The results of the interview had been disappointing to say the least, and now it appeared that Susan might be having strong second thoughts about his innocence.

"Doesn't look so good about my theories," he said, off-handedly.

Susan stared out the side window and made no reply.

"If this was a typical Hollywood thriller," Parker said, "I'd have no difficulty guessing the next scene."

The fog lessened so Parker sped up to sixty mph while Susan continued her vigil with the side window.

He continued. "Driving on this lonely stretch of road, the heavy fog obscuring everything, you'd suddenly realize that I did kill your father... and now it's your turn." He paused. "Is that what you're thinking?"

Susan switched the radio on and gave him a look reserved for the proverbial turd in the punch bowl. Before he could think of a response, her expression suddenly changed as she screamed.

A tremendous jolt rocked his side of the car accompanied by the sound of screeching metal. Parker had one brief glance of the car that sideswiped them before the Porsche went careening off the road, totally out of control. They roared over an embankment and became airborne.

"Hang on," Parker yelled, gripping the steering wheel.

The Porsche landed upright on all four wheels but at an angle. The car's terrific momentum carried it over into a long series of side rolls.

As the car kept rolling over and over, Parker felt like he was in a clothes dryer, peering out the little glass window. There was no sense of up or down, just an endless spinning sensation. The air around him filled with the sounds of shattering glass and tearing, crunching metal.

Then, quiet. They'd stopped. He wasn't sure if he had been unconscious or not. *It doesn't really matter. What matters is I'm still alive. But is Susan?*

Still shaking, he began to stretch toward her side of the car when he felt a tight, heavy pressure across his abdomen.

Something is definitely wrong!

He tried to keep the panic down as horrendous possibilities raced through his mind --- ruptured intestinal organs, torn major abdominal arteries, fractured pelvis --and then almost laughed when he diagnosed the problem. The series of rolls had so disoriented his sense of equilibrium that he just now realized the car was laying on its roof and he was hanging upside down. The abdominal pressure was his seat belt cutting across his stomach, suspending him in the air.

Parker again leaned toward Susan. He couldn't see her face in the limited light, just a blur of white. Suspended by her seatbelt, she was perfectly still. He reached over and gently shook her.

"Susan! Are you alright?" He felt some movement but heard no answer.

"Susan, speak to me! Are you hurt?"

She moved a bit more and this time emitted a low moan.

She's alive, thank God! Parker was amazed, though, with her next sound. A soft chuckle. He thought he was mistaken until he heard it again, only this time it grew into a laugh. Susan was becoming hysterical.

He grabbed her shoulder and shook her hard.

"Dammit, Susan! Answer me! Are you alright?"

Slowly the laughter died out and she took a deep breath. "Yes... everything seems alright... except I ache all over."

"Any one place that hurts a lot more than the others?"

"No, not really."

"In that case, tell me what was so funny. I could use a good laugh right now."

"Did you really shout, 'Hang on', just before we crashed?"

"Yeah," he replied. "Something like that."

"You mean as our car was forced off the road, shot over the embankment, and became airborne, you thought you should caution me to 'Hang on'... like maybe I might not think of it myself?"

Now Parker understood. The laugh was her joy of being alive. Life is never as precious as when you almost lose it.

"So how do we get out of this contraption?" she asked.

Parker pushed his seat belt release button, but it refused to respond. "Try your seat belt release," he told her. "It's the button on your left."

Footsteps approached the car.

"Hey!" Parker yelled. "We're trapped in here! We need help!"

Susan joined in. "Please, help us!"

The side windows of the car had shattered during the series of rolls, but had not fallen out. The back side window, broken in the fight at Big Sur, was obscured by duck tape. This, combined with the return of the dense tule fog, made visibility through the windows impossible. Their only view of the dim outside world was through a small portion of the front window that had snapped out during the crash. It was through that hole that Parker saw a set of feet appear and stop in front of the car.

"Hey!" he repeated. "We need assistance!"

No answer.

Leaning toward Susan, Parker said quietly, "Try and get loose quickly. This guy isn't here to help us."

"What are you babbling about?" She turned from Parker and peered toward the hole in the front window. "Hey, we need some help!"

A lit match landed on the ground in front of the front windshield.

Susan gasped. "What's he doing?"

"The gas tank's up front. I can smell the gas. It's probably all over the ground there."

Another match landed and fizzled out.

"You mean he's trying to burn us alive?"

"Not us," Parker replied as he struggled with his seatbelt release. "Me. What did the car look like that ran us off the road?"

"A black Trans Am."

"That's the same people that attacked me in Big Sur. We need to get out of here. NOW!"

His seat belt suddenly released, dropping Parker partially onto the roof. He tried to move only to discover that his legs were trapped by the steering wheel and a very deformed dashboard. *Ah, shit.*

Outside, another match dropped in front of them, then went dead.

Parker felt Susan struggling next to him. "Are you free yet?" he asked.

"Damn seatbelt won't release."

"Let me help you." I reached over, pressing the release button.

"We don't have time. Try and find my purse. See if it's on your side."

"Some guy is trying to fry us and you're searching for your purse! No one's going to notice a little smeared make-up in the morgue!"

"Find the purse!" she yelled.

What the hell, he decided. He groped around, but couldn't find it, so he switched his attention to freeing his legs. As he maneuvered them about, something fell past his face. The purse.

The fifth match landed on the ground, flickered a few times, then died out.

Parker handed Susan her purse. "If you're thinking of using your mace, don't! It's flammable."

The next match appeared, only this time instead of dying out, it began to burn brighter. Parker squirmed and kicked, trying to free his legs.

A tremendous explosion shattered the silence. Portions of the remaining front windshield blew out and Parker waited for the flames to take him. Only there were no flames.

What the hell? And then he understood. It hadn't been gas exploding, but rather a gunshot, amplified by the closed surroundings.

"Goddamn it! Now the bastard's shooting at us."

"Wrong. I'm shooting at him."

"Where'd you get a gun?"

"From my purse."

"I mean what are you doing with a gun?"

Susan finally got her seat belt to release. She lowered herself down to the roof of the car, leaving his question unanswered. After knocking out the remaining glass in the front window, she fired another shot. The sound was deafening.

"Did you see him?"

"No, I just wanted to make sure he stayed away." She knocked a hole in her side window with the butt of the gun. "It's clear over here. Check your side!"

Parker searched around for something to break the glass. All he could find was his ancient beeper. He used it to break out a section of glass, and peered out.

"Nobody on my side."

Susan started wiggling out through the front windshield. She stopped part way and lifted her hand to her nose. Parker didn't need to ask what she smelled. Gasoline. By now, the ground was saturated. With renewed vigor, he tried to lever the steering wheel up but without success. Next he tried to open his door, hoping to ease out that way, but it wouldn't budge.

Free from the car, Susan came over to his side window, gun in hand, and cautiously scanned the area.

"Whoever he was, he seems to be gone now," Susan said. "The gun probably altered his plans."

"Give my door a pull, will you."

It wouldn't open even with both of them pushing and pulling. Susan stepped back, looked at the bent car frame, and shook her head. "Nothing but the jaws-of-life will get this door open again."

She knelt down at his window. "I'm going for help; otherwise, you'll never get out of here."

Before he could reply, she thrust the gun at him through the side window. "Here. This will keep you safe until I get back."

"Now, wait a minute," Parker said.

"That man will be back, and you'll need more than words to dissuade him."

The gun felt cold under Parker's shirt as he watched her disappear in the fog. She was going to parallel the highway back the direction they had come for a mile, and then rejoin it and try to get help.

Parker changed his strategy and tried freeing one leg at a time. He was able to maneuver his right leg toward the passenger's side only to have its progress halted by the car radio which projected far back behind the dashboard. Wiping sweat from his face with his shirttail, he took a deep breath, willed his hands to stop trembling, and then began to dismantle the radio.

Working as fast as he could, he got the radio loose but it wouldn't slide out. He hammered, pulled, and finally it popped out, hanging only by a few wires. This allowed him enough room to slide his right leg free. With this added mobility, he was then able to extract his other leg.

Once free, Parker wasted no time. On his belly, he quickly made his way out the front window to the gasoline soaked ground under the front of the car. There he paused, He was alone.

He crawled the rest of the way, and then tried to stand only to crumple to the ground. His legs were useless. The prolonged, cramped, upside down position he'd been stuck in had cut off the circulation to his legs. It would be awhile before sensation and strength returned.

Feeling like a wounded animal, Parker pulled his way to some nearby bushes that offered a semblance of cover.

As he lay on his back, catching his breath, he heard movement behind him. Quietly, he rolled over and peered through the brush. In the darkness of the tule fog, a man crept up to the side of the car, lit a flare, and threw it under the hood. The gasoline ignited almost instantly. Parker quickly turned on his side, putting his back to the car, as a massive explosion filled the air, raining metal and dirt. He used the noise to cover the sound of him chambering a round. Then as the dust settled, he rolled out of his hiding place, gun extended.

Chapter Sixteen

"A person could get killed that way!" He was a bear of a man with a heavy beard, a Denver Bronco's cap, jeans, and a plaid Pendleton shirt, staring down at Parker through the open passenger door of his double rig.

"A person could get killed a lot of ways these days," Parker replied as he swung up into the warmth of the heated truck cab. "Thanks for stopping. I was getting a little desperate."

The driver put the truck into gear and they pulled back onto the highway.

"Thumbing a ride in this fog is real desperate!" the trucker remarked. He rolled down his window, spit out a stream of tobacco juice, and rolled the window back up. "No one can see you off the side of the road, so you have to get damn near on the highway to be noticed." He shook his head. "Yet these bozos out here can't even avoid hitting another car in the fog, much less some hitchhiker in dark clothes."

As the warmth of the truck interior seeped into him, Parker felt some of the chill from his extended walk in the fog wearing off. He'd spent an hour searching for Susan through the undergrowth and along the roadside, finally deciding she'd been picked up by someone. There would have been no reason for his attacker to search for her since he only wanted Parker. And he probably thought Parker was now a bile of ashes.

The driver peeled off his cap and brushed back his dark brown hair. Reaching into his shirt pocket, he pulled out a plug of chewing tobacco and held it out to Parker.

"Like a bit of chaw?"

"No, thanks," Parker answered.

"Don't really like the stuff myself, but it sure keeps me awake on these long hauls." He dropped it back into his pocket.

"I'll tell you what I do need."

The driver glanced over.

"The reason I'm out here is someone ran me off the road, then set my car on fire in an attempt to kill me."

He started chewing faster. "No shit?"

"I need to use your phone to notify the police."

The driver pulled his cell phone from a cup holder and passed it to Parker. "Have at it."

Parker called 911 and was routed to the Highway Patrol. He described the situation to the officer, finishing with his concern about his female companion who had vanished

"One of our patrol cars just picked up a woman with a similar story. Very likely that's the woman you're concerned about."

Thank God, Parker thought.

The officer continued. "Have your truck driver friend drop you at the Monterey County Sheriff's office. We going to need them on site, and they can bring you along."

With the sway of the cab and the roar of the diesel lulling his senses, Parker settled back in his seat and reflected on his narrow escape. Twenty-five minutes later, they were at the Sheriff's Station.

Climbing down from the rig, Parker thanked the driver profusely, and then entered the Sheriff's building. What followed was the typical bureaucratic nightmare. When he told them about his vehicular accident, they told him he needed to report it to the Highway Patrol. Parker mentioned he already had and that it was more than a car crash. A murder attempt had followed the crash, something the Highway Patrol didn't handle. When asked where all this occurred, Parker guessed just north of the small town of Gonzales, so a turf question arose. If it was in the Gonzales city limits, their police force would conduct the investigation, but if outside the city limits, then the Monterey Sheriff Department would handle the scene.

They were still debating the matter when a call came in from the Highway Patrol. They were at the scene of the accident. The young woman with them claimed it had been a murder attempt, so they wanted the Monterey County Sheriff's Investigative Division to get involved.

Parker rode in the sheriff's green and white down to the accident scene. The tule fog had lifted and he could clearly see two Highway Patrol cruisers and a fire truck parked along the east side of the highway, their colored emergency lights blazing. The sheriff made a U-turn and pulled in behind.

Parker followed the sheriff's detective, Bob Gemill, over to a group of officials clustered on the side of the road. Seemed like everyone knew each other. Gemill introduced Parker to the others.

"Where is Susan Beckman?" Parker asked, glancing around.

Officer Prentis of the Highway Patrol gestured to one of their patrol car. "She's in my car. Seemed pretty shook up, and cold, so I told her to wait there until the sheriff's investigator showed up." He looked Parker up and down. "When we first arrived, your car was still on fire and too hot to examine. Once the fire department got here and put out the flames, we realized there was no body inside." He shook his head. "Your lady friend was insisting we look for you, when we got word you were on your way to the sheriff's office."

"Oh, thank God, Park," Susan said, as she joined the group and gave him a quick hug. "When I saw the car on fire, I thought you were dead."

Parker started to explain how he'd escaped when Officer Gemill interrupted him. "Let's get your story on the record." He held up a digital voice recorder. After recording his name, date, and people involved, he nodded to Parker.

"Mr. McGraw, why don't you tell your side first, then we can hear from Ms. Beckman."

Parker relayed his tale, leaving out the stop at the state prison, and Susan's gun, since he had no idea if she had a permit. When he'd finished, Gemill asked Susan for her version.

Parker noticed Susan also left the gun out of her story, as well as the trip to the prison. She confirmed Parker's account and then he got to hear what happened after she left their car. She had crept a mile or so back toward Gonzales, then cautiously approached the main road. There, she put her thumb out and almost immediately an elderly couple picked her up. When they heard her story, the couple insisted she use their cell phone to call the Highway Patrol. After she told the Highway Patrol what happened, arrangements were made, and the Highway Patrol rendezvoused with Susan and the couple, then brought her back to the crash site.

Gemill dropped the recorder in his pocket, stared at Parker, and gestured toward the car. "Why don't you walk me though this, from where your car left the highway to where you watched the perpetrator throw the flare."

After Parker finished, Gemill asked, "You never got a good look at the guy who did this?"

"No. It was dark and I only got glimpses."

"How about you, Ms. Beckman?"

Susan shook her head. "I only saw his feet."

Gemill dictated a few additional notes into his recorder. Once finished, he led them back to his car, where he told them to wait. He went off to huddle with the two Highway Patrol officers.

Parker leaned in to Susan and said softly, "I didn't mention your gun since I wasn't sure you had a permit."

"Thank you. And no, I don't. After what happened to my father, I borrowed it from a friend to be safe," she replied.

"What a hell-of-a-night," Parker said.

"If we ever have to go somewhere together again, remind me to take separate cars," she said. "You seem to be a magnet for trouble."

Gemill walked back over to them.

"Could you have misinterpreted this whole thing?" he asked.

"What do you mean?"

"Maybe in the fog, the car accidentally hit you. The driver saw you go off the road and was concerned about your welfare. You mentioned it was dark, due to the heavy fog. He might have thrown the matches to put light on your situation in the car, not aware of the gas leak."

Parker vehemently shook my head. "We yelled out to him and he never responded. Then he came back with the flare."

"Possibly he didn't hear you, and wanted a brighter light."

Parker told him about his run in with that same car down at Pfeiffer Big Sur State Park.

"Did you file a report?" Gemill asked.

"No, I didn't. I thought it wasn't worth the trouble."

"Did the man tossing the flare look like either of those two guys?"

"Never saw him well enough," Parker replied.

Susan whispered. "Like I said. A magnet."

Detective Gemill gave Susan and Parker a ride home. They stopped first at Susan's father's house and Gemill searched it before letting her go inside. Susan and Parker agreed to talk in the morning.

When they arrived at Parker's house, Gemill pulled his gun and cautiously checked it out before holstering his firearm and waving him in.

"Thank you for everything, officer," Parker said.

"We'll see what we can find out about the other car involved with your accident, but I'm not optimistic." They shook hands and Gemill said over his shoulder as he left. "Be careful."

Parker stood in his living room, surveying his quarters. Everything looked so normal, he found it hard to believe that a few hours earlier someone had been trying to kill him.

His assailants, he figured, thought he was dead, but they still might check his home to make sure. As much as he wanted to go to bed, he had to insure his safety. He grabbed a bottle of water and sat down at his kitchen table to make plans for his protection.

Fifteen minutes later, he had formed a strategy, and a possible scheme to track down his attackers. He took a quick shower and then began packing. His clothes went into a sail bag along with his cell phone, cell phone charger, and a Buck knife. A ball of twine, a dozen empty cans, and a few items from the kitchen rounded out his shopping list. He carried all this down to the garage and put it in the back of his other car, an old Toyota Land Cruiser. Its rusty exterior belied its real charms: a frame that was nearly unbendable, a spare gas tank, and a rebuilt 326 Chevy engine with dual carbs and headers. Parker had put more than five thousand miles in Baja on this car, much of it off-road, and the Land Cruiser had never let him down.

Monterey harbor is protected from the swells of the bay by a long rock jetty. Within the confines of the harbor are two large wharfs. The first, officially termed Municipal Wharf No. 1, is colloquially known as Fisherman's Wharf, and is a major tourist stop because of its numerous restaurants and gift shops. Municipal Wharf No. 2, about half a mile away and running parallel to Wharf No. 1, is primarily a working pier where most of the fish caught in the area are off-loaded and prepared for shipping.

It was on Wharf No.2, an hour later, that Parker left the Land Cruiser near a heavy chain-link gate. Gathering up his bag, he unlocked the gate, and shuffled down the gangplank onto A dock. This dock was the first in a series of docks situated between the wharfs and protected from the ocean surges by a cement sea wall.

Parker was surprised, as always, at the sudden change in his environment when he went from land to sea. The sounds became foreign. Water lapping against pilings, the creaking of wood slips, the flapping of boat covers, and the constant banging of halyards against main masts.

The smells were also unfamiliar. The scent of varnish, drying salt water, old fish scales, and diesel fuel, all set against the subtle yet overpowering fragrance that was the ocean itself.

Continuing toward the end of A dock, Parker spied the silhouette of the *Sun Chaser* in its slip, its mast sticking high above the neighboring power boats.

The *Sun Chaser* was an Erickson 39', a relatively fast, comfortable, single mast, fiberglass sailboat, that Parker had purchased when he was living in Southern California, and had no other financial responsibilities. He'd even lived on board for a short time. When he decided to move to Monterey, his plan had been to sell it, but there were too many good memories attached to let it go. So instead, he'd taken a couple of weeks off, filled it with excellent food and liquor, found a crew (by the name of Rhonda), and sailed north. There were a lot more good memories attached to it by the time they reached Monterey.

Parker walked out the finger of the *Sun Chaser's* slip, threw his possessions into the cockpit, and climbed aboard. Unlocking the main hatch, he stepped down the companionway into the master cabin. The air was a bit stale but dry, thanks to the floor heater he used to minimize the dampness and the mildew. Parker switched on the lights and crossed over to the refrigerator, searching for liquid refreshment.

With a soft drink in hand, Parker went up on deck and stretched out in the cockpit. The wake of a late returning fishing trawler gently rocked his boat as he lay listening to the sea lions barking on the rock jetty. Lethargy was taking over, and his body cried for sleep, but he knew he had several unfinished chores. Downing the last of his drink, he shook off his weariness and dug the cellular phone out of his sail bag.

He caught Jeff Gilman just leaving his office.

"What's up, Park?" he asked.

"I want to add to my claim that someone is trying to kill me." Parker had his attention and Jeff didn't say another word until Parker had finished his narrative.

"Ms. Beckman was riding with you?" Jeff asked.

"Yes, and she can corroborate everything that I've said."

Jeff's voice exploded through the phone line. "What the hell are you doing with her? Can't you see how the prosecution will view this – the only witness against you is nearly killed in a car crash and you were driving."

"You're missing the point. Somebody was trying to kill me."

"Knowing Hall," Jeff said with a sigh, "he'll probably think you set this up to make her death look like an accident."

The line remained silent as Parker tried to control is anger.

"What did you think you would accomplish going to the prison?" Jeff asked.

"Hopefully evidence to prove my innocence since no one else in this town gives a damn."

"Park, I told you my PI would be all over this when he gets back. Let the professionals do their job." He paused, then as an afterthought added, "And promise me you'll stay away from Susan Beckman. Hall would have a coronary knowing you're hanging with her."

Chapter Seventeen

Parker finished unloading his car and stowed everything away on the boat. He knew he had one last job to do. With three attempts on his life, setting up a warning system didn't seem like an act of paranoia. Using his own version of a poor man's burglar alarm, Parker stacked some empty cans on the bow of a boat two slips over and tied a piece of string to the bottom can. He then stretched the string across the center walkway, keeping it at ankle level, and attached it to a water faucet on the other side. Parker kicked the string with his foot and found the noise of the falling cans to be more than adequate to alert him. Restacking the cans, he went back on board and slept like a baby.

In the morning, it took him a few minutes to realize where he was and why. He took his freshly-brewed coffee up onto the dock and dismantled his make shift alarm system.

The summer fog had rolled in during the early hours and hadn't yet burned off, leaving all the exposed surfaces on the boat damp with dew. Parker wiped off one of the boat cushions and stretched out with his coffee. Pulling his collar up against the morning chill, he caught a whiff of frying bacon riding on the gentle offshore breeze.

Parker walked over to Fisherman's Wharf for breakfast and by the time he returned he had a game plan. Not fully formulated but functional enough to get by. He'd play the loose ends as they developed.

After showering and changing, he started the plan in motion. Digging out his oars, Parker climbed into his dinghy and rowed twenty feet over to B dock. B, C, and D docks were completely separated from A dock where Parker berthed his boat, and therefore had a different gate. That gate was entered from the parking lot about a quarter of a mile away from the A dock entrance on the wharf.

Tying his dinghy in an empty B slip, Parker walked past C and D docks and exited through their gate onto the municipal parking lot. He took an Uber ride out to the airport where he rented a car.

He drove over to his house and collected a few more necessities for his stay on the boat. While there, he put a new message on his cell phone: "You've reached Parker McGraw. I'm unavailable at present but leave a message with your name and number, and I'll return your call." He added today's date so there would be no mistake as to when the message was made.

Parker locked his front door, and walked back up the hill to his rental car. Climbing inside, he laid his head back against the seat, took a deep breath, and slowly let it out.

The trap is set and now I just have to wait.

He called Susan, but got her leave-a-message connection. He told her he'd be unavailable for a day or two while he tried to sort out what was going on.

On the way back to the harbor, he stopped at a grocery store and a hardware store, all the while, trying to shake off his growing apprehension and regain some of the optimism he'd had earlier in the morning.

He parked the rental car in the municipal parking lot, gathered up his new accumulations, and made his way to the B, C, and D dock entrance. With a key left over from the days when his boat was berthed at C dock, he let himself in and walked down to his dinghy. After stowing his possessions in the stern of the small boat, he rowed back over to his boat.

Once the groceries were put away, he grabbed his tool box and bag of newly purchased electrical goodies and went up onto the dock. Parker set up an "electric eye", an invisible light beam which, if disrupted by someone walking through it, would set off an alarm. The alarm he installed in the *Sun Chaser* cabin.

Early the following morning, the burglar alarm jangled. Kicking free of his sleeping bag, Parker grabbed his Buck knife. Peering out the forward porthole, he saw his intruder was only Jonesy, a commercial fisherman who had his boat berthed down past the *Sun Chaser*.

Parker switched off the alarm system and flopped back on the bunk. With his heart going like the final leg of a 10K race, he knew there would be no more sleep so he got dressed, and walked down the wharf for a morning paper.

It was a glorious day. No wind, just scattered cumulus clouds against a light blue background. The pier stood empty except for the early die-hard anglers. Parker had heard that people caught fish off this wharf, but you could never prove it by him. Most of the guys he saw here set their poles and then climbed back in their cars to sleep, read, or suck down a few beers.

With the Sunday morning edition of the *Monterey Herald* tucked under his arm, a fresh cup of coffee in hand, Parker strolled back to the *Sun Chaser* to enjoy the morning.

That afternoon, he cleaned up, locked the boat, and rowed the dinghy back over to B dock. From there, he went out the dock gate to the municipal lot and climbed into his Land Cruiser. He drove over to Carmel and parked on the street above his house.

Parker sat for a while, but everything appeared normal. His cell phone had recorded several hang-ups but no messages. He finally got out of the car and walked down to the house where he scavenged up a sandwich and a glass of milk, then retired to the deck to enjoy it. So far he'd noticed no curiosity, but the day was still young. To make sure people knew he was around, he started a fire in the fireplace and used damp wood to really get it smoking. By five, he felt enough was enough. Closing the house, he cautiously walked up to the car.

On the drive back to the boat, Parker repeatedly checked his rearview mirror but no one seemed to be following him.

He was almost to the wharf when he drove through the tail end of a yellow light. It changed to red as he was half way across the intersection. Behind him, he heard someone laying on their horn. Glancing in his rearview mirror, he saw a white van with two occupants dodging through the intersection several car lengths behind him.

The guys in that van must have had a desperate reason to make the light... and maybe I'm that reason.

Parker made a quick right and then a left. The white van stayed in his rearview mirror. The bait had been taken and his plan was now in motion. He drove slowly to the wharf parking lot.

After locking up the Land Cruiser, Parker sauntered over to the B, C, and D dock gate, giving his hunters more than enough time to see where he was going. He unlocked the gate and walked onto the docks. By the time he reached B dock, the farthest from the parking lot, he knew they could no longer see him. Climbing into his dinghy, he altered his appearance by donning a baseball cap and a sweatshirt, then rowed over to A dock. He tied the dinghy to his slip and hurried along. When he stepped through the A dock gate onto the wharf, he put his dark glasses on before heading back to the parking lot. He'd gone about halfway back, when he stopped and scouted the area with binoculars.

The white van was empty. Sweeping the rest of the parking lot with his glasses, Parker saw no one familiar. He checked the B, C, and D dock area. Nothing.

"Where the hell are they?" he whispered to himself.

After ten more minutes of scanning with negative results, his apprehension changed to fear. His disguise was meant to fool a passing glance, not to withstand serious scrutiny. *Maybe they've already spotted me and now they're laying low, waiting for my next move.*

He glanced quickly around him, expecting to see the blond gorilla leap from behind a parked car, or his dark-haired companion charge around the side of a building. *What the hell was I thinking? I'm not a cop. I could get killed.*

Parker checked the area. *I need a safe harbor. Some place I'll be protected.* And then he saw it. The Rogue Restaurant, sitting smugly on the second floor of the only building nestled between the parking lot and the wharf. Up in the restaurant, his exposure would be minimal, and if they had spotted him, he wouldn't be leading them back to the *Sun Chaser*. Best of all, it had three exits and lots of witnesses.

Moving rapidly, but not so quickly as to attract attention, Parker hurried to the rear of the building and charged up the stairway to the back entrance. Before entering, he checked the surrounding area. Still nothing. He eased open the rear entrance door and... there they were. The blond and his dark-haired friend sitting at a table with their backs to him, staring out over the docks. Parker slipped quietly back down the stairway.

It was dark when they finally gave up their vigil. Parker had been in his rental car for almost two hours when he saw them come out of the restaurant, get into their van, and drive off. He smiled as he dropped in behind them. *What goes around comes around.*

He followed them over to Del Rey Oaks, a small bedroom community about fifteen minutes from the harbor. The van turned into a large apartment complex and the blond got out. After a few parting words with his friend, the blond walked off toward the apartment building while the van drove away.

Parker was tempted to follow the van then decided he'd pressed his luck enough for today. The blond disappeared into an upstairs corner unit. Checking the apartment number, Parker matched it with a name on the mailboxes out front: Bernard Johnson.

##

The following morning, Parker arrived back at Bernard Johnson's apartment house at six-thirty. At seven-fifteen, Bernard came out, got into a familiar black Trans Am, and headed east on Highway 68 toward Salinas. He'd only gone a few miles when he turned into the Monterey Research Park, a large, business park specializing in high-tech companies, medical facilities, and physician offices.

Parker tailed him up into the development which was on top of a hill. They drove through several blocks of new streets with open fields, some of which were marked with surveyor stakes and others with beginning construction. As they got further into the park, the rolling hills were replaced by asphalt and concrete. Bernard turned left onto a side street, went to the end, and pulled into the parking lot of a large, single story structure. Parker pulled to the curb one hundred yards back.

Grabbing his binoculars, Parker focused on the building, its appearance as exciting in design as a wood coffin.

They didn't waste any money on that exterior. Probably use single ply toilet paper in their bathrooms.

Parker shifted the lenses to a small unobtrusive sign set in a lawn the size of a welcome mat. White letters against a black background read 'Citadel Pharmaceutical Company'.

Directing the binoculars to the parking lot, Parker picked up Bernard walking toward the building. He had taken off his windbreaker and had a uniform underneath. As he walked, he was fastening on a wide black belt which had several objects dangling from it. Bernard was a security guard.

Parker laid his binoculars down, leaned back, and wondered about Bernard's association with Citadel. Was it entirely unconnected or did he do more for Citadel than act as a security guard?

Chapter Eighteen

"Karl, if we convict you, you'll be a three-time loser and you know what that means. A long time behind bars."

Ray Stone was enthralled by the bony, scrawny hands of the man seated in front of him in the interrogation room of the county jail. As Karl Knott tried to play cool, his hands told a different story. Entwined with one another then apart. Clasped behind his neck, then across his belly, then behind his neck.

During the rare moments the hands were still, Stone observed a slight tremor.

"You like it in jail, don't you Karl? Maybe this time you'll find a boyfriend." He smiled as Karl's tremor increased.

"Bet you wouldn't mind a little fix right now," Stone said, staring at the needle tracks on Karl's arms. "Well, I can't help that... but how about a cigarette?"

Karl's expression resembled that of a drowning man seeing a life-preserver coming his way. By the time he got the cigarette in his mouth, his hands shook so much Stone had to light it for him.

Karl cupped the cigarette in his hands, closing his eyes each time he took a deep drag.

Stone waited until the third drag. "This next conviction could be ten years or more, Karl."

"Look, here, Mr. Prosecutor. I ain't say'in nothin' until my lawyer gets here."

Stone slapped the cigarette out of Karl's mouth and leaned down so they were nearly touching faces. "You don't understand, do you, gutter ball," Stone yelled. "With what we've got on you, you're going' down for the long one. Do you really think some fuckin' public defender gives a shit what happens to you? No one cares how long you rot in prison! No one!" Stone watched Karl shrink in front of him, pulling his body into a ball. The tremor had returned tenfold. His eyes darted wildly around the room.

"No one," Stone said softly, "but me, Karl."

Stone waited for that to sink in. Waited for Karl's shakes to lessen. For his trembling body to look up at him. When he did, Stone continued. "And that's why I'm here, Karl. I do care about you. And I can prevent bad things from happening to you in jail." He paused. "Do you want to know why I care? Why I'm going to keep you out of prison?"

Karl nodded slowly, mesmerized by Stone's announcements.

"Because you're going to do me a favor."

##

Parker had to move his boat. Bernie and his dark-haired friend now knew his general vicinity, and it would only be a matter of time before they located the *Sun Chaser*. Parker legged it to a nearby store and bought some needed provisions. While climbing onto the boat, his cell phone rang.

"I thought you were going to call me yesterday," Susan said, with a touch of anger.

"When I told my lawyer what happened, he became adamant I avoid you. He's afraid if Hall found out I was hanging with you, he might yank my bail," Parker replied.

After a pause, she replied, "I can understand that." Another pause. "The real reason I'm calling is... to agree that there might be more to my father's death than I'd first appreciated."

"It's hard to ignore being deliberately run off the road and then someone trying to burn us alive," Parker said.

"Look. I'm trying to politely tell you that... maybe I was wrong, and you might be innocent."

Parker sighed. "Well, that's a step in the right direction."

Suddenly, Parker knew he wanted to see her again.

"What do you have planned today?" he asked.

"Nothing special. Why?"

"How about a quiet sail on the bay? Lunch, with cold beer included."

He could hear the smile in her voice. "Quiet sail, huh? With you that means either run over by a passing oil tanker or adrift in a sea of sharks." She paused. "Only if I can bring the lunch."

"You drive a hard bargain."

##

The wind held at a steady ten knots with only a light ocean swell. The warm weather had persisted, and as it was a weekday, theirs was one of the few boats on the bay.

"Is this merely a fun sail or do we have a destination?" Susan asked, sitting across the cockpit from him.

"I'm moving the boat to a new mooring," Parker replied.

"Where?"

"Stillwater Cove in Pebble Beach." Parker noted the jib luffing slightly and pointed the boat lower into the wind. "A friend of mine has a mooring there and said I could borrow it for a few weeks. It's a nice set-up. The cove is well protected from the ocean swells in the summer and there's a pier where I can tie my dingy when I go ashore."

Susan twisted around and stared at the shoreline. "How about a geography lesson while we're sailing. I've no idea what we're passing."

"Do you want the James Michener version or the one-page tourist size?"

"A bit of both."

Parker put out his right hand, palm down. "Think of my thumb as the Monterey Peninsula, extending westward into the Pacific Ocean. The area encompassed by my thumb and index finger is Monterey Bay. Down at the base of the thumb is the town of Monterey, with its wharfs and Cannery Row."

"I've always loved John Steinbeck's description of that area," Susan said.

"Well, it's undergone some major changes from when it was primarily devoted to fish canneries. Although Doc Ricketts' lab is still there."

Parker looked down at his hand. "So moving further out along the side of the thumb, we come to the town of Pacific Grove. At the tip and down the southern edge is Pebble Beach. My favorite memory of Pebble is one early morning, as the fog started to lift, I saw a herd of deer feeding on a fairway as a foursome of golfers played through

"How beautiful. Where is Carmel?"

"It's down at the southern base."

Susan cocked her head. "Someone told me that if you cut down all the trees in Carmel, what's left might be considered a slum."

Parker laughed. "There used to be a lot of 'Carmel charmers' that fit into the category of tear-downs, but many have been remodeled into small McMansions."

With the sound of the hull knifing through the water, the sails ruffling in the wind, and the warm sun offsetting the coolness of the occasional sea spray, they had all the ingredients for a perfect sailing outing.

Susan sat on the bow, her legs around the front stay. Dressed in Levis, tennis shoes, with sparse makeup, and long hair carelessly pulled back in a clip, Susan had metamorphosed into the girl next door.

After a while, she came aft and he let her handle the wheel.

"You're doing great. Have you sailed before?" he asked after a while.

"No, I've only been on power boats. This is my first time out on a sailboat." She glanced around and her grin widened.

Parker smiled and leaned back.

Susan watched his face. "You really love the ocean, don't you?"

Parker shrugged his shoulders. "At times I love its gentle soothing ways, then at other moments, I fear its harshness. Yet there is always this pull to get back to the water."

Parker reached over and loosen the jib line slightly. They were silent for a while, listening to the boat sounds, enjoying the feeling of power as the ship drove through the swells.

"Thank you for keeping me company," Parker said. "It's been a while since I've felt this relaxed."

"Me too." Susan said softly. "Why don't I fix us some lunch?"

"Sounds good to me. Consider yourself switched from guest to cook and go below."

Susan gave a mock salute. "Aye aye, Captain. But I believe the term these days would be chef." She laughed and went down into the cabin.

Parker stared after her retreating figure and smiled.

"Would you like another beer?"

Parker stretched his hand out for the cold bottle. Lunch had been a spinach salad with jumbo prawns accompanied by chilled beer.

"I'm impressed. Did you make all this yourself?" Parker asked.

"I can't take credit for the beer, but, yes, the rest did originate from my kitchen."

Parker adjusted the boat's course. "The only thing that originates from my kitchen is mold."

Susan grinned. "Don't get me wrong. I'm no Julia Child, but I love to cook when I have the time."

Parker glanced over at her, noting the flush from the sun on her cheeks. "And what is it that occupies your time?"

"Mainly my job. I have… an interior decorating business in San Francisco."

Parker gave a low whistle. "Impressive." He lifted his bottle. "To the lady with hidden talents."

Holding her drink up, Susan replied, "And to the most accomplished sailor I've ever sailed with."

Parker laughed. "And the only one you've ever sailed with."

They stowed the bottles away while Susan helped Parker bring the boat about. Once they had safely tacked and the jib line was secured, the beer came out again.

"I know a lot about your father and nearly nothing about you," Parker remarked.

"Single, working, love the outdoors, snow ski in the winter and water ski in the summer, on a continual diet, and now slightly inebriated a mile out to sea." She drained the last of her beer. "Your turn."

Parker stood up and bowed formally. "Single, out of work at present, love the outdoors which excludes prison, and still sober a mile out to sea."

Susan leaned back and gazed up at the mainsail. "Never married before?"

Parker found himself staring at her long slender neck and wondered how it would taste laced with salt and sun. He shook his head and directed his gaze seaward. "No, never married... I was engaged once."

Susan caught the inflection change in his voice and looked back at him with raised eyebrows. "Touchy subject?"

"Use to be." He finished the last of his beer then rolled the empty bottle around in his hand. "She reminds me of that old line from W.C. Fields: `A woman drove me to drink and I didn't have the decency to thank her'."

When he said no more, Susan asked, "End of topic?"

"Let's just say I let her slip away and by the time I realized my mistake, she'd married someone else." Parker stood up. "Why don't you take the helm while I go forward for a minute?"

After making a few adjustments to the lines, Parker returned to the cockpit and stretched out.

"Have you ever heard of Citadel Pharmaceutical Company?"

Susan shook her head. "No. Should I?"

Parker quickly outlined the events of the last few days, and where they'd led him.

"You think Citadel might be involved with all of this?" Susan asked.

"I have no idea," Parker admitted, "but for now it's the only lead I have."

Parker made a call to Dick Garden, who was involved with research projects for a large internationally known pharmaceutical company. He got lucky and caught Dick in his office. After getting the usual salutations and questions out of the way, Parker asked him what he knew about Citadel Pharmaceuticals.

"I've heard of the company, but that's about all. Rumor has it that they've got some new drug in clinical trials that's a definite winner, so the companies' stock is soaring. Other than that, I can't add much."

Parker explained what he needed.

Dick didn't waste time asking why. He told him someone would be back in touch within the hour.

Twenty minutes later, the phone rang. It was a Dr. Fred Spring, head of Research and Development for Dick's company.

Parker thanked him for phoning.

"My pleasure. I owe Dick a few favors and he speaks highly of you." Spring cleared his throat. "He mentioned questions about Citadel Pharmaceutical Company. Fire away."

"Not so much questions as information. I want an outline of who and what they are. After that, I might have a few questions."

"Splendid. Let me organize my thoughts for a second." After a short pause, he began rattling off information as rapidly as if reading it. His executive position clearly not a fluke.

Citadel was a relatively new (apparently fifteen years in this type of business was considered new) small company that had initially made generic drugs. Parker knew these were popular medications whose formulas, after a certain number of years, had come under public domain. These generic drugs could then be produced at a much lower price by other pharmaceutical groups since they didn't have to recoup the Research and Development costs incurred by the original company that discovered the drug.

Using the capital from generic drug production, Citadel had gone into developing their own drug lines. They'd produced several different medications, but most of them were the `me-too' kind of drugs: a close derivative of a particular drug that was already on the market. No one had paid much attention to them until recently when they'd discovered a new blood pressure lowering medication. In fact, it represented an entirely new class of antihypertensive medication. There was nothing on the market even remotely resembling it. The preliminary trials had shown it to be very effective with a minimal side effect profile.

Spring cleared his throat. "Usually this type of information doesn't get out, but rumor has it that someone in the company may have leaked the information to jack up their stock price. If that was the plan, they succeeded beyond their wildest imagination. Their stock soared, increasing its initial value tenfold, and it's still climbing. Even if the drug turns out to be a dud, someone has made a lot of money. On the other hand, if the drug lives up to even half of its potential, someone is going make a lot more money." Spring paused. "And that is a thumbnail sketch of Citadel."

"Thank you. That gives me a very clear picture of who they are."

"Any questions?"

"A couple. Have there been any accusations of foul play or illegal activity made against the company? And is there any association of ex-cons with the company?" Parker said.

"Some might interpret their stock manipulation, if true, as not quite cricket, but there have been no allegations of illicit actions otherwise." He paused. "I'm not aware of any relationship of the company with ex-convicts."

Parker thanked Dr. Spring for his time, and hung up. *So why does a security guard from a pharmaceutical company try and kill me? This makes no sense unless the two are not related.*

A V-shaped flock of brown pelicans passed low in front of the bow, rising and falling with the change in air currents, just skimming the tops of the waves. Parker found his focus pulled to their synchronization and tightness of their formation.

The ring of his cell phone broke the spell. It was Dr. Spring.

"Your last question stirred some cobwebs in my memory, so I made a few calls. The results might interest you."

"Anything you've got, I'm all ears."

"Well, my sources reminded me that there is one interesting side note about Citadel. They are one of only three drug companies in the United States doing drug testing in prison. And it seems they are the only one using a California prison for their testing site."

Chapter Nineteen

"May I speak with Warden Morris, please? This is Tyler Beckman calling," Parker said.

A sweet but firm voice replied, "I'm sorry. Warden Morris is out sick today. Can someone else help you?"

"Maybe you can."

"What is it that you need?" she asked.

"Does Citadel Pharmaceutical Company do drug testing at your institution?"

She hesitated a moment. "Let me check." Two minutes later, she was back. "There is a company with a facility here, devoted strictly to drug research. I'm not sure of the name, but I think it's Citadel."

Parker explained that his father had been an inmate at the prison, and had died shortly after being paroled. Warden Morris had been very cooperative in answering queries about his father's incarceration.

"Since my last visit with the warden, some urgent questions have arisen," Parker said. "When do you think he'll be back?"

"I'm not sure, Mr. Beckman. It's possible he could be out for several days."

"Is there anyone else I could meet with?"

She remained silent for a moment. "Why don't I make an appointment for you with Warden Morris tomorrow, and if he's still absent, I'll find someone else to help you."

Parker summarized for Susan what he'd learned from Dr. Spring.

"How does this all fit together?" Susan asked.

"There must be some connection. Bernard and his dark-haired companion attacked me in Big Sur. They're the ones that ran us off the road. Bernard works for Citadel. Citadel does drug testing at Soledad State Prison. Your father was confined at Soledad."

Susan stared questioningly at him.

"Yeah, I know," Parker said. "My psychiatrist friends would call this looseness of association. Very loose."

"What interest could a drug company have in my father?" Susan said. "And even so, it doesn't explain how someone else killed him, when you were the only person with him in that room."

Susan saw Parker's surprised expression. "Now don't get me wrong," she added. "I think you're innocent, but I'm playing the devil's advocate."

"Why don't we pretend the glass is half-full instead of half-empty," he said. "Compared to what I had a few hours ago, this seems like the case is half solved."

##

The drive to Soledad the next day was, in Susan's words, "delightfully uneventful". There were a few more clouds in the sky and the day not quite as warm, but all in all, Parker thought it another fine day.

Or maybe having Susan in the car would make any day a fine day.

Parker felt nearly normal when he awoke that morning. The effects of his injuries had essentially disappeared, allowing him an hour in the gym at the Beach and Tennis Club and then a thirty minute jog. Having been sedentary for so long, Parker found the ache of his exhausted muscles an enjoyable sensation.

He also felt good remembering last night. They'd ended up barbequing chicken on a small hibachi that he kept on the boat. Susan had rustled up some odds and ends in the galley and created an "eclectic salad". For the piece de résistance, Parker had discovered an excellent bottle of Chateauneuf-du-Pape that an old medical friend had left on board as a thank you.

Lit by the pastel colors of the fading sun, the meal had been excellent.

The evening concluded with a long lingering handshake on the Stillwater pier just before she got into an Uber car.

The drive to Soledad the next day breezed by and they arrived in no time.

"Warden Morris is still out sick," Morris' secretary said, "but one of the assistant wardens, Mr. Girard, will see you. One of his duties is to act as our liaison with the drug company doing research at this facility."

She led Parker and Susan down a nondescript hall to Girard's office.

A thin, short, impeccably dressed man rose from behind his desk to greet them. Mr. Stephan Girard was pleasant, almost deferential in his introductions as he escorted Susan to one chair and gestured Parker toward the other. Trailing an odor of pungent aftershave, Girard moved back to his desk and perched on the edge. He appeared to enjoy this elevated position.

"I understand that you have some questions regarding your father, Michael Beckman." He used the flat of his hand to smooth back his thinning hair. "I took the liberty of reviewing his file." He stared at Susan with what could only be described as a leer. "How can I be of service?"

Susan spoke first. "My father spent almost two years of his life in here..."

Girard interrupted, "Actually a year and eight months."

Susan continued, "...and I'm trying to find out as much about his stay as I can. It may help me to understand his actions after he was out of prison."

Girard frowned. "His actions?"

Susan glanced down. "He was killed in a drug transaction." She paused and then continued, her voice quavering slightly. "So anything you could tell us about his life here might help us understand what caused such an abrupt personality change after his release."

Girard walked over and placed his hand on Susan's shoulder in apparent sympathy. To Parker it looked like lechery.

Leaning down, Girard said, "It would be my pleasure to answer whatever I can to aid you in your loss."

Susan reached up and placed her hand on Girard's. "You're so kind, Mr. Girard. Anything would be helpful. Was he involved in special activities or programs? Things like that."

Reluctantly Girard pulled his hand away and walked to his desk, picked up Beckman's file and sat down.

After a quick review of the file, Girard looked up. "We offer several different programs at Soledad. There is a vocational training program to give the inmates a means of earning a living when they are released. In addition, we offer various high school and college courses. So much so, that an inmate could graduate from high school and finish four years of college, if he remained here that long. We also offer a number of arts and crafts." He glanced again at Beckman's file. "The records indicate that your father was not involved with any of these."

Susan shook her head. "Maybe if he had, things might have been different. I do remember that he mentioned one thing, and I thought it was very strange. He said something about being in a drug study." Her expression went quizzical. "Do you know what he was talking about?"

Was it Parker's imagination or did Girard suddenly sit up a little straighter. He opted for imagination since Girard already moved like he had a poker up his ass so how could he sit any more erect.

Girard turned a few pages of the file and then glanced up. "Yes, that is true. He was involved with not one, but two drug studies while he was here."

Parker spoke up. "I thought drug testing in prison was outlawed."

Smiling politely, Girard launched into an obviously well-rehearsed monologue on the subject of "research behind bars." He explained that a local pharmaceutical company had been allowed to take over a wing on the prison grounds. It contained several offices and a lab but it primarily acted as a housing facility for the prisoners involved in the drug testing. The type of studies done at Soledad were termed Phase I drug testing, which basically entailed giving a new drug to humans for the first time to see what toxicity it might have.

"I'm a little shocked that this kind of research is allowed in prisons," Susan said.

"It is unusual since the United States is the only country in the world that permits prison research. On the other hand," Girard said, "the vast majority of phase I studies are done not in prisons but in the general population using paid volunteers. Allowing prisoners to volunteer for the same studies that their counterparts in the outside world are paid for doesn't seem that incongruous."

"I can understand why money might attract some people to participate, but what draws an inmate?" Parker asked.

"It is surprising," Girard agreed, smoothing back his perfectly coiffured hair. "There are basically three reasons. First, meritorious good time. This is a reduction of their sentence by a certain number of days. Yet, they can get the same type of reduction for good behavior or for doing certain jobs around the prison. Second, meritorious compensation. This is a system of monetary payment which, again, is available to all prisoners by doing maintenance and other tasks within the prison."

"So prisoners could earn these same benefits in other ways," Susan ventured.

"Exactly," Girard replied. "It's the third reason that most researchers feel is the strongest impetus. And that is that while in the study, the inmates are housed in the drug facility, thus separated from the rest of the prisoners. Each of them has a room of their own, access to excellent medical and dental care, and is removed from the sociopaths and psychopaths that surround them in the day yard.

Inmates claim they feel safe for the first time since their incarceration because violent and psychopathic prisoners are not eligible for these studies."

"And our father enrolled in two of these studies?" Susan asked.

"Yes, according to my records, he did."

"Is it possible to find out the nature of those studies?"

Girard looked at her speculatively then slowly shook his head. "It's not possible, Ms. Beckman, because all records regarding the exact details of the drug studies are kept by the pharmaceutical company."

Susan smiled. "Please... call me Susan." She paused. "Is there someone in the prison administration who watches over the inmate's welfare in these trials?"

Girard puffed up like a rooster showing his plumage. "In fact, Susan, a major portion of my job is exactly that, the inmate's well-being in these trials. I evaluate and review all the ongoing research."

"I suppose there are other agencies that also supervise the studies," Parker said.

Girard glared at him. "All research trials here are reviewed by the FDA. On top of that, there are a number of other government agencies that periodically examine the study protocols and their results." He turned back toward Susan and puffed his feathers up again. "One of my functions is to make sure these various groups know when a study is complete so they can review its records for safety."

"But why does Soledad get involved in something like this. I'd think it would be one more bureaucratic headache," Parker asked.

Girard gave him an 'are-you-still-here' look and directed his answer to Susan. "We are involved for financial reasons. The drug company compensates us for allowing the studies to be performed here. It requires a significant amount of money to maintain this facility and, alas, we never seem to have enough. As fast as we get funding and build new space, it's filled to overcapacity. This chronic overcrowding has resulted in early prison releases and other publicly unpopular solutions. We saw this involvement with drug studies as a way, albeit a small one, to correct some of our chronic financial instability."

With an air of nonchalance, Parker asked, "Which drug company is doing the trials here?"

Girard reluctantly shifted his attention back to Parker. "Citadel Pharmaceutical Company. A very reputable organization, I might add." He tried to stare Parker down with the weight of his pronouncement, as if no other questions could be necessary.

Someone needs to knock this little prince down to a more earthly level and I'll be happy to volunteer even without benefit of `meritorious compensation'.

Susan verbally stepped in before Parker's dissatisfaction had a chance to progress. "Mr. Girard, I have a small problem that I hope you could help me with." Her voice, filled with respect, was heavy with implied suggestion.

Girard swiveled his chair toward her, responding to this hint of intimacy, and smiled.

She continued. "My father told me, shortly before he died, that he'd left some of his personal belongings with a friend, a Mr. Bill Harris. I have been unable to locate that individual. The name is not someone my father associated with prior to his time in prison, so I wondered if it could be someone he met in here?"

Girard nodded. "That seems a reasonable possibility."

"I know this is irregular but you have been so helpful, I was hoping you might bend the rules a bit, and let me know if a Bill Harris was in prison while my father was here."

"It would be a pleasure," he oozed the last word out, "to assist you. And I wouldn't be breaking the rules since the information is available to the general public, but only after going through a lot of bureaucratic red tape." He pressed down on his intercom and asked his secretary to see if there was a file on a William Harris and if so, to bring it to his office.

For the next few minutes, he and Susan occupied themselves with small talk. As for Parker, he felt if this self-important twit straightened his tie once more, he would rip it off.

The secretary dropped a file onto Girard's desk. He opened it, briefly perused its contents, and then compared it to Beckman's file. "It does seem that there was a William Harris in prison at the same time your father was here."

"So I was right. But I wonder how dad came to know him." Here it came, the big question. Susan slipped it in ever so innocently. "Could Mr. Harris have been in one of the drug studies with my father? Could they have met and become friends that way?"

Girard shrugged his shoulders. "Anything is possible."

"Could you take a peek in Harris' file and see if he was involved in either of the two studies my father was enrolled in? That might settle the question."

Girard again shrugged his shoulders and opened the two files. He looked back and forth between them, and as he did, his demeanor became more and more formal. When he finally looked up, his face was coldly impassive. "I see no indication that Mr. Harris and your father were ever involved in drug studies together." He closed the two files and put them in his out box. "I'm afraid it would be unethical for me to answer any further questions about Mr. Harris' imprisonment."

Susan stood up and reached her hand across his desk. "Thank you anyway, Mr. Girard. You have been so helpful." They shook hands and she enclosed his with both of hers, and held it longer than appropriate.

Under Susan's touch and stare, Girard lost his sudden frigidity. "Let me... walk you out."

They ambled out to the hallway and had gone about twenty yards when Susan's groan of disgust stopped them.

"On, no," she said. "I left my purse in Mr. Girard's office."

Girard turned back, but Susan linked her arm into his and brought him to a halt. She beckoned to Parker. "Tyler, could you fetch it. I want to talk with Mr. Girard... alone."

"Sure, sis." Parker wasn't sure what the game was, but he'd play along.

Girard made to protest, but Susan silenced him with a squeeze of his arm. "I'd love for you to tell me more about yourself... and your role here."

That was enough to silence any objections Girard had. He glanced at Parker. "Ask my secretary to get it for you."

As Parker walked away, he heard Girard verbally strutting his indispensability to the prison system.

The man has no sense of the word humility.

When Parker stepped back into Girard's reception area, his secretary was talking on the phone. Parker heard enough of the conversation to know she was speaking to a supervisor. Very apologetically, she put her caller on hold and looked up at Parker.

"Can I help you, sir?"

"My sister left her purse in Mr. Girard's office," he said.

Just then, her phone rang. Parker glanced down at her phone bank and saw multiple flashing lights. Apparently, she had a number of people on hold, including her supervisor.

She frowned and moved to get up, but he waived her back into her chair. "Go on with your calls. I'll get it."

She needed no second urging, and immediately resumed her conversation with the supervisor.

Entering the room, the first thing Parker noticed was the prison files lying in Girard's outbox. The temptation was overwhelming. He pulled out his cell phone, and quickly took pictures of the drug study information regarding both Beckman and Harris.

Parker had just stepped away from the desk when the secretary entered. Before she could speak, he said, "I can't seem to find her it."

They both searched and eventually discovered it far back under the desk.

#

"That was a nice move with the purse."

"So you got a peek at the files?" Susan asked.

"More than a peek. I took pictures."

"What did you find?"

"Your father was transferred to the drug research unit for two separate periods of time. I assume those dates correspond to the two different studies he was enrolled in. Using those dates, I reviewed Harris' file."

"And?"

"Girard is a lying slime. Harris was also in the drug research unit for several weeks. His dates of confinement correspond to the same dates your dad was there for his second study."

"Interesting."

"And just as interesting is why Girard would lie about it."

Chapter Twenty

On the drive back from Soledad, Susan asked Parker questions about drug studies and it became apparent that he needed to know a lot more about them. After dropping Susan at her home, McGraw returned to his boat and made a phone call to the Food and Drug Administration (FDA) in Washington.

His inquiry eventually connected him with Sarah Morganson, one of their public relations staff, where he made his plea.

Parker introduced himself, and said, "I've been enlisted to speak to the County Medical Society about the steps a new drug has to undergo before it's released to the public." He paused. "I was hoping you could walk me through the process, so I can make sure I'm up-to-date in my information."

"I'd be delighted," she replied.

"Start from when the drug company has a new but untested drug?" he asked.

"Sure," she said. "Even with a brand-new chemical compound, the lab chemists will have some predictions about its actions, based on the actions of known drugs with similar chemical structures. The lab would first do basic chemical tests on the new compound, followed by various animal studies. Once the company has a better understanding of the drug, including its potential actions and side effects from the animal studies, they would apply for an investigational new drug number (IND). This application would include a description of the new drug - its actions and safety records - along with the results of the animal studies supporting these claims. In addition to the application, the company would submit a detailed description of their phase 1 testing protocol."

"Phase I testing. Remind me." Parker recalled that phase I was the level of testing done at Soledad.

"There comes a time when the testing of a new drug moves from animal studies to human studies. Animal studies can never completely predict man's response to a particular drug. The biochemical variations between human and animal species are so great that both therapeutic effects and side effects can differ between the two. And the response among different animal species, even among different strains of the same species, can be variable."

"You mean that one strain of rats might experience a side effect that another strain wouldn't?"

"Exactly," she said. "You can see the problems that relying purely on animal studies would create."

"I can understand why the response in a rat may not be predictive but what about using species closer to man, like monkeys? Wouldn't they more closely approximate man's response?"

"That's true, Dr. McGraw. The problem with using primates is the relatively high cost of obtaining and housing them, not to mention the difficulty in procuring them. I'm afraid that the bottom line will always be the response of the drug in man."

"So phase I testing is the first time the drug is used in human beings?" Parker asked.

"Yes. Therefore, these studies involve relatively small study groups, usually no more than twenty or thirty volunteers per study. The main purpose of these studies is to examine the safety of the drug. How it's tolerated and what side effects it has. Volunteers for these types of study are usually paid and there are long detailed consent forms that the volunteer has to read and sign before he can enroll. As a further safeguard, the FDA generally reviews the phase I protocol and its consent form before the trial is initiated."

"Can a company do a phase I trial without it's protocol being reviewed by the FDA?" Parker asked.

"Yes, but we don't encourage it." She paused and when Parker had no more questions, continued on. "Before moving on to phase II trials, the FDA encourages the company to sit down with them and discuss the design of their phase II protocols. Although that isn't a necessity, they prefer to work with the drug company and make sure they're headed in the right direction."

"How many people are involved in those trials?" Parker asked.

"Phase II trials are designed to study larger populations, so about two hundred. In addition to looking at the questions of safety and toxicity, these trials examine efficacy and dose ranges.

"With the completion of this level of testing, the company is now ready to move onto phase III trials, the so called `pivotal trials'. At this point the FDA practically insists that the company review their ideas for phase III with them prior to writing the protocol. Phase III are the real clinical studies and include thousands of patients, usually at multiple centers. A mistake in the design of the protocol at this level of testing could be very costly and significantly delay, if not eliminate, the chances of the drug becoming licensed."

Uncertain what might be important, Parker wanted as much information as he could about the testing procedure. "Do you review the results of the trials in each phase before you allow the company to go onto the next phase?"

"We do and we don't. Usually the results of the preceding phase are briefly mentioned in the introduction of the protocol for the next phase. So in a way, we do hear about the results but they're not closely scrutinized until the company submits its new drug application, termed NDA."

"And when do they apply for that?" Parker inquired.

"Once all the phase III trials are complete, the company fills out the NDA and sends it in. The NDA is basically a summary of all the studies and data the company has collected on the drug. This information is used to support the company's request that the drug be licensed for release in the US."

They talked for a bit longer and then hung up.

##

Parker called Susan to summarize his conversation with the FDA, and share his plans for tomorrow.

"McGraw, if you'll excuse my French, you've got balls. I may be bold at times but nothing like that."

He laughed. "Wish me luck."

"You mean wish us luck, don't you? You're not doing this without me!"

Parker protested, but she was steadfast. "Don't even think of going without me and that's final. So what time do we leave?"

Parker surrendered. "I'll pick you up about three. Dress conservatively, in fact, matronly."

He spent the next few hours working on the *Sun Chaser*. Parker's belief in boat maintenance was deeply ingrained and based on a conversation he'd had years before with an elderly sea dog who'd been twice around the world. He could still hear the old mariner's harsh voice and smell the whisky on his breath when he remembered his advice.

"A house," the man had said, "needs a lot of care, but if you let it slide for a while, maybe you get a leaky roof or a clogged drain. Let your boat maintenance slide and you could end up with King Neptune as a roommate."

Toward dusk, Parker switched on some music, grabbed a beer, and retired to the fantail to watch the sunset.

He remembered he hadn't been home for several days, and reminded himself he needed to swing by and pickup his mail.

With that thought, something that had been nagging at the back of his mind clicked into place. With that thought, something that had been nagging at the back of his mind clicked into place. With that thought, something that had been nagging at the back of his mind clicked into place. "Mail! That's it! The mail!"

##

"You called me to talk about your mail?" Susan said with surprise.

"I'm not talking about my mail, I'm talking about Harris' mail that I grabbed from his mail box."

Her voice changed. "I didn't know you had his mail."

"Well, I don't now. It went up in smoke with my car."

"Oh, great."

"I remember, though, he gotten a postcard. I think the card had the word `Study' in the right hand corner followed by several numbers."

There was a pause on the other end of the line. "Maybe I'm a bit slow, Parker, but with the card gone and your memory a little hazy, how can it help us now?"

"It doesn't. But if Harris got a card, then maybe your father did too. And if he did, it could still be around."

Susan hung up to go search her father's belongings. Twenty minutes later the phone rang.

"Bingo!" Susan said. "I almost missed it. It was stuck to the bottom of another envelope."

"So what's printed in the right hand corner," Parker asked.

"The card is from our favorite place - Citadel Pharmaceutical Company. It's a reminder to come in for a follow up visit. And in the right hand corner is stamped, `Study: Chem 19'."

Chapter Twenty-One

"And who may I say is calling?"

Parker smiled back. "I'm Dr. Peter Joyce, from the FDA. And my companion is Ms. Grimbottom, president of the local chapter of PETA."

The shapely blond secretary tried not to smirk as she asked Parker and Susan to have a seat and lifted the phone to contact Mr. Amaray, the president of Citadel Pharmaceuticals.

Parker felt Susan's elbow jab him as they sat down on one of the nearby overstuffed couches. "Grimbottom?" she whispered.

Parker had arrived at Susan's at two o'clock, and was pleased to see she'd followed his instructions as to dress. With her hair drawn back, no makeup, granny glasses, and baggy plain clothes, he thought she looked the part of the perpetual hippie searching for another cause.

Within a few minutes, a tall, thin man wearing a light blue shirt with a narrow black tie, under a long white lab coat, came down the hall. When he entered the lobby, the secretary nodded in their direction.

The man approached, his hands in his lab coat. Parker and Susan stood up.

"Hello. I'm Dr. Onge," he said, "vice president of Citadel." His tone was noncommittal.

Parker held out his hand. "Dr. Peter Joyce, field inspector for the FDA." Onge's hand was ice cold and his grip limp.

Parker gestured toward Susan. "This is Ms. Grimbottom, president of the local chapter of PETA."

Onge offered his limp handshake to Susan and then he led them through a maze of hallways to his office.

The office, like its inhabitant, was a plain, no-frills room, with a large gray metal desk as its centerpiece. Papers, journals, lab notebooks, and bulging manila folders covered most of the desk top.

There were four metal filing cabinets against one wall with more manila files stacked on top of several open drawers. The rest of the wall space was devoted to bookshelves, filled haphazardly with bound and unbound journals.

Onge directed them to matching gray metal chairs while he cleared away some of the wreckage on his desk.

Onge had gray-black hair sitting on a long thin face. His hairline had receded far back along the temples, leaving a lone tuft stranded on his forehead. Watching him clear his workspace, Parker noted multiple psoriatic lesions on the back of his hands.

When he finished the desk reorganization, Onge settled into his chair and regarded them with what Parker now realized were perpetually raised eyebrows and half-mast eyelids. "To what do we owe this visit, Dr. Joyce?"

"As you may know, the FDA periodically makes on-site visits to research facilities. Usually, these are announced, but occasionally, as in this instance, they are not."

Onge removed his black rimmed bifocals. "No, I wasn't aware of such visits." Methodically, he cleaned the lenses. "What is the purpose?"

Parker bent forward, his face serious. "Dr. Onge, there has been a lot of poorly-done, even falsified, research published in some highly regarded research journals lately. Just last year, the *New England Journal of Medicine*, that bastion of respectability which acts as the source for much of the lay press' medical information, had to retract several articles. The reason? Dishonest research. The author had concocted his results to make the data fit his hypothesis. As another example, thirty research articles in various journals were retracted two years ago due to data manipulation by another physician."

Onge snorted. "I'm aware of this, but what does it have to do with Citadel?"

"If you allow me to finish, I'll tell you."

Onge flinched as if struck, and Parker mollified his voice as he continued. "In parallel to this, but in no way connected, there's been a growing public dissatisfaction with the FDA. Accusations that we move too slowly to approve new therapies, as in the instances of the AIDS medications and certain cancer drugs. Others claim that we are inefficient in our screening of potential new therapies and as a result drugs or treatments get passed that are later shown to have dangerous side effects. Witness the potential for cancer and infertility seen with the copper seven IUD."

Parker settled back in his chair and took a deep breath. He was on a roll, and looking over, he thought even Susan seemed impressed.

"So in order to combat this combination of slipshod, sometimes falsified, research data and our fading popularity," Parker said, "we have decided to do more field visitations, especially surprise ones. The hope is that researchers, knowing that we might stop in at any time to review their ongoing studies will be less likely to try and submit bogus results or falsify reports. In addition, it gives us a head start in licensing new potential therapies by reviewing the work in progress, even before the company applies for a new drug application."

Onge nodded. "Makes sense, I guess. Nice to know that the FDA is aware of its shortcomings and trying to correct them. I doubt, though, that this is the most productive manner for those corrections." He nodded toward Susan. "And Ms. Grimbottom's role?"

"This is another facet of our attempt to improve the FDA's public image. We are firm supporters of the tenet that animal research is a necessary, indispensable, element of medical research. The animal rights activists, on the other hand, have also become a firmly entrenched element."

"A loud, obnoxious, and uninformed element," Onge interjected angrily.

Parker waved his comment aside. "Be that as it may, they remain a very permanent influence in the field of animal research. It is our hope that by allowing representatives of the local activist group to join us on our investigational visits, two things will result. One, the laboratories will be more attentive to the question of animal rights, knowing that they may have an inspection at any time. Two, the animal rights activists may be pacified when they see that the animals are treated with dignity and respect for their rights. We hope, as a side benefit, they may also come to realize that research would be impossible without animal studies."

Onge faced Susan. "What do you see as your role here, Ms. Grimbottom?"

Susan smiled. "It's not to break open cages and free imprisoned animals, Dr. Onge. I'm not so much an activist as an animal rights awarenist."

What the hell is that? Now I was impressed.

Susan proceeded. "I'm aware that animal right violations do exist, but in many cases the violators are more than happy to correct them once they are pointed out. Our groups' long term goal is not to work against animal research but rather make it under the most humane circumstances, and only when it is definitely indicated. That means not using animals for any half-ass... err, half-baked study which comes along."

Onge, wearing a half smile after Susan's slip, turned toward Parker. "Although your goals are laudable, Dr. Joyce, the likelihood of reaching them seems very small. But since I really don't have much to say in the situation, why don't we just get on with it."

Parker and Susan stood up just as Onge remarked. "Of course, there is the matter of your identification. So far, I have only your word as to who you are." Clearing his throat, he looked back and forth at each of them. "There are numerous labs who would love to get some inside information on our recent research, so you will understand my reticence to open the lab to just anyone who walks in."

Susan gave Parker a "help me or your ass is grass" look before she turned toward Onge. "I'm afraid I don't have any identification with me."

Parker had known this would be a problem, especially since his identification forger friend was out of town. He quickly spoke before Onge could reply. "I'm sure that authenticating my credentials will confirm both of ours, since Ms. Grimbottom is with me."

Parker reached into the inside pocket of his suit coat and pulled out a business card. He extended it to Onge. After several minutes of studying the card, Onge looked up.

"Not very impressive," he said. "No special seal. No photograph. Just this simple white card." He dropped it on his desk. "One could get this made up anywhere."

Not just "anywhere". It took me three stops to find a cooperative printer.

Onge continued. "Truthfully, I have no idea what the business card of an FDA investigator should look like. So if you don't mind," Onge added, "I'll give your Washington headquarters a call to verify your credentials. Any problem with that, Dr. Joyce?"

"Please do, Dr. Onge."

Parker glanced at this watch, and then at Susan who seemed to be edging toward the door. "Shall we be seated, Ms. Grimbottom? This might take a while."

Susan hesitantly returned to her chair and gave Parker another one of her looks.

While they sat, Onge used his computer to look up the FDA number in Washington. As Onge punched in the number, Parker noticed Susan fidgeting on the chair next to him. His attention was pulled back to Onge as he spoke into the phone. "Hello. I'd like to verify the credentials..." He halted in mid-sentence, glared at the phone in disgust, and hung up.

"Is there a problem?" Parker asked.

"Damn answering machines!" Onge looked up. "Two hour time difference so it's after five in Washington and your headquarters are apparently closed for the day."

Thank God for government employees. If there is one thing they don't do, it's answer phones after five.

Onge went back to his computer. "I'm going to look you up on their web site." After several key strokes, he leaned forward. "There is a Dr. Peter Joyce shown here, but his picture doesn't look much like you."

Parker smiled. "That's an old photograph when I was sporting a full beard."

Onge leaned back, a picture of doubt.

"Would you like to call our local facility in California?" Parker inquired. He heard Susan choke.

Onge agreed and Parker pointed out the toll-free number on the bottom of his business card. Onge dialed it several times and each time quickly hung up. He glared at Parker. "It seems to be continually busy, Dr. Joyce."

"Well, I think we have two options open to us, Dr. Onge. You can accept my credentials at face value and we can go on with the visit. Or I can come back on a different day after you've had a chance to verify my credentials."

"The latter would be my preference," Onge said.

"Let me finish the second option before you make your decision," Parker said. "If I come back on another day, my next opportunity to be in this area won't be until next Wednesday, a week from now. Since this is supposed to be a surprise visit, I obviously can't allow you time to prepare for my visit. Therefore if you chose option two, I will have to insist that the entire complex be closed until my return."

Onge was aghast. "But that's not possible. We are in the midst of numerous projects. We can't suddenly shut down, especially for that length of time."

"Let's make a compromise," Parker suggested. "My purpose is merely to make sure your trials are properly designed. Reviewing your phase I protocols will tell me that. Ms. Grimbottom is only concerned about how you treat the animals. Show her the animal cages, and she'll be happy."

"And that will be enough?" Onge asked.

"More than adequate."

Onge drummed his fingers on his desk for a full minute, stood up and told them he'd be right back. The door had no sooner closed when Susan reached over and grabbed Parker's tie and pulled his face up to hers. She whispered ever so softly, "You knew that the business card wouldn't be enough, didn't you?!"

Parker nodded.

Her vocal intensity rose slightly. "You knew he would call Washington, but it would be after-hours, didn't you?!"

Parker nodded again.

Now her voice was really rising. "And when he tried the California office, the line would be busy?!"

"The number I gave him was the information number for the IRS. It's always busy." Parker arched his eyebrows and smiled.

Susan's voice went to full timbre. "Yet you never warned me about any of this!!" She ended her exclamation with a shove that sent him and his chair over backwards. As he fell, his head struck the edge of one of the shelves on the bookcase behind him, knocking it loose. Twenty heavy bound, dust covered, volumes of *The Journal of Clinical Investigations* poured down on him.

Stunned, lying under this avalanche of books, Parker heard the door open and Onge's voice. "My God, what's happened?"

Susan's voice drifted down to him as he felt books being pulled and pushed aside. "Dr. Joyce leaned too far back in his chair and fell against the bookshelves."

When most of the books had been lifted off, Parker grabbed Onge's outstretched hand and stood up. He dusted himself off and straightened his hair. Onge's voice interrupted any further ministrations.

"Dr. Joyce, I'd like to introduce you to our company president, Mr. Amaray."

Parker swiveled in the direction of Onge's gesturing hand. He found himself staring into the cold, back orbs of a tall, well-built man in his late forties. With jet black hair combed straight back and a small Johnny Depp mustache on his tanned, handsome face, the man radiated power, capability, and authority.

Parker, with disheveled hair, dust-stained clothes, and tie askew, felt like something that Amaray probably cleaned off the bottom of his shoe from time to time.

Amaray offered a well-manicured hand which Parker shook, noticing his diamond-studded gold cuff links as he did.

"It's good to meet you, Dr. Joyce," Amaray said. Up close, there was a suggestion of ruthlessness in Amaray's face that wasn't obvious from a distance.

"The pleasure is mine, Mr. Amaray," Parker replied.

Amaray made no comment on Parker's less-than-pristine appearance, except to inquire if he'd been injured. With assurances by Parker that he was fine, Amaray shifted the force of his presence onto Susan. Parker detected a flush in her face as they were introduced and it seemed like an hour before Amaray released her hand.

Amaray turned back to Parker. "Dr. Onge has informed me of the situation and I see no problem with you inspecting our phase I protocols. I'll be interested in your findings. Dr. Onge will hand you over to our chief lab technician and I will escort..." He looked at Susan, "Ms. Goodbottom is it?"

Parker corrected him. "Ms. Grimbottom."

Susan gave him another of her withering looks.

"Yes, Ms. Grimbottom, to our animal area and let our resident animal handler show her around."

Susan smiled up at Amaray. Even dressed like an aging hippie, she was a knockout. "Please call me Susan."

His return smile revealed a perfect set of teeth. "Only if you call me Randall."

Amaray offered his arm, which Susan obligingly took, and lead her to the doorway. He paused and glanced back. "Dr. Joyce, your face seems familiar. Have we met before?"

Parker realized that he'd lost his limited disguise with his fall. The center part in his hair had evaporated, and his newly purchased brown rimmed glasses were under the pile of books. "No, I'm sure we haven't, Mr. Amaray," he mumbled as he bent to find his glasses.

Onge delivered Parker to the chief lab technician, a Mr. Gary Sato, who guided him through the research facility. It was an impressive layout, with at least ten thousand square feet of space devoted solely to research. He was introduced to several technicians and PhDs during the walk and given a brief overview of some of their ongoing studies, concentrating on the phase I trials.

When the tour was completed, Parker asked Sato if he had a list of drug studies which had been done over the last year-and-a-half.

"Is there some certain study that you are interested in or something in particular that I can answer?" Sato was most accommodating.

"No. I'd just like to see what you've been doing. Maybe pick out a few phase I trials and review their protocols, their record keeping, and their patient safety considerations."

After a ten minute wait, Sato produced a list of about twenty ongoing and completed studies. Parker noticed that all of the studies were designated by a series of four letters, followed by a number. He asked Sato to explain.

"That's our in-house method of keeping track of the various projects. Nearly all of our studies revolve around a specific drug or chemical, so the initial group of letters is an abbreviation for the name of the drug that is being tested. The digits that follow designate the particular study being done on that drug, each one being given a different number."

"Are those numbers in the order in which the studies are completed?"

"No, they're in order of when the studies were started because we may begin another study before its predecessor is complete or even run two studies simultaneously."

Parker checked the list and found 'Chem 16' and 'Chem 17'. He pointed these out to Sato. "What do these two indicate?"

"The letter prefix 'Chem' refers to the drug chemopandilin. The numbers 16 and 17 refer to the sixteenth and seventeenth study that we did using that particular chemical."

"Tell me more about this chemo... whatever."

Sato smiled. "Chemopandilin. It is classified as a psychotropic drug and is supposed to suppress violent, antisocial behavior."

Parker studied the list again then gave it back to Sato. "Are you sure that all your recent studies are listed here?"

Sato looked the list over, slowly and methodically. "Yes, everything seems to be here." He looked up. "Why do you ask?"

"There hasn't been a Chem 18 or Chem 19?"

"Not to my knowledge. I've only been here about six weeks though, and all the studies using that particular drug were before my time. But I'm sure that Chem 17 was our last evaluation of chemopandilin because I remember checking that when I compiled this list."

Parker took the list back and scanned it. "This says that Chem 17 was completed almost a year ago. Isn't it strange that no further studies have been done on the drug since then?"

Sato shrugged his shoulders. "It's my understanding that we have stopped all further studies on chemopandilin."

"Why is that?"

"The company has decided to put all its efforts in a different direction."

"What direction is that?"

Sato regarded Parker with surprise. "I felt sure that the FDA knew." He shook his head. "We have discovered an antihypertensive drug that has an entirely new mechanism of action and, as such, represents a brand new class of antihypertensive agents. We are calling it, Normopressor."

"Yes, now I remember reading about it."

"I think you'll be more that reading about it in the future," Sato said excitedly. "This is one of the most thrilling drug discoveries of the decade. Our preliminary trials show Normopressor to be much more effective than any other drug on the market, and its side effect profile is practically nil."

"I remember a mention of your stock value."

Sato's expression changed to one of wistfulness. "Ah, yes. Our stock values have jumped unbelievably since the drug's discovery."

"What happened to your predecessor? I'm surprised he'd leave with a drug like that in the pipeline."

Sato shifted his eyes on to Parker. "That was Mr. Ludwig. He's dead."

In order to keep up pretenses, Parker reviewed several other phase I protocols along with their raw data before concluding his official visit. Sato returned him to Dr. Onge's office where he found Susan in a heated discussion with Onge over animal rights. She was warming to her new role. His entry cut their conversation short.

Onge shifted his attention to Parker. "Well, I trust that all was in order, Dr. Joyce. Is there anything I can answer or show you that Mr. Sato didn't cover?"

Parker bowed his head toward Onge. "I commend you, Dr. Onge, on the professionalism of this entire facility. Very nicely run." He paused. "There is one thing, more a point of curiosity than anything else. What happened to Sato's predecessor?"

Onge's head jerked up and for an instant Parker thought he saw fear on Onge's face before he quickly bent back down to organize the papers on his desk. Once they were aligned, he straightened up and spoke, his tone matter of fact and his face now expressionless. "He was killed in an automobile accident. Anything else, Dr. Joyce."

"No, everything seems to be in order." Parker turned to Susan. "How about you, Ms. Grimbottom? Any improprieties that you want to mention?" *Such as with randy Randall?*

She stared at Parker for a long moment before replying. "No. There were no improprieties of any sort to report."

They both thanked Onge, who in turn, offered to walk them to the front entrance since it was now after hours and the doors would be locked.

Walking with them down the hall, Onge suddenly halted. "Oh, good. I see the security guard is at the door. He can let you out. So if you don't mind, I'll excuse myself now."

They had only gone a few feet when Onge called after them. "Dr. Joyce! Ask Bernard, the security guard, to come down to my office after he lets you out. Thanks."

Parker glanced toward the front entrance and recognized the hulking figure of Bernard Johnson. Luckily his back was turned. Parker grabbed Susan by the arm and quickly explained the problem.

"He knows who you are? Great!" Susan said.

"I need a distraction and you're the only distraction available."

"Why do I listen to you? I've must have a death wish!"

Parker pulled her close and whispered his plan.

Once again, they proceeded toward the door, only to halt after a few steps. In a loud voice Parker said, "Darn! I left my notes in Dr. Onge's office. I'll be right back." With that, he moved off in the direction of Onge's office. Susan continued on, calling loudly over her shoulder, "I'll wait for you at the door."

Parker went back down the hall until he was out of sight, waited for a few minutes, and then trudged back toward the entrance. In the distance he could see Susan standing in the open doorway having a discussion with Bernard. Parker moved quietly to his left as he drew near them, trying to come up behind Bernard. As he got closer, Susan's voice became louder in an attempt to muffle his approach.

Just a few more steps and I'm out the door before Bernard can see my face.

He didn't make it.

Some sixth sense alerted Bernard and he turned suddenly, staring directly at Parker. Quickly covering the lower half of his face with his hand, Parker simulated a coughing paroxysm. Still coughing, he turned his face away from Bernard as he passed through the door. Susan moved to his side, slapping him several times on the back while they continued walking toward the parking lot.

Parker started the car, wondering all the time if Bernard had recognized him. As they drove out of the parking lot, Parker glanced over at the front entrance. Bernard was still standing out front, watching them leave.

"Did he recognize you?" Susan asked.

"Is the pope Catholic?"

Chapter Twenty-Two

The western sky was dark with a thin rim of orange on the horizon as Susan and Parker drove down the coast to Big Sur. Parker banked left into the Ventana Inn driveway and slowly accelerated up the hill to the restaurant. They were early so they strolled around the grounds and had a drink on the restaurant veranda. By the time they were called for dinner, they were both famished.

Parker had the fresh ahi and Susan the sea bass. They were both excellent and so was the bottle of German white wine they had with it. In the afterglow of the meal, while drinking Amaretto coffees, they rehashed their sojourn to Citadel.

"I'm afraid that nothing I saw or heard was of any significance," Susan said.

Parker sipped his coffee. "I found my time productive, and it raised a number of questions."

"Like what?"

"Let's start with the missing studies. Sato assured me that the last study done with chemopandilin was Chem 17. Yet your dad got an appointment card reminding him of a follow up visit for a study listed as Chem 19."

Laying his credit card on the bill, Parker took a last swallow of coffee. "So why doesn't the company have any record of a Chem 19 study or, for that reason, a Chem 18 study since the studies are supposed to run in numerical order?"

"Maybe someone made a mistake on the number on my father's card and it was supposed to be 17 not 19."

Parker shook his head. "No, I reviewed the protocol for Chem 17 and the study subjects were rabbits. And in Chem 16, the study population was rats. No, all the studies on chemopandilin up to and including Chem 17 were animal studies."

Susan sighed. "So in summary, we have two men, my father and Harris, whose only apparent connection was in a drug study that Citadel claims never happened."

Susan left for the bathroom while McGraw signed the bill. As he sat waiting, he mulled over his reservations about Citadel in the role of bad guy. *Why should Citadel lie about some obscure prison drug study? And why would a company on the verge of making millions bother to frame a small-town physician?*

The night air was actually balmy when they stepped out of the restaurant, an unusual occurrence for the central coast. Enjoying the warm night air, Parker thought it was a shame to waste such an evening on a long drive home.

He opened the car door for Susan and after she climbed in, he made his proposal. "How about relaxing in a hot tub before we go home?"

She glanced up at him. "Sounds delicious, but where?"

They drove over to the hotel portion of the Inn, parked in the shadows, and got out. Parker cleared his throat. "There is one small detail I should mention. The hot tub here is reserved for hotel guests so we'll have to sneak in."

Susan laughed. "I've always wondered how physicians entertained their dates."

Parker grabbed her hand. "Come on. You'll love it."

She hesitated. "What will I wear? I'm not into nude hot tubbing."

"Susan, feel this night air. This is an evening for adventure, for romance. It's not a night for inhibitions, for clinging to social mores."

She remained in her seat.

"Okay. I'll see if I have something in the trunk you can wear." Walking around to the back of the car, Parker loudly remarked, "I don't understand it. Those lines always worked before." He heard Susan's soft laugh as he opened the trunk.

They walked onto the spacious grounds and strolled toward the pool area where the spa was located. Parker put his arm around Susan but assured her it was for appearances sake only.

"This hotel is frequented almost solely by honeymooners, and couples who want a romantic getaway. If we don't act like star-crossed lovers, we'll stand out like a sore thumb."

"Right, McGraw."

"Do I detect disbelief in your voice, Ms. Beckman?" Parker stopped and squeezed her tight. "You don't think I really enjoy having my arm around you?"

They walked past several rental units. Although very dark, the path was lit by knee-high shaded lamps.

"So you're forewarned, there is a security guard here at night. Allegedly, there are lowlifes who try to sneak into the hot tub," Parker said.

"McGraw, if we get arrested for this..." She didn't get a chance to finish for Parker had seen a figure coming up the path toward them.

"It's the guard!" Parker whispered. Before she could reply, he pulled her into his arms and kissed her. She started to pull away but by now the presence of someone else on the path was obvious. They continued to kiss waiting for the figure to pass, and when it did, it was not a security guard but rather an elderly woman. Susan pulled away, but slowly. She gave him another of her looks but this time there was the hint of a smile.

Parker held his hands up in front of him. "Hey, anyone can make a mistake. I thought it was the guard." *And if it had been, I would have really been shocked since they've never employed one before.*

As they strolled on further, Susan slipped her arm into Parker's and rested her head on his shoulder. He was going to compliment her on getting into their role then decided it wasn't the time for levity.

They arrived at the small house which enclosed the hot tub. He directed Susan into the female dressing area while he went into the male changing room. After putting on his bathing suit, Parker stepped into the hot tub. A long hall-like structure connected the two dressing areas, with several bends to assure visual privacy. The whole complex had a roof, except for the center length of the tub which opened out on a large wooden deck.

Parker slowly made his way along the tub until he meet Susan. The moonlight glistening on her wet hair, casting partial shadows across her face, gave her a sultry sensuous appearance. Neither spoke for a while, content to soak in the simmering water, listening to the night.

"Let's go out on the deck. It has a panoramic view of the hillside," Parker suggested.

"I'll pass since all I'm wearing is this wet t-shirt, and we don't know each other that well."

"Isn't there some way we can speed up introductions," Parker asked with a grin.

They had a splendid time and all too soon it was time to go.

##

Despite the early morning hour the following day, Bob Clancy was already at his desk at Merrill-Lynch. He was happy to hear from his old friend, Parker, even if he only wanted information.

After listening to Parker's requests, Clancy said, "Yeah, the information is probably available, but I'm not sure I can obtain it on such short notice."

"If anyone can do it, you can, Bob."

"And if anyone can sling the bullshit, you can, Park." There was a pause. "To get this information in just two hours is really going to be tough."

Parker gave a hoarse laugh. "What's the bottom line?"

"The use of your boat for a night and two bottles of wine."

"In your dreams, Bob."

"That information is looking harder and harder to come by."

Parker sighed. "One bottle and you bring your own sheets."

"You're a born Yankee trader, Park."

It was pushing three hours when Clancy called back, but he had the information. Finding the right people had taken time, he explained, but they'd been able to answer all of Parker's questions. And the answers where exactly what Parker had hoped for.

Parker's next call was to Soledad to make an appointment to see Girard. Girard's secretary explained that his calendar was full for today but there were some openings next week.

"Actually, it's Ms. Beckman and I that want the appointment. Could you please check with Mr. Girard before making any decisions?"

She was back in a flash and, miraculously, there was no difficulty in obtaining an early afternoon meeting.

The last call was to Susan, and Parker caught her just getting out of the shower. He told her he had some errands to run and would be out of town for most of the day.

"How about dinner tonight?" he asked.

There was a pause.

"Your out-of-town business, does it relate to my father's death?" she asked.

"It does, but this time you're definitely not going, so don't even ask."

"Well, that's plain enough."

#

"Oh... Mr. Beckman. I thought the meeting was to be with you and your sister." Girard was not enthralled that Parker had walked into his office without Susan. He recovered quickly.

"But of course, I'm more than happy to see you." He made a show of checking his watch. "Unfortunately, I have a very full day so I can only spare a few minutes." He gestured to a cushioned chair. "Have a seat."

Girard sat and leaned back in his chair. Parker decided to go for the jugular.

"You lied during our last conversation, Girard. You told me that Harris hadn't been in any drug studies, when in fact he'd been in the same drug study my father was involved in."

"I'm sure you're mistaken, Mr. Beckman."

"Don't bullshit me, Girard. Both Harris and my father got notification cards from Citadel telling them of the termination of a study called Chem 19. Yet when you reviewed their files, you denied any such connection between the two of them."

Girard rose. "Our meeting is over, Mr. Beckman. You know where the door is."

Parker stood and walked over to Girard's desk. "I want some questions answered. Now!"

Girard's left hand moved toward his intercom.

"Okay, then let's talk about your financial relationship with Citadel," Parker said.

Girard's left hand stopped its inching. He glared up at Parker. "My relationship with Citadel is that of a liaison between them and the prison. Nothing more!"

Parker sat on the edge of the desk, staring down at Girard. "Nothing more? How about the Citadel stock you own?"

Girard paled and some of his assuredness drained away. "Any... anyone can own Citadel stock. There's no crime in that," he stammered.

McGraw could see Girard was a house of cards that just needed a wind to blow him down. "Yeah, that's true. But how does someone with your salary afford seventy-five thousand dollars of that stock?"

Girard slumped back in his chair, the intercom forgotten. "I had money saved up, and... a small inheritance."

"Sounds good to me, Stephen, but I'm not so sure how it will sound to your supervisors and maybe to a Grand Jury."

"How did you find out?"

"Since you work closely with Citadel and would have access to privileged information, you're classified as an insider. All insiders who own stock have to be registered with the bank that is acting as the transfer agent." Parker hated to give up the next bit of information, but he had to destroy Girard's confidence.

"When Citadel… gave you the stock, they had to register you because of your insider status. A friend of mine found out the transfer agent for Citadel and got a list of insiders owning stock. Your name was there."

They sat in silence. Girard, once the proud peacock, now looked like a plucked chicken. When he finally spoke, his voice was flat and listless. "What is it you want, Beckman?"

"I want a list of every man that was involved in that drug study with Harris and my father." Parker leaned forward in his chair. "And I want those names now, before I leave."

"That's all?"

Parker nodded. "That's all."

"But why?"

"Three men, including my father, have died because of that study and I intend to find out why."

# #

Surprisingly Girard had been able to get a list of all the prisoners involved in the Chem 19 study fairly quickly. There were a total of ten names, including Beckman and Harris.

After leaving Soledad, Parker had driven about thirty minutes when he noticed that he needed gas. He pulled into a service station, and while filling up, used his cell phone to call Jeff.

"Park, where the hell have you been?" Jeff said when he came on the phone. "I've left messages all over town. Don't you ever return calls?"

"Sorry, Jeff. I've been busy."

"What could be more important than talking to your lawyer?"

"Mea culpa. Mea culpa."

"Don't give me that religious mumbo jumbo. We need to meet."

"Let's get together tomorrow morning. In the meantime, I've got a list of eight ex-cons that I need you to check out. Maybe through your law enforcement connections."

"Sure. They've nothing better to do than answer to my beck and call."

"Jeff, these names may hold the key to Beckman's murder."

"I'll see what I can do, Park. But I need to have something more specific in mind when I ask for information. 'Check them out' is too broad a category."

"See if they're still alive."

Chapter Twenty-Three

The offshore fog bank had moved in, leaving Pebble Beach damp and misty. Parker rummaged through his duffel bag in the back of his rental car and found an old sweatshirt and a baseball cap, both of which he slipped on to ward off the cold. He locked the car, smiling at his luck in findings an empty parking spot in the Beach and Tennis Club lot, and headed for the Stillwater Cove pier. As he walked onto the pier, he passed a man hurrying off. Normally, Parker wouldn't have paid much attention, except that his man had red hair and a handlebar mustache which reminded him of an old medical school friend. Parker was staring at him as they passed and for an instant their eyes met. A flicker of something in the man's eyes... recognition... surprise... Parker wasn't sure, and then he was past. Parker glanced back, but the man continued on without breaking stride.

Parker strolled down the gangway onto the dock where his dinghy was tied. He scrambled into the small boat and moved to the stern to start the outboard motor. He placed one hand on top of the motor and grasped the starting cord handle with the other hand. He was about to give it a yank when his subconscious alarm bells began to clang. Stepping back from the engine, he tried to focus on what was wrong and then it hit him. It'd been hours since he'd used the motor so the engine housing should be cold and wet.

So why is it warm?

Parker went in search of the kid who watched over the pier and ran the shore boat. He found him sitting on the beach, finishing a bag lunch.

"Hey, Jimmy," Parker called down from the pier. "Have you seen anyone using my dinghy?"

Jimmy jumped up and walked over. "Only that friend of yours."

Parker felt a tightening in his spine. "What friend?"

"Your friend, Hal... somebody."

Death has a List

"Why don't you refresh my memory of what my old buddy, Hal, looks like?"

Jimmy stood and thought for a bit. "Well, he's about your size and age. Seemed friendly. And, ah... oh yeah, he had reddish hair and a mustache."

"And he used my dingy?"

"Yeah, he came down onto the dock, climbed in, and started up the outboard," Jim explained. "He acted so sure of himself, I didn't say anything. When he was pulling away, I decided I should check. He yelled back that he was an old friend of the doc's, so I left it at that."

Going back to his dinghy, Parker pulled the engine cover off the outboard motor but couldn't find anything out of the ordinary. He even probed around in the gas tank, but again nothing. Despite this, Parker elected to row out to the boat instead of using the engine.

As he neared the *Sun Chaser*, he altered course and slowly circled it. He saw nothing out of place. No limpet mines clamped to the hull. No dynamite strapped to the mast. He pulled up to the bow of the boat and inspected the mooring line and the buoy. All clear.

Instead of rowing to the stern, he climbed onto the bow. *If it is booby trapped, it's unlikely to be at this end of the boat.* He crouched on the foredeck, resting only on the balls of his feet, ready to move at an instant, while he visually examined the boat. Inconsistencies is what he was looking for. Something that shouldn't be there.

The deck appeared unchanged from the morning. The lines and the self-furling sails where were they should be. No footprints on the wet deck surface. It all looked fine. Then he saw it. The first inconsistency. The forward hatch was slightly open. He had definitely closed it before he'd left for Soledad. It was so common to encounter wet weather that even on nice days, he always closed the hatches.

Walking on cat feet, he eased over to the hatch and bent to examine it. After prolonged scrutiny, he concluded it was safe.

"Would you bet your life on it?" he asked out loud. *No, I guess I wouldn't.* He decided to find someone who would.

# #

"It would have blown this boat to kingdom come and then some."

The man speaking was kneeling over a narrow, twelve inch length of what appeared to be Play-Doh, the putty-like stuff that children play with. It was laid out on a tarp on the pier. A small red box was stuck in the putty, with several wires heading from it toward a larger black box. The wires were not attached.

"What is all this?" Parker asked, staring down at the tarp.

Pushing a scratched pair of wire rim glasses up the bridge of his nose, the man glanced up at Parker then pointed to the black box. "That there's the triggering mechanism. And these wires, which are unhocked, run from it to the detonator, that red box imbedded in the putty."

"And the putty-like stuff is some kind of plastic explosive?"

"You got it."

"Where did you find it?" Parker asked.

"It was attached to the inside of the door leading into the cabin. If you'd opened it that would have been all she wrote." He glanced down at the deadly creation spread out before him and then up at Parker. "I'd say someone has you on their shit list."

Parker drifted over to the end of the pier where Monterey Police Detective Hall was conferring with several uniformed men from the sheriff's office. Parker had called Hall first, telling him his fear about a bomb on his boat. Surprisingly, Hall hadn't ridiculed his concern, but instead had been serious from the start. He'd advised Parker to keep everyone away from his boat and to make sure that any nearby boats were empty. In turn, Hall said he would contact the sheriff's office, who had the jurisdiction for Pebble Beach, and "get the ball rolling".

That simple phrase, Parker discovered, had included the bomb squad, several trucks from the fire department, an ambulance, two squad cars, one unmarked police car, and multiple official looking vehicles belonging to Pebble Beach's private security force. If that wasn't enough, a van with a local TV news station logo on its side had just driven up. It was quickly becoming a circus.

Hall noticed Parker standing nearby. He excused himself from the group he was talking with and sauntered over, his eyes on the ground.

"Now do you believe that someone is out to get me?" Parker asked when Hall was next to him.

Hall didn't reply, choosing instead to turn and watch the scene out on Parker's boat. A small Coast Guard boat was tied to its side. Several figures were visible on the *Sun Chaser's* deck. Parker knew there were more below deck. They were fingerprinting the scene and whatever else the police did in this type of situation.

When Hall still didn't reply, Parker raised his voice. "Someone tried to run me down with their car. When that failed, they forced me off the road and incinerated my vehicle. Now this." He stepped in front of Hall. "How much longer are you going to ignore the obvious?"

"Well, maybe someone is trying to kill you. Or maybe someone is just trying to make it look that way," Hall replied.

Parker grabbed the lapels of Hall's jacket. "What the hell are you talking about, Hall! No one's trying to make it look like anything. They're trying to kill me, goddammit."

Hall tore Parker's hands off his coat. Slowly, methodically, he straightened his shirt and jacket, then in a low, menacing voice said, "Don't ever touch me again."

He took a few more deep breaths and his angry contorted face relaxed.

Parker tried to reign in his own frustration. He'd made a major error grabbing and yelling at Hall in front of his cohorts, but he couldn't believe Hall's persistence in ignoring these episodes. And he couldn't believe how close he'd come to dying... again.

They stood silently, side by side, for almost a full minute before Hall spoke.

"If you think you can act like a rational person instead of..." he mumbled some term, "maybe we can continue our discussion."

Parker let out a sigh. "I'm sorry about grabbing you. This whole thing is making me a little crazy."

"Maybe things are what they appear... and maybe they aren't." He paused, watching for Parker's response before he proceeded on. "Let's objectively examine these incidents."

"Yeah, let's do that."

Hall held up one finger. "First, the hit and run. It was late at night, and the lighting on that street was very poor. It's entirely possible that the person driving didn't see you."

"He was aiming right for me and had his lights off."

"Another reason that he didn't see you. He could have just started his car and forgotten to turn on the lights."

"Why didn't he stop? He knew he'd hit me. If he was so innocent, why drive off?"

"For any number of reasons, Dr. McGraw. He had an invalid driver's license, no insurance, it was his parents' car and he wasn't supposed to be using it. The possibilities are endless." Hall raised another finger. "Second, the accident in the fog."

Parker shook his head. "It wasn't an accident. It was deliberate."

Hall scowled at him. "You asked me my opinion, doctor, and I'm trying to show you that an objective evaluation of these episodes can have more than one interpretation."

Rubbing his hand across his face, Parker said, "What the hell, Hall. Give me the rest of this fairy tale."

"The road you were on is notorious for fog-related car collisions. Your crash was not unusual." He paused in anticipation of another outburst. Parker remained silent, so he continued. "The incineration of your car could have been spontaneous since there was extensive gasoline spillage at the scene. Or it could have been that a clumsy Good Samaritan accidentally ignited the gas while trying to investigate the wreck for survivors."

"And today's episode. I can't wait to hear your explanation of this one."

Hall stepped back and leaned against the pier railing. "I want to ask you a few questions first." He pulled a pen and a small notebook from his inside coat pocket. "Who knew you moved your boat here?"

"No one, but there aren't that many moorings on the peninsula. If someone was persistent enough, they could find me."

"Who knew you'd be gone today?"

"Only the guy I went to see at Soledad State Prison. A Mr. Girard."

Hall glanced down at his notebook. "How about the guy with the red hair and mustache? Ever met him before?"

"Never."

"Then how is it that he knew which dinghy was yours, that you were a physician, and that you'd be gone for a prolonged period?"

Parker shrugged. "Maybe he was watching the boat, saw me come in, and drive off."

Hall wrote something in his note pad. "You spoke with the bomb specialist, didn't you?"

"Yes. He explained the device to me."

"So you're not familiar with explosives?"

"Very unfamiliar with them," Parker answered.

The roar of the Coast Guard cutters' two powerful engines filled the quiet cove. Everyone turned to watch as it pulled away from the *Sun Chaser* and slowly motored toward the Stillwater pier.

"There is something that the specialist didn't tell you," Hall said softly. "I asked him not to tell anyone."

Parker turned back toward Hall. "What's that?"

"One of the wires running from the triggering device to the detonator wasn't attached."

"Which means?"

"Which means the bomb was a dud. It would never have gone off."

Parker plopped back against the pier railing next to Hall. They watched silently as the Coast Guard boat pull up alongside the pier.

Why the hell would someone go to all the trouble of setting a bomb on my boat and not make sure it was wired properly? And why was Hall telling me this when he'd withheld it before?

Hall put his pen and notebook away. "We were talking about an objective evaluation of the facts."

"And how would you objectively weigh that fact?" Parker asked.

Hall looked intently at Parker. "Whoever set up the explosive device was very... unfamiliar... with explosives."

Chapter Twenty-Four

The view from the deck of Parker's suite that evening at the Highlands Inn was fantastic. He could see the southern side of Point Lobos, with its extensive kelp beds. The kelp kept the ocean surface like glass, so the water mirrored the deep blue of the cloudless sky which contrasted nicely with the fresh white of the surf exploding against the rocky shoreline.

Stretched out on one of the deck lounges, Parker let the setting sun warm his face. The fog, so chilling earlier, had pulled back and now sat in a high bank several miles offshore.

After Hall had essentially accused Parker of planting the bomb, he'd taken a different tack and advised Parker to find a new place to stay since his boat was now compromised. Parker couldn't figure Hall at all, but he'd had to agree with his suggestion.

Hall had one of his technicians confirm there wasn't a tracker on Parker's car, and Parker made sure no one followed him out through the Pebble Beach security gate.

After living in the cramped quarters of a boat for the last several days, a spacious, luxurious suite seemed the solution, and the Highlands Inn fit that description nicely.

Rising from his cushioned seat, Parker stepped into the vaulted ceiling living room, stacked some wood on the grating in the stone fireplace, and settled into a leather couch. He picked up his cell phone and called Jeff's office, leaving word with his secretary to have Jeff meet him in his hotel suite tomorrow, where they could talk over breakfast.

Parker fetched a soft drink from the adjoining kitchenette, crossed the living room, and slid open the partition to the connecting bedroom. He stretched out on the king-size bed and called Susan. She answered on the second ring.

He decided not to mention the bomb scare. "About tonight, why don't you meet me at the Highlands Inn in the lobby bar, about seven? Okay?"

It was now about five, which didn't leave much time for what had to be done. Parker shed his clothes and showered. As he was drying off, he stared at the Jacuzzi tub nestled in the bathroom corner and hoped he'd get a chance to use it.

He drove his rental car out to the airport and exchanged it for a larger, heavier built car. As a precaution, he had the rental woman change his agreement and put collision on the policy. She was more than happy to oblige since this was one of their big money makers. *Maybe not this time.*

Leaving the airport, he drove to Susan's street, where he parked several houses away and waited. Susan came out fifteen minutes later, climbed into a red BMW, and drove off. Parker followed her from a discrete distance. She'd only gone a few blocks when a black Trans Am pulled out from a side street and slid in behind her.

The appearance of the Trans Am confirmed Parker's suspicion. Susan's house was under surveillance.

I must have led them to Stillwater after I dropped Susan off the other night. He squeezed the steering wheel hard. *Well, they're not going to find me tonight.*

Susan came to a stop sign, and turned right heading for Highway One. The Trans Am followed and Parker was right behind it. The street they'd turned on sloped downhill and then flattened out. When they neared the flat, Parker hit the gas and pulled out around the Trans Am. As he passed, he suddenly swerved into the Trans Am, striking the front of their car and sending it off the road. The sound of shattering glass and crunching metal filled the air. Parker looked in his rearview mirror and saw the Trans Am wrapped up in a chain link fence with steam pouring out from its hood.

Death has a List

He'd thought about pulling them over and questioning them, but the odds they'd try to assault him where much higher than the chances they'd admit anything. So he'd done the next best thing.

##

"Hey, Detective Hall. Got some interesting news for you."

Hall looked up from his work as Cordoba dropped into a chair, leaned back, and stuck his feet up on the edge of the desk. Hall grimaced and moved his framed picture away from Cordoba's size eleven boots to the other corner of his desk.

"What've you got?" Hall asked as he resumed his writing.

Cordoba grinned, exposing white, straight teeth. "A little tidbit about our doctor friend."

Hall set his pen down and fixed his eyes on Cordoba's brown face.

"Remember how the good doctor said he'd never met Beckman nor had any dealings with him?" Cordoba said.

"Yeah."

"Well, 'no es verdad', as my old man would say."

Hall shook his head. "Cordoba, I know your father doesn't speak Spanish and I imagine the closest you've ever come to Mexico is probably a Taco Bell."

Cordoba laughed. "Ah, come on. It goes with my image."

"Save it for the ladies and the promotion board." Hall paused. "So he lied to us. Tell me more about the good doctor."

"I just got a tip from the D.A.'s office. Some perp, Ray Stone was interrogating for drug dealing, by the name of Karl Knott, knew Stone was the prosecuting attorney in the McGraw case. He wants to make a deal. If they drop the charges against him, he'll provide evidence for the McGraw case."

"Such as?"

"He saw McGraw and Beckman together... the week before the murder."

##

A fire crackled in the immense Carmel stone fireplace as Parker crossed the polished wood floor of the Highlands Inn lobby. In the far corner, several large picture windows offered a spectacular view of the fading sunset to the accompaniment of a grand piano beautifully played.

Susan was sitting alone in an overstuffed couch, staring out at the waning light. Parker thought her exquisite. The surroundings, built at a cost of millions, seemed inadequate as a backdrop to her beauty. Parker had almost reached her side when she caught sight of him. Her smile was instant and the welcome in her eyes unmistakable. Or so Parker told himself.

She was wearing a white, nubby cotton sweater-dress with a deep V-neck line, cinched at the waist by a wide brown belt. The whiteness of the material emphasized her tan and gave her a fresh innocence that her curvaceous figure belied. Sitting down next to her, Parker said, "Now I understand the phrase 'Beauty is its own excuse for being'. You look lovely."

Susan laughed. "Is that another of your patented lines?"

"In this case, no." Parker smiled, then caught the server's attention and ordered drinks.

"You're looking fairly debonair yourself tonight," Susan said as the waitress left.

"'Fairly'? Hours in the bathroom. Half a month's salary on the clothes. Shoes buffed and rebuffed. A thirty dollar haircut. And all I get is a 'fairly' rating."

Susan rolled her eyes. "The rating would be higher if it was for bullshit." She straightened her dress. "So what did you find out today?"

Parker spent the next thirty minutes, and two rounds of drinks, bringing her up to date on his sleuthing. The conversation with Girard, his involvement with Citadel, the list of prisoners, the call to Jeff.

They discussed and re-discussed Parker's day until they'd exhausted their ideas. The only clear conclusion was that Citadel needed more investigation.

"That's enough discussion about murder and drugs. It's all I've lived with the past two weeks. Let's talk about other things tonight," Parker said. "Tell me about you. I now know your family intimately, but I know nothing about you."

"Okay, but at the first yawn, I stop," Susan replied.

"Deal."

"I grew up in the San Francisco area, where I went to a school of interior design. When I graduated, I decided to take some time off before starting an interior decorating business."

"Good idea," Parker said.

"My boyfriend and I moved to Sun Valley. Summer there was pretty quiet but he managed to find work in construction, while I got a job assembling ski boots at a local factory. I lasted one day."

"What happened?"

Susan shrugged her shoulders. "Anyone can confuse their right with their left?

"Happens all the time."

"My job was to attach buckles to the ski boots. I just happened to attach them to the wrong side of the boot. I was encouraged to find work elsewhere."

"Encouraged." Parker laughed. "Sounds better than fired."

They ordered another round of drinks as Susan went on to describe her first serving job at a posh restaurant in the Sun Valley Lodge. One of her tables ordered a bottle of expensive champagne, so she'd fetched the desired vintage from the wine cellar and brought it back to the table. She unwrapped the wire around the cork but couldn't get the cork to budge. Hoping to get better leverage, she'd put the bottle between her legs and with all her strength pulled on the cork.

"Realize I'd never opened a bottle of champagne," she said.

The maitre d', appalled at her methods, rushed over to the table just as the cork popped out. Champagne exploded over the entire group at the table. Susan turned the bottle away from them and unwittingly sprayed the approaching maitre dei.

"I suppose you were again 'encouraged'?" Parker said laughing.

"Oh, most definitely." Susan grinned at Parker. "And I suppose you're life has been free of <u>faux</u> <u>pas</u>?"

Parker chuckled. "Oh, I've had a few indelicate moments."

They were leaning back in the couch, catching their breath, between stories, when Susan put her head on Parker's shoulder and asked him about dinner. He checked his watch.

"What kind of place did you have in mind, Ms. Beckman?" He found her perfume overpowering, drawing him like a moth to a flame. Her proximity increased the effect.

Susan rolled her head on his shoulder so that their faces were almost touching. Her words came out softly, "Some place romantic, McGraw."

Parker bent the rest of the way and pressed his lips against her's. For an instant, Susan resisted then she placed her right hand on his neck and pulled him closer, pressing her lips into his.

As they eased apart, the piano player began "This Guy's in Love with You". Hands entwined, heads together, they nestled back into the couch to listen.

The song was nearly over when Parker started nuzzling and kissing her neck. Slowly, Susan pulled away. "Don't think I've forgotten about the dinner you promised me," she said.

He smiled and snapped his fingers. "Now I remember why we're here." Signaling to the server, he closed out the check. "The restaurant here has a great reputation, if that's okay with you?"

"We can seat you and the Madame in an hour," said the restaurant hostess. "Would you care to wait in our bar?"

Parker smiled at her and shook his head. "Thanks, but no thanks." He looked at Susan. "Let's go into town. I know a nice romantic place without a wait."

"I hope you're not thinking of driving?"

Parker laughed. "Drive? I can hardly walk. We'll use Uber." As they descended the entrance stairway, Parker stopped and slowly began to grin.

"That's an evil grin, McGraw."

"All the better to smile at you with."

"And me without my red riding hood."

"Actually, I decided where we can go for dinner."

He led Susan across the entrance driveway to a winding path set amongst the housing units.

They started up the trail. Susan, her head against Parker's shoulder, asked, "Where are we going."

"To a romantic hideaway for dinner. My room."

"Just for dinner?" she whispered.

Parker stopped, took her in his arms and kissed her. He could feel every line of her figure as she pressed her body against his. With their mouths hungrily enjoined, tongues exploring, the intensity of their passion was overwhelming. Intoxicated with alcohol and lust, Parker was entertaining thoughts of ravishing her there on the walkway when he heard a gentle cough behind him and a voice that said, "Excuse me. Can we get by?"

Hand in hand, they continued up the walkway to Parker's suite. After showing her around, Parker opened a bottle of Mumm's champagne he'd brought from the boat. Sipping the champagne, they checked over the menu then phoned room service.

Parker led her out onto the balcony where they stood, glasses in hand, admiring the night and the sound of the distant surf.

"This is beautiful," Susan said, leaning against him. Parker placed a finger on her chin and tilted her head up.

"At the risk of sounding redundant, you're beautiful." He bent and kissed her. It was a long slow kiss, directly from the heart.

The evening had become chilled, so they adjourned to the living room where Susan offered to demonstrate her fire starting abilities, acquired after two cold winters in Sun Valley.

The fire was crackling and flaming when the waiter arrived with their dinner. He set an elegant table, displaying the courses beautifully, but Parker's mind was not on food.

Susan went into the kitchenette to wash her hands and Parker followed to get ice water for the table. Even with their backs to each other, Parker was conscious of every move, every sound that Susan made in the confined kitchen space. Several times they inadvertently touched, and each brush was like an electric shock.

Parker reached around for water glasses and came face to face with Susan who was just leaving. They stood millimeters apart, staring into each other's eyes. Susan, the firelight glinting off her long hair, said slowly, "I seem to have lost my appetite... for food."

Parker pulled her to him, kissing her with all the pent up fervor the night had created. He ran his hands, caressingly, up and down her body, feeling everything and wanting it all. Caught in a tide of passion, Parker gave into his desires, clawing at her clothes, ravishing her body with his hands and his mouth.

Susan's response was no less intense, smothering him with her mouth and her tongue, even tearing off his shirt buttons when they wouldn't unfasten. All the time, her voice urging him on, moaning her need for fulfillment.

Parker lifted her in his arms with some vague idea of carrying her to the bedroom. He made it only as far as the living room. There on the thick carpet, with the firelight illuminating their naked bodies, they made hungry, passionate love. There was none of the hesitancy of first love; none of the embarrassment of first exposure, there was just feverish carnal lust.

And when they were finally spent, and their ravening fires consumed, they made love again, but this time with slow methodical movements, gentleness now replacing the unbridled cravings of before.

Chapter Twenty-Five

There is no better way to rid oneself of a hangover than to exercise. The sweating, the aching muscles, the pounding heart all burn off the residual effects of the night before.

At least, this is what Parker had told himself when he'd gotten up early and spent twenty minutes stretching and doing abdominal exercise, all the time trying not to vomit. He was now thirty minutes into his run and finally losing the blurred disconnected feeling he'd awoken with this morning.

The run took him through the tree-lined, narrow streets that snaked along the hillside above the Inn, where he strongly doubted any of his foes would see him. He was nearly up to full par when he stepped back into the suite and plopped on the couch. Through the sliding door, he saw Susan sound asleep on the bed, her long hair fanned out over the pillow.

Noticing the empty champagne glasses and the clothes strewn across the floor, he smiled.

They'd eventually gotten around to dinner, which they enjoyed in the terrycloth robes that went with the room. Later, they adjourned to the Jacuzzi bathtub where they spent a relaxing hour, sipping on Amaretto, talking, and gently necking. One thing led to another and this time they did make it to the bed but only after their attempts at lovemaking in the tub nearly flooded the room. Sometime after that, the oblivion of sleep took over.

Sitting down on the bed next to Susan, Parker kissed her exposed shoulder. "Come on, beautiful. Time to get up."

She groaned, grabbed the pillow next to her and pulled it over her head.

Parker lifted the pillow. "Susan, my lawyer is coming over in an hour."

"Just close the bedroom door." She pulled the pillow back down over her head.

Parker lifted it again. "He's got some interesting news about your father's case." He let the pillow fall back in place and went to the kitchen to make coffee. A few minutes later, he heard sounds of life in the bathroom.

He rapped on the bathroom door. "How do you like your coffee?"

A raspy voice answered. "Black."

Parker was pouring the coffee when Susan appeared, dressed in a terrycloth robe. Glancing at the clothes strewn about on the floor, she shook her head then sat down on one of the bar stools.

"Good morning, Ms. Beckman." Parker set the coffee in front of her. "And how are you today?"

She groaned. "Terrible. How much did I drink last night? No, wait. Don't tell me, I'll just feel worse." Holding the cup with both hands, she sipped the coffee.

After a few sips, she looked up from her cup. "I have a vague recollection that you took advantage of me last night."

Parker gave her a smile. "Several times."

She laughed, leaned across the counter and kissed him. "I hope I enjoyed it."

Parker grinned. "Don't just take my word for it. Ask the neighbors."

She threw a dish towel at him. "Cute, McGraw." She turned and stared at the remains of her clothes. "What the hell am I going to wear?"

"No, problem. I'll have room service press your things... but that may take a while."

"So what do I wear while your friend is here?"

Parker looked her up and down. "You look great just as you are."

She glared back at him. "Somehow the idea of meeting your lawyer in my bathrobe is not appealing."

Walking out from behind the counter, Parker sat on the stool next to hers. "I do have something you could wear, but..."

She eyed him suspiciously. "But what?"

He stepped off the stool and put his arms around her. "But it's going to cost you."

Susan slid off the bar stool, allowing her robe to gape open, exposing a generous amount of cleavage. She placed her arms around his neck and in a sultry voice said, "I'm sure we can work something out."

##

Jeff arrived as the room service waiter was laying the table with three place settings. "Who's joining us?" he asked.

"Susan Beckman." Parker nodded toward the bathroom. "She's getting dressed and should be out in a minute."

Jeff raised his eyebrows. "Michael Beckman's daughter? I thought we'd agreed you'd stay away from her."

"I never agreed. I just didn't argue."

Jeff took a deep breath and blew it out. "She's getting dressed in your bathroom?"

Parker nodded again.

"Stupid question, because I know the answer, but I hope I'm wrong. Why is she getting dressed here instead of her own home?"

"She spent the night here."

Jeff rolled his eyes up and leaned back in his chair. "Park! Are you crazy? How is this going to look to a jury?"

"How is what going to look?" Susan said, emerging from the bathroom.

She was wearing one of Parker's long-sleeve, dress shirts and a pair of his Levis with the pants cuffed. Rising, Parker introduced Susan to Jeff.

Jeff stood and stared, his eyes widening. It was a long moment before he spoke. "Nice to meet you... Ms. Beckman."

Parker broke the uneasy silence that followed. "Let's eat. I'm starved."

They made the usual small talk over the beginning of a meal and Parker noticed that Jeff remained strangely reticent, not his usual gregarious self. As the meal neared its end, Parker asked Jeff about his findings.

"Let's wait until we're finished," Jeff replied.

When breakfast was over, they settled back with coffee. Parker set his cup down. "Okay, Jeff. The floor's yours."

Jeff placed his cup carefully on his coffee plate and turned to Susan.

"Ms. Beckman, at the risk of sounding rude, I'll have to ask you to leave. No matter how Park feels, you're not part of our defense team."

Parker sat up in his chair. "She stays, Jeff. Anything you have to say, I want her to hear. We're in this together."

Susan shook her head and stood up. "No, Park. If Mr. Gilman feels that way, I'd be uncomfortable staying."

Standing, Parker grasped Susan's arm. "Wait, please." He turned to Jeff. "If she goes, I go."

Jeff shrugged his shoulders. "Well, it was my duty to warn you, but if that's the way you feel, then why don't you both sit down and we'll get on with business. That is, if Ms. Beckman will forgive the remarks I had to make."

Sitting down, Susan smiled. "There is nothing to forgive unless you keep calling me Ms. Beckman instead of Susan."

Jeff politely half-smiled back. "Okay, Susan."

Reaching into his briefcase, Jeff removed a sheaf of papers, laying them on the table in front of him. "Susan, you're aware that Parker gave me a list of eight ex-cons to check on?"

She nodded.

Turning to Parker, he continued, "Before I talk about them, I want to know where you came up with these names, Park."

"Those are all of the convicts involved in a specific drug study, Chem 19, done at Soledad."

"Drug study? Soledad?" Jeff looked perplexed. "I think I need some updating."

Parker told him about the events of the last few days, finishing with his interview with Girard.

"Let me get this straight," Jeff said, his eyes wide. "Susan's father and William Harris from Big Sur, along with the eight names on this list were all involved in the same drug study at Soledad, something called Chem 19. But the drug company that oversees these studies, Citadel Pharmaceuticals, claims that no such study was performed. In fact, their records show that the last test was designated Chem 17. They deny the existence of a Chem 18 or 19." He paused to catch his breath. "Have I got it right?"

"Right on track. And that brings us up to the list of names," Parker said. "What have you got?"

Jeff spread the papers out in front of him. "The information that I have is derived from parole board records. Because these ex-cons were scattered all over the state, it required a lot of man hours to dig this up."

"I already told you we're even, Jeff."

"Oh, we're not even, Park, but that's not the point of my remark." He picked up one of the pages. "The first name is Andy Norris. He died in a car accident when his vehicle went off the road, two weeks after being released."

"Any witnesses or anyone in the car with him?" Parker asked.

"No, to both questions." Jeff checked his sheet again. "The second name is Harry Winn. A nice friendly guy who beat up the social worker that came to his house. Before the police could arrest him, he was found in a back alley, dead from a stab wound. The police felt this was a mugging since his wallet and watch were gone. There's a possibility, though, of a witness."

He picked up a second page. "The next is Melvin Loomis. One week out of prison, he was struck by a car and killed."

"Hit and run?" Parker said.

Jeff nodded. "The fourth is Dan MacKey. Three weeks out of prison, he just up and disappeared. His family filed a missing person's report but so far he hasn't turned up. The fifth is Ken Lewis. He committed suicide one week after his release. His landlord found him hanging in the bathroom."

Susan wrapped her arms around herself and shivered. "This is getting creepy."

"Oh, it gets even creepier," Jeff said. "The sixth name is Jose Ramos. He disappeared three days after his parole. Someone called in a tip that they'd seen him crossing the border into Mexico."

"That sounds plausible," said Susan.

"Not when you realize he was born and raised in Los Angeles, all his relatives resided in southern California, and he didn't speak Spanish."

"Are any of the people on that list still alive?" Parker asked.

"Hold your horses, Park." Jeff grabbed the last paper from the table and perused it quickly. "The seventh name is Jack Hyams. Does that name ring any bells?"

Parker had heard the name before, but he couldn't place it. He looked at Susan, but she just shook her head.

Jeff continued. "Old Jack went berserk in a Macy's shopping center two weeks after his parole. He killed five people and wounded another nine before he was shot down."

"Now I remember," Susan said. "Wasn't he shot by an off-duty policeman who happened to be in the store?"

"Yes, he was. Otherwise he might have killed even more people." Jeff scanned his paper. "So who's next? Ah, yes. Our eighth and last name. The lovely Fred Quinn. Just before his release, he got into an altercation with the guards, killing one and serious injuring another. He's now in solitary confinement at San Quentin, awaiting trial." Jeff gathered up his papers, put them into his briefcase, and settled back in his chair.

"Do you realize that seven out of those eight names are either dead or have disappeared?" Susan said.

"It's even more impressive," Jeff said, "when you add your father and Harris. Nine out of ten of the convicts involved in Chem 19 are dead or have disappeared, which is probably the same thing. The odds of that being a natural occurrence are a million to one. Wouldn't you agree, Park?"

Parker nodded. "What I don't understand is why the parole office didn't get suspicious when these ex-cons, all recently released from Soledad, started dying off."

"My sentiments also," Jeff said getting up and walking over to the kitchen counter. He poured himself a cup of coffee and leaned up against the counter. "But there were a number of reasons why they wouldn't. For one thing, my reference to several different parole boards being involved. When a prisoner is released, the location where he's settled will determine which parole office will follow him."

"And these guys were settled all over so that a number of parole offices were involved?" Parker ventured.

"Exactly. So no one office would see the trend. Instead, each office would record a random death or disappearance. Second, there was really nothing unusual about any of the deaths or disappearances when viewed separately. Lastly, society in general doesn't take that much notice if an ex-con dies or drops out of sight."

Susan broke the silence that followed. "So where do we go from here?"

"Simple," Parker replied. "We take it to Hall and have him investigate it."

Jeff laughed. "Park, you're a dreamer." He paced around the room. "First off, it's not Hall's job to investigate further. He already has his murderer, and has given his case to the D.A. Second, this is evidence of what? Evidence that a group of ex-cons, involved in a drug study the pharmaceutical company denies ever existed, had a higher than normal mortality rate. Forget it. Hall would laugh us out of his office. And even if he believed us, we still can't explain your purported killing of Susan's father."

"But they have the manpower to investigate this a lot more thoroughly than we can?" Parker's voice had an edge to it.

"Look, Park. This information confirms your suspicions that Citadel and Chem 19 are key to solving Beckman's murder. But we need a lot more before we can go to Hall."

Parker groaned. "Maybe you're underestimating the man."

"Maybe I am," Jeff said calmly, "but I don't see Hall busting down doors to prove your innocence and destroy his own case at the same time."

Susan walked over and put her arm around Parker. "Jeff's right. Until there's more, we need to wait."

Jeff looked at both of them. "Okay. So we agree. For now we'll sit and let my investigator check into it. He'll be back in two days." He closed the briefcase.

"Chem 19 is the answer," Park said. "And I'll bet its secret is somewhere in the Citadel building."

"I agree." Jeff said, picking up his briefcase. "I'll get a court order for Citadel's records. I'm sure there is a paper trail proving Chem 19's existence." He shook hands with Susan and then asked Parker to walk him to his car.

Parker and Jeff went down to the parking lot, where Jeff turned to him. "We need to talk about Susan."

"Come on, Jeff. I'm not going to argue the pros and cons of the situation."

"The problem is... she is not Michael Beckman's daughter."

Chapter Twenty-Six

"You've never met Susan Beckman before, so how do you know this?"

Jeff leaned against his car and stared down at his spotless wingtips. "When I was reviewing the police records on the case, there was a picture of Michael Beckman and his daughter in the file. The woman in that picture isn't the same one that's in your room. The two have similar hair color and facial resemblance, but that's all."

Parker was stunned. For a moment, there was no sound, no light, no nothing. Then slowly his surroundings came back into focus. He felt weak and listless, like a building whose internal supporting structures had collapsed leaving only the exterior standing.

"Why didn't you say something before?"

"I wanted to see what her game was. Why she'd attached herself to you."

"But now she knows about Citadel, Chem 19, and what happened to all the participants."

Jeff put his arm around Parker's shoulders. "All of that is public knowledge. Nothing she learned is going to hinder our case."

"It's my own stupid fault," Parker mumbled. "I should have been suspicious when she agreed to work with me so easily."

They were silent for a while.

"Look, Park. You can go back to your room, tell her to get out, curl up in bed, and cry yourself to sleep."

Parker looked up.

"Or you can get raving, pissed-off mad. That bitch has been using you from the start and now it's time to use her. She's involved in this somehow. Find out how." Jeff shrugged his shoulders. "Maybe you'll get some answers and maybe not, but at least you'll be doing something productive, instead of hibernating with your bruised ego."

Minutes passed while Parker stared at the ground then slowly he straightened up. He'd lost some of his hang-dog look.

"You're right. It's time I start doing the using."

"Now that's the Park I know." Jeff patted him on the back. "When my investigator returns, she'll be one more thing for him to check out."

After Jeff drove off, Parker went back into the suite and found Susan stretched out in the bedroom, sound asleep. His borrowed shirt and Levis were draped over the couch. He stood next to the bed and stared down at her.

"Damn you," he said softly. He bent and gently brushed a loose strand of hair off her face.

Quickly, he bundled up a few odds and ends, then wrote a short note: I'll be gone all day and then have plans for tonight. I'll call you tomorrow.

The fog in the Highlands had burned off by the time Susan's red BMW came whizzing past Parker's rental on its way toward Carmel. He pulled out from his hiding spot and fell in behind her. It was an easy tail job for she went straight home. Parker took up a position at the end of her street, and settled down to wait.

The afternoon sun gradually warmed the limited confines of his rental car, making Parker drowsy. He rolled the side window down, hoping the faint ocean breeze would cool the car's interior and keep him awake. Leaning slightly out the side window, he found he had a better view of Susan's car and her front door.

He still thought of her as Susan since it was the only name he knew. Drumming his fingers on the steering wheel, Parker stared at her front door. *Who is this woman? And where the hell does she fit into all of this?*

A car backed out of the driveway next door to Susan's and drove away.

At least now I understand some of the inconsistencies that have been bothering me. Things I let slide as I got emotionally involved.

Parker had attributed Susan's willingness to meet with him to his persuasive manner. Not now. If he hadn't called her, she undoubtedly would have tracked him down.

And the visit to prison when she'd become nervous while meeting St. Jude. Of course she'd gotten nervous. St. Jude had mentioned having a picture of the real Susan Beckman. Fortunately for her, it was when the real Susan was much younger. Jeff had said the two were somewhat alike, so it's not surprising that St. Jude, told he was meeting Susan Beckman, had accepted her as such.

And the reason she couldn't explain the lack of family contact with Michael Beckman while he was in prison? She wasn't family.

The gun in her purse and her dexterity with it, were no longer enigmas. With the type of game she was playing and the people she was playing with, she needed a gun.

But what is her game? She couldn't work for Citadel. If she did, they wouldn't have run my car off the road with her in it. But maybe they didn't know she was with me. And if she works for Citadel, why did she seem like such a stranger to the employees and to the layout? Well, maybe she's a new employee. Or maybe she's just a good actress.

Remembering last night, Parker winced. *There's no maybes about her acting ability.*

Several hours later Susan came out, climbed into her car, and drove off. Parker followed her into downtown Carmel where she parked on a side street. Unable to find a parking spot, he left his car in a yellow zone and hurried after her.

The sidewalks were congested with the usual summer tourist crowd, making it all the easier for Parker to tag along behind. They'd gone about two blocks when she abruptly veered into the Hog's Breath Restaurant.

One of the more celebrated restaurants in Carmel, the Hog's Breath is famed not so much for its bill of fare, as for one of its previous owners, Clint Eastwood. The entry to the restaurant is a walkway, running between two buildings into a large sunken brick patio in the back. The patio has tables and chairs scattered amongst several brick fireplaces with a small enclosed bar at the very back.

Parker knew if he used the entry walkway, he'd be on display for anyone sitting in the patio. So instead of following Susan, he hurried over to the street behind the restaurant, and used the back entrance. This little known passageway wound through a maze of shops behind the restaurant, then entered at far end of the patio, next to the small enclosed bar.

Parker peered cautiously around the corner of the bar building. The patio was crowded, with nearly all the tables occupied. At first, he couldn't find Susan, then he saw her at a far corner table. She was sitting with someone and already had a glass of wine in front of her. Parker leaned further out and caught a glimpse of her companion.

The shock was as physical as a gut punch. Turning back, he fell against the bar wall.

Damn. I should have known.

Closing his eyes, he willed his breathing to slow, and forced himself to calm down. Several moments passed before he peered out again.

Susan and her companion were having what appeared to be a very heated discussion. After a bit, her companion stood up and dropped several dollars on the table, then bent down and kissed her on the lips. When he straightened up, the sun glinted off his red hair and handlebar mustache.

Pulling back from his vantage point, Parker leaned against the wall and swore intently under his breath.

Now, there's no unanswered questions about the bomb attempt at Stillwater Cove. The location of my boat, when I'd be gone, which dinghy was mine -- they'd all been supplied by Susan.

When he looked out again, the red-haired man was disappearing up the stairs.

Parker didn't waste time. He bolted back through the rear passageway, out onto the sidewalk, and around to the front of the restaurant. He planned on following the red-haired man, but when he reached the restaurant entrance, the man had disappeared.

Standing, catching his breath, Parker decided he'd had enough of lying and deception.

He marched down the entry way into the Hog's Breath. Pausing at the top of the stairs, he scanned the patio. Susan's table stood empty. She was gone. *Damn it to hell!*

He drove to her house, but her car wasn't there. After waiting an hour, he decided to call it a day.

# #

Settled back into the lounge chair on his hotel-room balcony, Parker stared at the note he'd left Susan. Across the bottom, she'd scribbled, "I'm tied up tonight also. Talk with you tomorrow."

He crumpled the note up and threw it toward the trash can just inside the door. Of course he missed. Just that kind of day.

"So what's the key to this whole mess?" he said out loud. "The one thing that everything else turns on?" He took a sip of bottled water he'd gotten from the kitchen.

"Chem 19. But that bit of knowledge is of no help to me unless the records of the study still exist." Another sip, then a slowly spreading smile.

"And I'll bet they do. No true research scientist is going to perform nineteen studies on a drug and then toss out the records of the last two trials. Even with negative results, there's potential for important conclusions. Maybe even a basis for designing future studies. No, those records still exist. The question is where?"

He stared at the bottle in his hand.

"Maybe my friend Girard might know." He checked his watch. It was 6:30pm. Girard would be home by now.

Parker brought the phone out to the balcony and called Girard's cell phone. He'd forced Girard to give him his number at their last visit employing the same threats he used to get the list of prisoners.

Girard answered immediately and then realized who was on the line. "Beckman, if you don't stop this harassment, I'll call the police!"

"That's bullshit and you know it. But if you're tired of talking to me, then why don't I talk with your wife. Does she know about your bribe? Your financial indiscretions? Or maybe I'll just tell her I'm an irate husband and you've been playing around with my wife."

There was no sound for almost a minute, and then Parker heard a sigh. "Okay. What do you want?"

"Where does Citadel keep the records for its drug studies?"

His voice was flat, monotone. "They keep them at their main facility."

"There are no records kept at the prison?"

"None."

Parker ran the Citadel lab layout quickly through his mind, and tried to think where he would hide records. He came up blank. "Any guess where they might store the records of the Chem 19 study."

A pause. "Was that the study your father was in?"

"You know it was, asshole."

"I have no idea."

You're not even a good liar, you son of a bitch.

"Why don't I talk with your wife, Girard? Maybe she has an idea."

There was only the sound of heavy breathing for the next few moments, then his voice faint and empty. "Amaray has a storage closet in his office. I've seen him lock important papers in it."

"Good boy. What about his house?"

"I've never been there."

"Girard, I'll be talking with my lawyer and we will be getting a court order for those records Monday. I'll keep you out of this, if in return you keep this conversation just between the two of us. Deal?"

# #

"I need to speak with Mr. Amaray, right away."

"One moment, sir," a cultured male voice said. "I'll see if Mr. Amaray is taking calls at this time."

A minute passed.

"I've told you never to call me at home, Girard!"

Girard's voice quavered. "I didn't know what else to do. Tyler Beckman called and he knows about the stocks you gave me, and the drug study his father and Harris were involved in. He's going to get a court order Monday to search your lab for the drug study records."

The phone went silent for so long that Girard thought he'd been disconnected. "Mr. Amaray! Are you still there?"

"What does Tyler Beckman look like?"

After Girard's short description, Amaray gave a harsh laugh. "Relax, Girard. Your Mr. Beckman and our FDA inspector, Dr. Joyce, are both Dr. McGraw, and he won't be seeing anyone next week. Now tell me more about your conversation with him."

# #

Parker eased his rental car to a stop fifty yards down the street from Susan's house. Her car now sat in the driveway, and a white van stood at her front gate.

His plan had required no imagination. She'd be busy tonight so while she was gone, Parker planned to search her place in an attempt to determine her real identity and her role in his case.

Hours passed with no activity except a couple of late night dog walkers and a few passing cars. Parker checked his watch for the umpteen time. Eleven PM. Apparently Susan had lied and had no plans for the evening.

He had decided to call it a night when her front door opened and a man walked out. As the man turned back to the house, apparently to say something, the light streaming from the door illuminated his red hair and mustache. He walked to the white van and reached inside. Examining whatever he'd retrieved, he went back to the front door and held the item out. Susan stepped into the light, took it from him. The two of them hugged then red hair walked back to his van and drove off. Parker debated about following him, but settled instead for the license plate number. Ten minutes later, Susan's lights switched off and she emerged from her front door. His plans to search her house were immediately cancelled. She wasn't heading out for an evening on the town, unless black jeans, black hoodie, dark tennis shoes, and a small backpack over her shoulder were de rigueur for the night set.

##

Parker lay motionless in the high weeds of the empty lot, hoping the sheriff's car would move on. The calls on the cruiser's radio carried easily across the silence of the moonless night, reminding Parker that any sound he made would carry just as easily back to the patrol car.

Parker had tailed Susan to the parking lot of a popular restaurant. It lay situated a mile away from Ryan Ranch, a business park scattered over several hundred acres, much of it undeveloped. Citadel Pharmaceuticals sat in this same business park. A quick walk over some rolling hills and through a few empty lots brought one right to Citadel's doorstep.

Guessing Susan's destination, he gave her a ten minute lead and then followed. He had been crossing one of the open fields, a block from the lab, when the sheriff's car had suddenly materialized. Immediately, he'd dropped to the ground but he wasn't sure if he'd been fast enough. The car pulled up to the curb not thirty feet from where he lay and stopped.

The quiet was broken by the creak of the sheriff's car door opening, followed by the scrape of leather soles on asphalt. This was soon replaced by the crackling of dry weeds as the person stepped from the street into the field and began to move in Parker's direction. Parker could heard the footsteps moving closer and closer. Desperately, he pressed his face into the dirt and tried to muffle the sound of his breathing.

A few more feet and he'll be standing on top of me.

The footsteps stopped abruptly. A soft metallic sound broke the night stillness. It was a familiar noise but Parker couldn't place it. His ability to concentrate was lost in his struggle to control an overpowering urge to leap up and run.

His senses were so acute that the rivulets of sweat running down from his forehead seemed more like rivers. He was still adjusting to that feeling when he noticed a new sensation - drops of rain pelting his head. Only it wasn't drops of rain. And then he identified that metallic sound and knew why the cop had stopped. He was taking a leak and much of it was splashing up on Parker.

It seemed to go on forever before the now identifiable metallic noise repeated and the man moved away.

The cruiser's lights disappeared around the corner before Parker relaxed his vigil and sat up. He tried using the sleeve of his sweatshirt to clean off what he could, but he still reeked.

Not a very auspicious beginning, he thought, staring across the fields at the large, single story building that was Citadel Pharmaceuticals.

Parker rose to a crouch and cautiously approached. A high chain-link fence enclosed an area on the left side which apparently served as a delivery dock. Parker saw several strands of barb wire running along the top of the chain-link fence. All the windows he could see were covered with wire mesh, except for the large bay windows which sat on either side of the glass entry doors. There were lights on inside, but they seemed to be hall lights for none of the offices or lab rooms were lit up. Not surprising since this was the weekend.

He had no idea how Susan planned on getting inside, and for that matter where she was. Moving with caution, he crept toward the building. Seeing no one, he slipped carefully around to the right side of the structure and... there she was, a pencil light in her mouth, its light directed down to a door handle.

Parker crept up behind her. "Not sure this is legal, Miss Beckman."

She jumped with surprise, dropping her light. Seeing who it was, she swore softly and said, "What the hell are you doing here, McGraw?"

"Following you. My guess is you're here for the Chem 19 records."

She wrinkled her nose. "Is that some kind of earthy cologne you're wearing," she asked.

"Eau de Policeman."

Bending, Susan grabbed up her light and returned her attention to the door handle. With obvious experience, she placed two small metal tools in the key hole and began to manipulate them. Parker had seen enough movies to know these were the lock-picker's instruments of choice: a pick and a tension wrench.

"Even if you find the Chem 19 records, you won't be able to use them in court since they won't have been legally obtained."

"They aren't meant for court," she replied curtly, still working on the lock.

"You're wasting your time," Parker said. "I'm sure they have a security system that will alarm the minute you open the door."

"Ah, duh," Susan said over her shoulder. "Be useful, McGraw. Watch out for that security patrol."

Thirty seconds later, Susan said, "I've got it." Holding the door handle with her left hand, she dropped her tools into her backpack and pulled out a small hand-held radio.

"What's that for?" Parker asked.

"It's going to get us past the alarm." She held up the radio. "When I open this door, the sensor on the other side will detect it and transmit a radio frequency signal to the main control panel."

"Which triggers the alarm and we are toast."

"Let me finish. The signal the sensor sends is very weak, just a couple of milliwatts. I used Google to find out what frequency the sensor for this security system transmits at."

"That info is on the internet?"

"Yep. Just need to know where to look. So I set my radio to transmit at the same frequency, only I increase the signal it sends to 5 watts. This will jam the control panel, masking the sensor signal when I open the door. After I close the door, the sensor stops sending a signal, and I turn off my radio. The alarm will never see the sensor warning."

"How did you know which security system they use?"

"They made a typical mistake and displayed a window sticker from the company. This warns the world they have a security system, but tells the crooks which system they have to defeat."

Parker stood and stared at her. "Who the hell are you? I know you're not Susan Beckman."

"We don't have time for that. It's enough to know that I'm on your side." Using the hand holding the radio, she slipped her arm through the back pack strap and pulled it over her shoulder. She gave him a questioning look. "Are you coming or not?" With that, she turned the door handle, then pressed and held the send signal on the radio.

Once inside, Susan swung the door shut and then let go of the send signal.

"Did it work?" Parker asked, glancing nervously around.

"We'll know in a minute."

Chapter Twenty-Seven

They waited, ready to bolt at the first shrill of the alarm.

"How do you know it's not a silent alarm," Parker asked.

"I don't but that would be unusual. Alarms are designed to scare the individual away since it often takes a while for the police to arrive."

"While we're waiting, answer me a few questions, like why did you try and kill me?"

Susan shook her head. "I may have lied about a few things, McGraw, but I've never tried to harm you."

"Then why did your boyfriend plant a bomb on my boat?" he said vehemently.

Susan leaned up against the wall. "Okay. Let's talk about the bomb on your boat."

"Yeah, let's!"

She closed her eyes as she spoke, her tone one of resignation. "The guy with the red hair and mustache, his name is Mark. He didn't plant the bomb, he disarmed it."

"He what?"

"He found the bomb and disconnected one of the wires," she said in the same quiet voice.

Parker was speechless. After a bit, he said: "What was he doing on my boat in the first place?"

She opened her eyes and pushed away from the wall. "That can wait. It's enough to know that neither he nor I have any intention of harming you." She paused. "I'm not your enemy, Park."

Susan glanced down at her watch. "Come on," she said grabbing his arm. "We'll finish this discussion after we get out of here."

They moved rapidly through the dimly lit corridors until they reached Amaray's office. The door was locked but Susan had it opened in minutes.

She entered, crossed to the windows, closed the mini-blinds and pulled the curtains. Parker then switched on the lights.

Susan glanced around and gave a low whistle. "Not bad. Couldn't land a jet in here, but a prop plane should be no problem."

Parker was just as surprised. He'd been expecting a slightly larger version of St. Onge's sparse retreat, not a page out of *House Beautiful*. It was a long rectangular room with a beamed ceiling arching over a thick Berber carpet, and antique wood furnishings. Parker ran his hand over the polished surface of a huge mahogany desk.

"What a place," she said.

"It's more like a palace," Parker said, surveying the room.

Susan pointed to a small closet door in the corner. "You tackle the closet and I'll take the desk."

Parker grabbed her arm as she passed him. "This is a mistake. Even if we find the Chem 19 records we can't use them or any knowledge we gain from them. What do they call it? Fruit from the poisonous tree?"

Susan shook her arm free. "If you thought your court order was going to get these records, think again. Even if they still exist, Amaray and company were never going to turn them over. Besides, our discovery of the Chem 19 postcards and the deaths of the volunteers was unearthed long before we came looking for these records so that information might still be useable for your case."

"Then what's tonight's purpose?"

"We are wasting time, McGraw. Go check the closet."

From a distance, the closet didn't appear to be a Fort Knox. *So much for appearances,* Parker concluded after he inspected the door. It was solid hard wood with two dead bolts that looked battering ram proof. He was pondering his approach - maybe a bazooka - when Susan eased him aside.

"You take the desk, Park. This is woman's work." She pulled her lock-pick tools out and bent over the first lock.

Shaking his head, Parker walked back to the desk. He spent the next ten minutes sifting through the contents of each drawer. Nothing.

He arrived back at the closet door just as Susan popped open the second deadbolt.

The door opened easily on well-oiled hinges, revealing an interior much larger than one would estimate from the outside. Four tall filing cabinets lined one sidewall, while several cardboard file boxes were stacked up against the other wall.

"If what we're looking for isn't here, then I doubt it still exists," Parker said looking around.

By silent agreement, Susan began to search the file cabinets while Parker sallied forth into the contents of the boxes.

They'd been at it for about twenty minutes when Parker started to get anxious. He was on the second to last box and still nothing.

"Park?"

He looked up from the papers he'd stacked on the floor.

"I think I've got something. Take a look," Susan said.

She handed him two manila folders, each bulging with loose papers, then went back to her inspection of the file cabinets. Parker carried the folders over to Amaray's desk, spreading the contents out on the polished wood surface.

After a moment, he smiled. *She did have something. The raw data from the Chem 19 study that linked her father with Bill Harris. The study that Citadel denied ever existed.*

He poked through the papers, searching for the study protocol, a several page document which would describe the reasoning behind the study and how it was to be performed. He found it on the bottom of the pile. Setting the protocol in front of him, he settled back into Amaray's desk chair.

He was on the last of the study papers - the patient data reports - when Susan came over and sat on the edge of the desk.

"So? What have we got?"

Parker set the last page down. "What we've got is a big fat zero."

"There must be something."

"I agree, but I can't find it. The Chem 19 study was designed as a simple Phase I trial to test the safety of chemopandilin administered to human subjects for the first time. The study was targeted for twenty patients but for reasons not mentioned here, enrollment was halted at ten."

"Maybe someone grew two heads or a couple of fingers fell off," Susan said. "There must be some reason they stopped the study and went to all this work to keep it secret."

"Well if there is, the answer's not here. From all I can gather, the drug was well tolerated. No nausea. No dizziness. No anything. Not even a skin rash." He shook his head. "I guess I shouldn't be surprised since the drug was tried in a number of animal species before it was tested in man."

"If the drug is safe in animals, shouldn't it be safe for humans?"

"There's no guarantee. That's why they perform so many studies on other species. And that's why such small groups are used when they first test the drug in man." Parker shuffled through the pages.

"Why is that?"

"The biochemical variations between human and animal species are so great that even if a drug causes no side effects in animals, it may still do so in humans. This biochemical variation can, in fact, be so different that the potential for side effects may vary even within the same species."

Susan bent forward, clasping her arms across her chest. "You said something like that before. One strain of rats may develop a side effect and yet another strain may remain unaffected."

Parker nodded. "Probably the best example of varying response to a drug is the story of thalidomide. Have you ever heard of it?"

She shook her head.

"Thalidomide was first marketed in Europe as a wonder drug for morning sickness. The only species tested before human use was rats, and there were no apparent ill effects. Somehow, on the basis of those limited tests, the company decided that the drug was so safe that it could be sold over the counter without a prescription. The long term result of their carelessness was an estimated twenty thousand deformed children and eighty thousand infant deaths worldwide because the drug had severe effects on the developing fetus during the first three months of pregnancy."

"Oh, my God!"

"What demonstrates my point is that even after thalidomide was known to cause birth defects in humans, it was hard to prove it in animal species. Dogs, hamsters, guinea pigs, hens, even most strains of rats and mice, had no apparent ill effects from the drug. It was only in a certain strain of New Zealand white rabbits that the deforming effects on the fetus could be clearly demonstrated. Realize that these studies were done after the effects of thalidomide in humans were known."

They sat in silence for a while and then Parker rose from his chair. "You're finished with those filing cabinets?" he asked.

"Yes. Are you done with the boxes?"

"No, there is one left." Parker entered the closet and lifted the top of the only cardboard box left unexamined. He had little hope of finding anything.

"What have you got?" Susan asked when he emerged a few minutes later.

Holding up a large manila folders Parker replied, "Chem 18."

Removing the papers from the Chem 18 folder, Parker organized them into separate piles. Separating out the protocol section, he read it slowly and then read it again. Shifting his attention to the stacks of results and observations, he quickly combed each page before moving to the next

Leaning back in his chair, Parker rubbed his face and yawned. "It's basically the same study as Chem 19 only done with dogs."

He positioned the Chem 18 papers in front of him. "Since Citadel numbers its studies in the order they start them, we can assume this one was done prior to Chem 19."

"Don't assume anything, Park."

"Yeah, you're right." He reached over to the Chem 19 file and checked the date that the first patient was enrolled and compared it to the date the first dog was exposed to the drug.

"Here's something odd. The dog study was to last for four months. Two months of observation on the drug and then two months of further observation off the drug."

"So?"

"Well the human study, Chem 19, started just two months after the dog trial was initiated. I'd have thought they'd wait for completion of the dog trial before moving on to the human trial."

Susan glided back to her chair and plopped down. "So Chem 18, the dog study, was the eighteenth animal trial?"

"No. Many of those numbers refer to purely chemical studies, such as examining the structure of chemopandilin and seeing how it behaves under varying chemical conditions. I would guess they only studied three or four different species before the dog study."

"Is that enough?"

Parker shrugged. "I guess so. I'm just surprised they went to all the work of starting a study and then didn't wait for the results before advancing."

He went back to examining the observation data. There had been a total of ten dogs involved and no mention of side effects, at least nothing that was labeled as a side effect. Parker read on and as he got into the third month of the study he got a hint of something he'd missed on his first pass through the records. It was only a hint but it gave him a glimmering of why nine men had to die and what kind of monsters they were dealing with.

"Susan, we need to leave. Now!" Jumping up, he grabbed the Chem 18 and Chem 19 files.

"Park, your expression scares me. What did you find?"

"Enough to know we have to get out of here."

Susan went out the door first and Parker right behind her. They stepped into the hallway and came to a dead stop. Bernard, Citadel's security guard, and his dark-haired friend were blocking their exit. What's worse, Bernard held a .357 Smith and Weston Magnum pointed at them.

"Going somewhere?"

Chapter Twenty-Eight

There was no way to get comfortable. Every time Parker leaned back in his chair, the handcuffs gouged into his wrists. When he sat forward, the awkward position made his back ache. Susan appeared to be just as uncomfortable, perched on the edge of a chair, her wrists cuffed behind her.

"Could we stand and stretch for a few minutes?" Susan asked.

Carlos, Bernard's dark-haired companion, strolled over to Susan. His slap was unexpected and nearly knocked her off the chair.

"Keep your mouth shut!" He raised his hand to hit her again when Parker's voice stopped him.

"What's the matter, Carlos? Balls still sore from our last meeting?" he taunted.

Carlos slowly twisted around and gave Parker a look of hate that gradually evolved into a sneer. "You're a lucky man, doctor. Mr. Amarary said not to hurt you... until after he talks with you."

Bernard called from his seat on the couch. "No, Carlos. He said not to hurt him... much."

Carlos smiled wickedly at Parker. "Hear that, asshole?"

Without warning, he swung hard at Parker, but Parker was ready. He pulled his head back as the hand whistled by harmlessly. While Carlos was still off balance, Parker kicked him hard in the pit of the stomach. A brutal, well placed kick. Parker expected Carlos to crash to his knees, maybe even empty his dinner onto the floor. Instead, Carlos staggered backward a few feet, making only a slight "oof" sound, his facial expression not one of pain but rather of surprise. Gradually it shifted to one of malevolence.

Ah, shit! It's definitely not my day.

Carlos walked up to Parker, grabbed him by the hair, and hit him with a straight overhand to the face. Then he hit him again.

"Well, if it isn't our favorite FDA inspector, Dr. Joyce."

Parker shook his head, trying to clear the haze. At first, he saw two blurred figures, but by degrees they merged into one - Randall Amaray.

"Why don't we find Dr. Joyce or Mr. Beckman or Dr. McGraw or whatever he's calling himself tonight, a place to sit," Amaray said.

Bernard and Carlos yanked Parker up from the floor, and tossed him into a chair. Pulling a handkerchief from his pocket, Amaray passed it to Bernard. "Clean him up. I don't want blood on my office furniture."

Amaray settled into his high-back desk chair. "You're a man of surprises, Dr. McGraw. We weren't expecting to hear from you until next week, and never thought you'd try a break-in." He glanced over at Susan. "And we surely hadn't anticipated Ms. Beckman, AKA Ms. Grimbottom, would accompany you."

"How is Girard these days?" Parker asked.

"A very frightened little man. I'll be sorry to lose him." Amaray flashed his white teeth. "He's been most accommodating."

"Does he know he's an accomplice in multiple murders?" Parker replied.

Amaray leaned back in his chair. "Murders? I'm not sure I understand, Dr. McGraw."

"Don't play innocent, Amaray. You and your lovely employees arranged the death or disappearance of eight of the ten convicts that were enrolled in the Chem 19 study. The police killed the ninth one for you. And probably the only reason that the tenth remains alive is that he's in solitary confinement and can't be touched."

Bernard gestured to the files on the corner of the mahogany desk. "He was carrying those when we caught him."

Amaray opened the files and for the first time, Parker realized that Onge had entered the room. He looked down at the papers Amaray was inspecting. Amaray shoved the files away. "Damn it, Onge. I instructed you to get rid of these."

Onge cleared his throat. "There might be a use for the drug someday. If so, these results could prove invaluable."

Rising, Amaray grabbed the front of Onge's coat with both hands, lifting him up onto his toes. "I'll say this once more. Those files go! I want them burned to ashes, and the ashes flushed down the toilet." He shook Onge. "Understand?!"

"Yes. Yes, Mr. Amaray." Onge paled. "I wasn't arguing."

Parker's voice broke into the prolonged silence. "Why didn't you wait for the results of the dog study before going on with the human study?" It was a shot in the dark but if his supposition was right, it was the key to the whole tragedy.

Amaray stared at Parker, then turned back to Onge who was nervously looking at his feet. Amaray pushed Onge forward. "Go on, tell him. It doesn't matter now."

Nervously, Onge straighten his coat and realigned his shirt.

And why not. You should be presentable when you rationalize multiple murders.

Onge cleared his throat. "I felt chemopandilin could have a major role in the stabilization of society in the future. Our country is presently faced with ever increasing statistics of crime, especially violent crime. Our jails are filled to capacity and as fast as we build new ones, they're filled." He started walking back and forth in front of the desk, as if he were lecturing to a class.

"It's apparent that rehabilitation for most of these violent criminals, many of whom are sociopaths or psychopaths, is not successful. Yet we keep putting them back on the streets in the hope that this time they've learned their lesson and will behave." He shook his head. "I don't have to enumerate the countless tales of degeneracy that have disproven that assumption.

Onge stopped his walking and stared at Parker. "So the problem remains. What to do with this type of criminal? We can't rehabilitate them. We can't keep them in jail. The courts would never allow permanent incarceration. Our court system exists to protect the criminal, not the victim. It..."

Amaray cut him off. "Get to the point, Onge."

Onge paused. Caught up in the passion of his beliefs, he'd apparently forgotten the circumstances that had brought them to this room.

"Sorry." He arranged his thoughts. "The point is that we have a growing element in our society that is uncontrollable, incompatible, and with our present approach, unsalvageable." He checked to see if he had everyone's attention. Parker nodded, hoping it would encourage him to keep talking.

He continued. "An unsolvable problem. Unsolvable, that is, until we discovered chemopandilin. It seemed to hold all the answers. Its action is to suppress violent, antisocial tendencies. It calms the maniacal, savage passions that these criminal elements harbor, allowing them to channel their energies into more acceptable pursuits. An added benefit is a sense of euphoria, a wonderful feeling of contentment, which goes with the medication.

"After a loading dose, given over a week, the drug's effects last several months. In short, we had the perfect answer to one of society's major problems."

"You'd put them all on the drug?" Susan asked.

Onge smiled. "Of course, my dear. They'd be started on the drug in prison, and instead of visiting a parole officer each month, they'd visit a parole doctor who would administer their monthly or bimonthly maintenance dose of chemopandilin."

Susan started to speak, but Onge halted her with a raised hand. "You're going to ask about compliance in taking the drug. No problem. The feeling of contentment is so addictive it would keep them coming back for more." He grinned at the ingenuity of it all. "The perfect solution."

"Almost perfect," Parker interjected.

Onge shook his head sadly. "You're right, Dr. McGraw. Almost perfect. We tested rats, mice, guinea pigs, and cats. Using stereotactic neurosurgical procedures, we would place electrodes into the animal's brain and stimulate their rage center. We would then try to suppress the response with the drug. It worked beautifully... until we tested it in dogs."

"There was no mention of neurosurgical procedures on the dogs in the Chem 18 study," Parker said.

"True. For that study, we decided not to surgically induce personality disorders, but rather try to create a semblance of our own social situation. Half the dogs we selected were tame house pets, chosen to represent the normal elements of society. The other half, representing the criminal element, were dogs known to be vicious and uncontrollable, all slated for destruction. Both groups were given the drug and as expected the house pets were unchanged, while the vicious ones became docile and friendly. Another unqualified success, or so I thought at the time."

"Until Ludwig was killed," Amaray added.

Onge nodded. "Yes. Poor Ludwig."

"Who was Ludwig?" Susan asked.

Standing, Amaray came around and leaned on the edge of the desk. "Hans Ludwig was our chief lab technician."

"I though he died in a car accident," Parker said.

"He did die in an accident, but it didn't involve a car. He was killed by one of the dogs," Amaray replied.

"One of the vicious dogs?" Susan asked.

Amaray shook his head. "No, by one of the house pets. One of Onge's allegorical normal members of society. The episode was regrettable, but by then Onge had already started Chem 19 and that was unforgivable."

He looked disgusted and Parker knew why. The ground work for multiple murders had been laid.

"The dog study had gone as expected," Onge quickly added, "so I saw no reason to wait several more months for its completion before starting studies in humans." His voice had taken on a defensive sound. "I had very strong hopes for the drug, and..." he glanced quickly at Amaray, "I still do."

Amaray's fist struck the desk top. "This company is finished with chemopandilin, Onge. So get it out of your mind. Now!"

Desperate for information, Parker quickly asked another question to keep Onge rolling. "So, by the time that Ludwig was killed, you had enrolled how many prisoners in Chem 19?"

"Seven. And three more by the time the other dogs changed."

"Changed?" Susan asked.

Onge nodded. "Several more of the tame animals became exceedingly vicious. At that point, we knew there was a problem so all further Chem 19 enrollment was stopped."

"And you hoped that the same change wouldn't occur in your human guinea pigs, who if I remember correctly, were all nonviolent criminals... somewhat analogous to your tame house pets," Parker added.

"Oh, my God," Susan whispered, the implications obvious.

"We more than hoped. We prayed." Onge wrung his hands. "For several weeks all went well - but the dogs had also been fine for the initial few weeks. Our first suggestion that the same effect might be occurring was Fred Quinn."

"Didn't he kill a prison guard in a fight?" Parker asked.

"Yes, he did. I personally reviewed his prison and pre-prison records, as well as his psychological screening test done prior to his study enrollment. There was nothing that even hinted at a violent streak." Onge rubbed his face as his eyes remembered past happenings. "Jack Hyams, one of the friendliest, pleasantest men in the study, in jail because of some minor infraction, confirmed our nightmare. Shortly after his release from prison, he went on a killing rampage in a department store."

Susan's expression registered shock, but Parker knew this was nothing compared to what was coming.

Amaray took over from behind his lacquered desk top. "Onge, by pushing up the starting date on the Chem 19 study, had put us in an impossible situation. This conversion of a normal placid personality into a raging psychopath was not specific for dogs. It was happening to the Chem 19 prisoners. We reviewed and re-reviewed the pretest profiles on all the prisoners. We even tried to find out about the earlier lives of the study dogs, hoping to find some common denominator that might predispose someone to this adverse reaction. Despite all of that, there was no way to predict who would become violent nor when the violence would occur.

"One of the dogs remained normal for as long as five months after his last dose before the change occurred." He made an empty gesture with his hands. "We were trapped with no way to turn."

"Why didn't you just report your findings to the FDA and let them help you?" Susan asked.

Amaray's laugh was short and harsh. "Help us? Help us do what? We couldn't predict who might become violent, so what were we to do? Put all these guys in solitary confinement and watch them?"

Susan shrugged. "That's one solution."

"So how long do we watch them? A month? A year? Or maybe a lifetime since there was no way of knowing if this drug, like LSD for example, might exert its effects years later."

He waited for Susan's response. There was none.

"And when they were released, as they would have to be someday, what if they became violent like our department store killer. The lawsuits against this company would be staggering. That is in addition to the lawsuits that would have already been filed because of the need to keep these men locked up, along with the litigation filed by the surviving relatives of the victims of Quinn's and Hyam's assaults."

"Don't you have some kind of malpractice insurance to cover this type of thing?" Susan asked.

Amaray brayed his brutal laugh once more. "I presented our problem to a lawyer acquaintance of mine, purely as a hypothetical situation. His `guestimate' of our liability was in the hundreds of millions. He started to drool just thinking about the chance to prosecute." Amaray shook his head. "No one has enough insurance to cover that kind of catastrophe."

"Not to mention," Parker said, "that instead of becoming millionaires from your new antihypertensive drug, Normopressor, you'd become paupers by the time the lawsuits were settled."

Amaray stared at Parker for a moment then smiled. "Yes, I'm afraid that fact did play a heavy role in our eventual decision."

Susan's voice broke the ensuing silence. "What decision?"

The room remained quiet so Parker spoke up. "If you have a problem that can't be solved, then the next best thing is to eliminate the problem... all ten of them. After all, who'd miss a few ex-cons?"

Amaray flashed his perfect set of teeth. "I'm not sure I would have put it so crudely, Dr. McGraw, but I'd agree with your evaluation."

Onge cut in. "Science has to go on, Dr. McGraw. And at times, someone has to pay for its advancements. You as a physician should understand that."

"Don't cover your actions under the cloak of scientific advancement," Parker replied vehemently. "Call it what it is. Greed! The only thing that stood between you and the riches from your new drug were those ten convicts. And now they're gone."

"No, Dr. McGraw. I'm afraid you're wrong," Amaray replied, his hand delicately sweeping unseen dust from his desk top. "We still have two obstacles left in our pathway. But they're short-lived, so to speak." He smiled then beckoned Bernard toward Susan and Parker. "Show them the part of the facility they missed on their first visit."

Carlos and Bernard pulled them roughly to their feet and lead them toward the door. Susan yanked her arm free and spun around. Bernard reached to pull her back, but Amaray waved him still.

"Is there something else, Ms. Beckman?" Amaray inquired.

Susan tossed her hair back. "Yes, there is. Who killed my father? You or McGraw?"

Having more than a passing interest in the answer, Parker swiveled around to hear his reply.

Amaray paused, then half-smiled. "Why Dr. McGraw, of course. I thought you knew that, being the main witness against him. Anything else, Ms. Beckman?"

Susan slowly turned around and walked toward the door. There was nothing else.

They were led through a maze of corridors finally stopping in front of a stout looking wooden door. It had a small window about eye level just above the door handle, reminding Parker of the doors in his elementary school.

Bernard turned the handle and pulled the door open. He ushered them into a narrow hall lined by a solid wall on the right and a chain link fence on the left. An open doorway could be seen at the end of the hall. Bernard shoved Parker forward. He started shuffling toward the distant doorway when he heard a blood curdling snarl to his left. He spun away from the direction of the snarl and saw a huge shape leaping at him.

Even if he'd had his hands free, Parker knew he was no match for the savage German shepherd hurling toward him. He braced for the inevitable.

Crash!! A tremendous clatter as the dog went full force into the chain link fence.

Shit! He's on the other side of the fence. How'd I miss that? Parker shook his head and took a slow deep breath. *Get it together, buddy, or you're dead.* Looking around, he noticed that the chain link fence had gates every so many feet, each opening into a separate enclosed dog run.

Bernard, still laughing at Parker's reaction, pointed at the snarling dog throwing itself at the fence. "Here, meet Queeny. Ain't she a lover?"

Parker thought her the most vicious creature he'd ever seen, until its companion in the next cage appeared, leaping up on the fence, its fangs bared, saliva dripping from its jaws. It was an enormous Doberman pinscher, and what made the dog even more frightening was that it made not a sound. Someone had trained it to be quiet when it attacked so its victim would have no forewarning. Forewarned or not, whoever this animal chose as a victim would have no chance.

Bernard gestured at the Doberman. "Can't forget our resident killer, now can we. This beauty is the one that mauled Ludwig."

Parker was shocked. "You mean this dog was one of the house pets in the study?"

"Actually, they were both regular teddy bears at one time." He put his hand out toward the Doberman who lunged up against the wire trying to bite it. "Midnight here was the friendliest dog I've ever played with."

"You played with that monster?" Susan asked as she shuddered.

Bernard chuckled. "Yeah, it's hard to believe when you see him now. He was Ludwig's favorite. He'd leave Midnight's cage door open and let him wander about while he was in the lab at night." Bernard shook his head. "Real shock when Midnight killed him."

"Cut the crap. Let's get this over with," Carlos said as he hauled Parker toward the end of the hall.

They stepped through the doorway into the adjoining room. It was large, with a high ceiling, and linoleum flooring. It had probably served as a lab at one time, but was now entirely empty, except for an open shower stall in one corner. Parker noted that there were no windows, and that the only way in or out was through the doorway they'd just entered.

Bernard pushed Susan into Parker and they both went down hard onto the floor. Parker rolled over and sat up as the two turned to leave the room.

"Bernard!" he yelled. "You won't be able to excuse our murders as accidents. People knew we were coming here. If we turn up dead, there'll be a lot of unanswerable questions. There's no way you won't get implicated in our murders."

Bernard and Carlos glanced at each other then laughed.

"You got it all wrong, doc," Bernard replied. "This time it will be an accident." They both laughed again.

"Shooting us can't be masked as an accident," Susan yelled.

Bernard solemnly regarded her, a look of innocence on his fleshy face. "Shoot you? You must have us confused with the villains in this story." He grinned, evil dripping from his yellowed teeth. "We're going to save you. Right, Carlos?"

The smile on Carlos's face made Bernard's appear saintly in comparison.

Bernard continued. "The dogs will 'accidently' get loose and attack you. We will arrive on the scene and shoot the dogs in a belated attempt to save you. Of course, the handcuffs will be removed from your mutilated corpses before the police arrive."

"That won't explain our presence here," Parker replied, grasping for anything.

Grinning at his desperation, Bernard said, "Dr. Amaray has already worked that out. It's not surprising that a suspected cocaine trafficker, like yourself, might break into a pharmaceutical company searching for drugs. As for the woman, they'll figure she's an accomplice and let it go at that."

Once again they turned to leave. Parker remembered a look that had passed between Bernard and Amaray in the office when Susan had asked her last question. He took a wild guess.

"Bernard! One more question before you go. How'd you pull off Beckman's murder? It was genius, no question about it. I'd think you'd be proud of it instead of letting Amaray sweep it under the rug." *God, I hope he's as vain as he sounds.*

Bernard stood in the doorway staring back at them, his face blank.

Did I guess wrong? Did I really kill Beckman?

"Sorry, doc. Don't know what you're talking about."

"McGraw!" Susan yelled. "You killed my father and you can't blame it on that brainless eunuch over there. I was in the next room. I know what happened." She gestured with her head toward Bernard. "That dildo in the doorway couldn't find his zipper in a lighted room, much less engineer my father's death."

Bernard strode over to Susan. "Fuck you, bitch. I killed your father and now I'm going to enjoy listening to you die." He ended his sentence with a vicious kick to her side and walked out of the room.

Parker had heard a snap-like sound when Bernard kicked her. Worried, he rolled over to her side.

"Susan, are you okay?"

She looked up, tears streaming down her face. "We got the son of a bitch." She winced with pain. "We got him to admit that you're innocent."

"Thanks," he whispered.

Her answer was lost in the sound of the dog pen gates opening and the wooden door beyond slamming shut.

Chapter Twenty-Nine

Parker remembered a story of a frail little woman, driven by desperation and adrenaline, who had lifted up the front end of a car to free her child trapped beneath. *My desperation and adrenaline can't be any less.* But no matter how hard he tried his hands remained firmly locked in the handcuffs behind him.

He rolled onto his chest, got on his knees, and stood up. In the distance, he heard the dogs rush out of their pens, snarling and barking, and knew they'd be here any second.

His plan was to cover Susan's body with his own the moment the dogs appeared. It was a sacrifice which would merely delay the inevitable, but he had nothing else to offer.

The seconds ticked by and the doorway remained empty. He could hear the shepherd howling. Intermittently, there was a loud scratching sound. It took a moment before he identified the source. *The dogs are scratching at the wooden door, trying to get out. They don't know we're down here. We've got a reprieve, until they smell us.*

Parker's eyes strayed from the doorway to the door-less shower stall in the corner of the room. Its sole purpose to rinse off lab personnel in case of a chemical spill.

Susan lay curled on her side, in obvious pain, calling softly, "Help. We need help."

Parker dropped to his knees beside her. "Be quiet! The dogs will hear you," he hissed.

She stopped her moaning and glared up at him.

"Get up! Now!" he screamed in a whisper.

The urgency in his voice caught her attention. She climbed to her feet while Parker helped as much as he could with his hands cuffed behind him.

The dogs had stopped the assault on the wooden door and now he could hear them roaming in the hallway outside of their room.

"Follow me!" he whispered.

He led her into the open shower stall which extended all the way up to the raised ceiling.

"Watch me," he whispered. Putting his back against one wall of the stall, he lifted his right foot up and placed it against the opposite shower wall, then his left foot. He looked at Susan. "Start climbing."

Slowly he began to inch his way up the stall walls. First, he moved his legs up a bit, then he slide his back up. It was slow but steady going. Parker used his hands to help support him and give him leverage each time he inched higher.

Susan got the idea immediately and followed suite. She was moving up at a good pace when she lost her footing, and slid down to the stall floor with a loud thump.

There was no need for Parker to urge her on. They both knew the noise would bring the dogs.

The Doberman raced into the room, but didn't immediately see them.

Although Susan had instantly started climbing, she was still too low to be safe. The Doberman turned toward the sound of her shuffling.

As it bared his teeth, the drawn back lips resembled a smile, and then the beast came for her.

He took two long strides and leaped, his jaws wide with anticipation. Susan screamed as he sunk his teeth into her thigh, getting clothing with his bite but no flesh. His jaw, fixed on Susan's pants, acted as a pivot point so that his body swung back and forth like a pendulum dangling from her leg. A loud tearing sound occurred and the portion of Susan's pants gathered in the animal's mouth tore free, dropping him to the floor. The dog landed on his back with a loud whack, and lay stunned. His immobility lasted only seconds, but enough for Susan to regain her balance and resume her upward climbing.

She was higher, but not out of reach when the Doberman launched himself at her again. There was no question he'd get more than pants in this attack.

Parker watched the dog leap toward Susan. Leaning forward, he prepared to descend when a streaking figure crashed into the lunging Doberman.

The shepherd, driven by the same unbridled intensity that had caused it to smash against the pen fence earlier, had charged toward Susan and collided with the springing Doberman, causing both of them to tumble down.

By the time the dogs untangled themselves, Susan was safe.

"I don't think I can last much longer, Park. My legs are giving out."

Susan wasn't the only one with exhausted legs. Parker's leg muscles had developed a burning ache after only a few minutes of supporting him against the shower stall walls. He waited for the muscle cramps that would herald the end of his legs' holding ability and the beginning of his descent into the waiting jaws of the dogs circling beneath them.

The dogs, after repeated attempts to reach them, had resigned themselves to prowling around, with the shepherd intermittently letting out hideous growls and snarls.

"We're only putting off the inevitable," Susan said, her voice reflecting her fatigue and despair. "Amaray's two killers will be back soon and they'll just stake us out again for the dogs."

"I have an idea," Parker said softly. "For now, don't speak, don't move, and, especially, don't look down at the dogs.""

After that, she asked no further questions. They both remained silent, avoiding any eye contact with the animals. Parker prayed his supposition was correct.

The dogs continued to pace below them, but the shepherd's snarls and yelps were less frequent.

The pain in Parker's legs had become almost unbearable. He knew that Susan's couldn't be any less. *Dammit! She's right. We're just delaying the inevitable.*

Parker felt himself slip ever so slightly. He looked over at Susan and realized with a shock that she had also moved down several inches during the last few minutes. Their legs were exhausted. Their strength gone. *This is it. Any minute we'll be low enough for the dogs to reach us.*

The shepherd let out a blood curdling shriek and leaped with its teeth drawn - but his target was neither Susan nor Parker. Rather it was the Doberman. Within seconds, the two were in a life and death fight and the humans were forgotten.

"Park. What's going on?" Susan asked quietly.

"The two are so violently antisocial," Parker whispered, "they can't even be around each other without fighting."

"But one of those dogs is bound to win sooner or later," she said. "Then we're back to square one, except with one dog instead of two."

"That's why we're not waiting." Parker started to slide down the wall. "Come on," he whispered. "We'll sneak out while they're distracted."

When he reached the stall floor, he flexed and un-flexed his leg muscles several times before trying to get up. His thigh muscles hurt like hell but he was gradually able to stand. Stepping past Susan, who was going through the same maneuvers, he peered around the edge of the shower stall wall. The dogs were fighting in one of the far corners and couldn't see into the stall.

He turned back to Susan and helped her up.

"Quietly, head for the doorway," he said into her ear. "You first, I'll follow. If something happens to me, don't stop!"

Once more he checked the dogs. They were in the same corner locked in their deadly struggle. He motioned for Susan to start for the door while he watched the dogs.

She stepped out of the stall and inched her way toward the doorway. The dogs never took notice and Parker could understand why. If either of them let their attention wander, the other would kill it instantly

When Susan was safely out of the room, Parker slipped out of the stall and followed after her. It seemed a year later before he passed through the relative safety of the distant doorway.

Susan was at the end of the hallway crouched against the wooden door. Parker hurried as fast as his aching legs would allow. When he got closer, she motioned him to get down. He crouched and silently crept to her side.

"What's the problem?" he asked softly.

She motioned with her head. "Amaray's two goons are on the other side of the door. We're trapped."

Parker slowly rose up to the small oblong glass window set in the door and took a quick peek. Carlos and Bernard were up against the far wall, having an animated discussion.

Moving away from the window, Parker leaned up against the dog pen fence.

"Now what?" Susan asked.

Parker was silent for a moment. "Stand up and turn your back to me. Put your hand in my front pocket and pull out any dollar bills you feel."

Susan swiveled around. Using one of her cuffed hands, she reached into his right front pocket and brought out several bills. Parker stretched his arms around and pulled a twenty dollar bill out of the bunch.

"Perfect!"

Susan glanced at the bill in his hand. "I doubt that will buy our way out."

Parker smiled. "It just might. With a little luck."

"Based on the night so far, you can forget about luck!"

Parker told Susan his plan and the part he wanted her to play. "Why don't we go back and face whichever dog is left. I think that would be a better gamble."

"Just do your part," he muttered.

The sounds of the dog fight were fading so their time was running short. Once one of the dogs became victorious, he would come looking for them, and Parker wanted to be on the other side of the wooden door when that happened.

He set the twenty dollar bill on the floor, and pushed it toward the door with his foot. Taking a quick peek through the door window, Parker saw that neither guard was looking toward the door.

"Now!" he whispered.

While he watched them through the corner of the window, Susan slid the bill under the door until only about an inch was still showing on their side. Turning his back to the door, Parker bent forward and reached upward with his hands to the door handle and very quietly twisted it open.

Susan stood up and they both braced their backs against the wooden door, all the while keeping their eyes glued to the tail end of the twenty dollar bill. Droplets of sweat ran off Parker's face making a small puddle on the floor.

Every second passed like a minute, as Parker stood watching the bill, trying not to think of all the possible miscalculations that might occur now that the plan was in action.

What would Bernard and Carlos do when they saw the money? Open the door to investigate? Or grab the bill and then open the door? Such a small decision, but our lives are hanging on it.

And there was also the time element. Would Bernard and Carlos see the bill before the surviving dog found them or would the dog come howling down the corridor first? If the latter happened, Parker planned on opening the door and charging out with the dog behind them, leaving their fate to the winds. Unfortunately, if the surviving dog was the Doberman, their first warning of his presence would be when he attacked them, for his approach would be silent.

Parker didn't dare look at Susan for fear of missing his cue. How long they stood there, sweating, straining against fear and apprehension, each lost in their own thoughts of mortality, Parker had no idea, but it was the longest wait of his lifetime.

Without preamble, the bill disappeared under the door. Immediately Susan and Parker shoved the door open with all the force and power their pent up nervous energy could produce. A loud smack sounded as the door hit something but they kept pushing until it was completely open.

Rushing out into the hallway, Parker saw that Bernard had been knocked out cold. He lay on top of Carlos, who was trying to free himself of Bernard's dead weight.

Parker charged over and delivered a kick aimed at Carlos's head. The kick, though, was rushed and Carlos was able to partially dodge it. Before Parker could follow with another kick, Carlos had gotten his hands free from under Bernard and easily deflected Parker's foot. By the time Parker tried a third kick, Carlos was completely free of Bernard and quickly rolled away from the attempt.

Jumping to his feet, Carlos assumed a martial arts position, backing cautiously away. That is until he realized that Parker's hands were still cuffed behind him. Straightening up, Carlos dropped his defensive stance and chuckled wickedly.

"So we change the scene. Instead of being killed by the dogs, the burglar is killed by the security guard who was trying to protect himself after his partner was injured." Carlos sneered, "Don't think I won't enjoy this, asshole. And I'll make sure you get to enjoy it, too. Nice and slowly."

Circling around Bernard's inert figure, he advanced toward Parker. His first punch Parker ducked, but the kick that followed caught Parker in the chest and knocked him up against the corridor wall. His chest felt like someone had whacked it with a baseball bat.

Leaning on the wall, trying to catch his breath, his arms bound behind him, Parker had no false expectations. *It's going to be a slow agonizing death unless I can goad him into ending it quickly.*

As Carlos moved toward him, Parker pushed away from the wall, and slowly slid to his right. Suddenly, he feinted to his left. Carlos, over anxious, went with the fake and Parker kicked him hard in the thigh. Carlos stumbled and went down on one knee. Keeping his eyes on Parker, he carefully rose up.

"Not nearly enough, doc," he said with a soft laugh.

He moved in fast, sending a round house kick toward Parker's left side. Parker couldn't dodge it, but he did manage to blunt its force with his left shoulder. He was feeling pleased with himself when he walked into an overhand to the jaw. He was still dazed when Carlos hit him twice more in the face and then kicked him in the abdomen. The blow to the belly doubled Parker over. Carlos brought his knee up into Parker's face, sending him backwards into the concrete wall, where he struck his head then slid to the floor.

It took a moment before Parker opened his eyes. Everything was blurred and there was a salty, metallic taste in his mouth which he recognized as blood. Idly, he wondered if the blood was from his broken nose, his smashed lips, or a combination of the two.

Carlos was drawing back his fist to hit Parker again when Susan kicked him. She tried to kick him in the groin but her foot missed its mark. Carlos tossed Parker against the wall and turned toward Susan.

"So you want to get involved, huh?" Grabbing the front of her jacket, he viciously backhanded her several times across the face before throwing her against the other wall. She went down like a rag doll.

Revenge for Carlos' handling of Susan generated energy in Parker he would never have thought possible in his state. He levered himself away from the wall, and while Carlos was still turned, enjoying his handiwork with Susan, he kicked him viciously in the side. Stunned, Carlos went down but not out. Parker kicked him again in the side as he clumsily tried to rise, then kicked him very hard in the head. Carlos slumped to the ground motionless.

Keeping a cautious watch on Carlos, Parker staggered over to Susan. Her eyes were open and she was trying to sit up.

Parker bent down. "Susan! We've got to get out of here. Try to get up!"

Parker was trying to help her stand when she screamed. An iron grip on Parker's shoulder swung him around into the oncoming path of a right handed freight train. His lights blinked briefly, then went out.

Parker awoke to a recurrent stinging sensation on either side of his face. It was Carlos slapping him.

"Wake up, asshole. Don't want you to miss the rest of the show."

He pulled Parker to his feet, propped him against the wall, and methodically began to beat him, mainly working on his midsection, occasionally switching to his face. He stopped briefly when Parker vomited and then went back to his work. All that kept Parker standing was the wall behind him and Carlos's left hand holding his shirt.

Carlos was pulling back his right hand to deliver another blow when Susan fell against him.

"Stop it. You're killing him," she pleaded.

He flung her against the opposite wall, without letting go of Parker, and laughed. "That's the idea!"

Turning back to Parker, he smiled. "Are we having fun yet, doc?"

Parker mumbled an answer.

Carlos shook him. "Say again, ass-wipe. I didn't hear you."

Carlos leaned forward to hear the reply and Parker smashed him in the face with his forehead. Carlos jerked back in pain and Parker kicked him in the balls. It was a hard sweeping kick, fueled with loathing and hate, expending the last of Parker's energy reserves.

My last hurrah.

Parker stood there, swaying, ready to die, when he saw a flicker of motion behind Carlos. With his last ounce of strength, Parker half stumbled, half fell into Carlos, hitting him in the chest with his shoulder and knocking him back through the open doorway, into the dog pen hallway behind him.

Totally spent, Parker slid to his knees and then face down onto the floor. "Susan!" he croaked. "Shut the door! Don't let him out."

Groaning, Susan rose and fell against the door, pushing it closed. Within seconds, Carlos was shoving against the door, and his power was such that it began to slowly open.

"Park! I can't hold it." Susan's voice was desperate.

"You have too!" he mumbled, too spent to move.

She braced her feet against the floor and used all the strength her fear could generate to keep the door from opening any further. It still wasn't enough as the door continued to gradually inch open.

Suddenly, the pressure on the door let up. From behind it came a series of agonizing, terrified screams.

Susan glanced over at Parker. "My God. What's that?"

Parker rolled on his side, facing her. "The dog's got him," he whispered hoarsely. The flicker of motion that he'd seen beyond Carlos had been the Doberman. He had finished his fight with the shepherd, then peeked around the end of the hallway, wondering about the noise. "Don't let up on the door."

There were several more pushes against the door, amidst screams of pain and terror. Finally the bumps against the door stopped, and shortly after that, the screams.

Chapter Thirty

Lifting his head, Parker watched Susan move across the hall as if in a dream. She was the only object in clear focus with everything else a surrealistic blur. He lowered his head back down, closed his eyes, and tried not to think about pain. Not the pain from his mangled face. Not the pain from his shredded lips, now plastered to his teeth with dried blood. And not the pain from his abdomen which felt like there were iron spikes imbedded in the muscles. And last of all, not the pain of simply breathing. Breathing that felt like a knife thrust into his side with every inhalation. He tried not to think of pain, but there wasn't much else to think of.

Susan's hand, gently shaking his shoulder, brought him back to full consciousness.

"Park. How are you doing?"

Parker gazed up into Susan's bruised countenance and wondered again who she really was.

"Park, I'm going to roll you over so I can get your handcuffs off. Okay?"

Parker wondered why she was speaking to him as if he was a child, when she moved him and the pain eliminated all other thoughts. His involuntary cry of agony tore his lips from their sealed position and set them bleeding again.

Susan stroked his face and dabbed his lips with her shirt sleeve. "I'm sorry, Park. I had to move you to get to the cuffs." He felt her fumbling around behind him and then his hands were free.

He tried to talk but the words came out garbled.

Susan gently propped him up against the wall. As she sat back on her heels, Parker saw Bernard start to move behind her. *Oh, God. Not again.*

"Bernard! Bernard!" he mumbled.

She leaned forward. "I can't understand you, Park."

He pointed past her to the now rising hulk.

Death has a List

Alarmed, she turned quickly. "Oh, him." She laughed softly. "Don't worry about old Bernard."

Was she crazy? Don't worry about a man the size of a house whose goal in life was to end their lives?

Susan stood up and walked over to Bernard who was now on his knees. She raised her foot and shoved him back down on the floor. Her casualness and his clumsiness were now explained. His arms were handcuffed behind him.

Without his hands for support, Susan's shove sent him face down into the floor. She bent over him and grabbed his hair. Turning his face toward her, she put the barrel of a .357 Magnum to his forehead. Her voice devoid of emotion when she spoke. "If you move again, even an inch, I'll blow you away." She jabbed the barrel against his forehead. "Did you get that, scumbag!?"

Bernard nodded quickly, letting his whole body go limp to confirm his compliance.

Fetching the handcuffs she'd recently removed from Parker, she applied them to Bernard's ankles and then returned to Parker's side.

She thrust the gun out to him. "Take this. I'm going for help and you're in no shape to come with me."

Parker smiled and pushed the gun away. "Not this time," he said hoarsely. "You keep it."

Susan laughed. "Macho to the end, right?" She lifted the left side of her jacket and Parker saw another gun stuck in the waistband of her pants.

"I found Carlos's gun near the wall. He must have dropped it while you two were struggling. Here. You take Bernard's."

This time Parker accepted the gun. It felt cold but comforting in his hand.

"Stay here and leave everything to me. I'll be back as soon as possible." She started to rise then paused. "I used Bernard's keys to lock the dog lab."

And then she was gone, sliding silently down the hall, gun in hand.

Clutching the Magnum, Parker rested his head against the wall, closed his eyes, and tried to relax. His fatigue began to overwhelm his pain. Slowly the tenseness drained from his body as he felt himself drifting off to sleep.

Scrape.

The sound jerked him awake. Quickly, he stared around. The halls were empty and Bernard was lying to his right were Susan had left him.

Relax, buddy. It's all over.

Closing his eyes, Parker settled his head against the wall. He was on the edge of a deep slide into oblivion when he heard it again, this time closer.

Scrape.

Suddenly he knew what the sound was. Immediately, he twisted to his left. As he moved, he felt a harsh scratch across the right side of his face then heard a loud smack against the wall where his head had been. He kept rolling, finally stopping about ten feet from where he'd lain. Gingerly he sat up and looked back. The pain of his rapid movement was lost in the realization of how close he'd come to death.

The scraping sound had been Bernard, slowly working his way over to where Parker had been slumbering. The kick from his booted feet had missed crushing Parker's head by just a few inches. With his hands and feet cuffed, Bernard had lined up his target but couldn't see exactly where the kick went when he lashed out with his feet. As it was, Parker's face still burned from the scrape of the boot as it went past.

Parker pointed the gun at Bernard and pulled the hammer back. "How'd the lady put it, Bernie - 'Blow you away' - wasn't that the expression?"

Bernard's eyes widened.

"But I'm not going to kill you," Parker added.

Bernard's expression relaxed, replaced with a look of relief mingled with scorn. Bernard clearly wouldn't hesitate to kill if the situation were reversed.

Parker lowered his aim from Bernard's head to his groin. "No, I'm going to blow your balls off instead." He grinned. "But don't worry, you won't die."

He steadied his gun hand with his other hand, sighting down the barrel.

"No! No!" Bernard screamed as he scrunched up in a ball, trying to protect his genitals.

Lowering the gun, Parker snickered. "Tell you what, Bernard. I'm feeling generous today, what with all the kindness everyone has shown me. So if you crawl on down to the end of the hall, I might give you a second chance."

He was in motion before Parker finished, resembling a mammoth garden snail as he inched along the floor.

Once more Parker settled back against the wall to wait for Susan's return when an unsettling thought occurred to him.

She didn't leave to get help. She left to get her own ass out of here and leave me with the blame. He slapped the floor with his hand. *Son of a bitch! With charges of murder and drug dealing already pending against me, I can just see trying to explain away a dead security guard and a burglarized office to the police. I'm sure my version of the facts will have little in common with the fairy tale that Amaray, Onge, and Bernard will relate. And with Susan gone, I've got no one to corroborate my claims.*

Amidst groans and grunts, Parker leveraged himself up the wall into a vertical position. *Definitely time to go. I just hope it's not too late.*

He yelled over at Bernard. "If you've moved from that position when I return, you'll be singing in the boys' choir! Comprende, shithead?"

Bernard nodded.

Parker agonizingly pushed himself away from the wall and lurched off in search of Susan, or proof of his innocence, or an exit - whichever he could find first. He wasn't particular.

The building was honeycombed with halls and offices. Parker's recollection of the exact route from Amaray's office to the dog pen was a bit vague. He'd had more pressing concerns on his mind at the time.

He staggered up and down multiple dimly lire halls and corridors without success. No Susan. No exit. No Amaray's office.

After pausing for several minutes at an intersection, Parker suddenly realized where he was. He'd stood in the same spot just a few days ago. The front door exit was down and around the corner to his left while Amaray's office was up the hall to his right.

Parker looked toward the exit on his left. Freedom and at least temporary safety. He glanced right, toward Amaray's office. Capture and imprisonment, offset by the remote possibility that the proof of his innocence still existed.

He checked the load in the Magnum and went to the right.

The Amaray's office door was partially open. He heard a constant humming noise from within but he couldn't recognize the source. Gun in hand, he eased the door open and stepped inside.

The noise was coming from a paper shredder in the corner of the office. Both Amaray and Onge stood over it feeding paper as fast as the machine would accept it.

Parker lifted the gun, took careful aim, and fired twice. A slow drawn out death, with a lot of pitiful sounds, but finally the machine gasped its last whirl and died.

Amaray was the first to recover from the shock. "Well, Dr. McGraw. This is an unpleasant surprise."

"Put the rest of the papers over there," Parker gestured with the gun toward the desk, "and move back to the wall."

Onge cautiously approached the desk, dropped his papers on top, and quickly backpedaled to the wall. Amaray remained stationary.

"I want your papers also, Randall. You can put them on the desk or I'll take them off your corpse. I really don't give a damn which way we do it."

Sirens sounded in the distance, drawing closer.

Amaray laughed. "You're finished, doctor. I suggest you use this time to escape, not to argue over worthless papers."

Parker cocked the gun hammer. "One way or the other, dirtbag."

Amaray began to argue but something changed his mind, and he laid the papers softly on the desk before moving back against the wall. Parker knew what had convinced him. He'd seen what was mirrored in Parker's face: a man so pushed by fatigue and desperation that he'd kill without hesitation.

Using his free hand, Parker gathered up the piles of paper on the desk, stuffed them in his shirt, and backed toward the door. The sirens were no longer audible.

Stepping into the hall, he pulled the door closed, and made for the exit as fast as he could. Through the large plate glass windows, he saw no less than four police cars parked in front. The glare from their red and blue flashing lights lit the whole scene and gave it a menacing quality. A feeling of death permeated the air. Parker didn't want it to be his.

He eased back around the corner and hobbled toward Amaray's office. He decided he'd use them for hostages until he could explain his side of tonight's occurrences. Hopefully, there was enough documentation left in the papers he had to support his explanation. Because if there wasn't...

The door to Amaray's office was closed.

He knew if they spoke to the police before he did, it might turn into one of those armed and dangerous, shoot to kill situations. At the very least, he'd be so buried in jail that by the time ,anyone listened to his version, Amaray and company would have been able to cover their tracks.

He turned the handle and entered. "Okay, guys. Over in the corner."

The room was empty. His luck had run out.

Chapter Thirty-One

"This is the police! Come out with your hands above your head!"

Parker opened the door and used his foot to shove the Magnum out into the hallway floor.

"I'm coming out! I'm unarmed." With that, he edged cautiously into the hall, his hands stretched above his head.

Immediately, he was surrounded by police - large burly men wearing bulletproof vests. They pushed him up against the wall, spread his legs and patted him down for other weapons. Finding none, they jerked his arms behind him, handcuffed him, and someone began to recite him his rights.

Parker caught the eye of a young blond policeman standing nearby. "Get me the officer in charge. I need to speak to him now!"

The officer gave Parker a look of surprise followed by doubt.

"He'll want to hear this, believe me," Parker added.

The officer disappeared as Parker was brought into the lobby. The room was crowded with six uniformed policemen, three people in plainclothes, several firefighters, and two paramedics.

The blond officer reappeared followed by a tall, sinewy man dressed in dark pants, white shirt, and gray sport coat.

"I'm Detective Quik. Officer Maloney says you may have some important information for me," he said in a gruff, no nonsense tone.

"Yes, that's right. There are some papers in my shirt..."

Before Parker could finish, Quik reached into Parker's shirt and removed the papers. Turning, he extended them toward someone behind Parker. "Are these the research papers he stole?"

A hand snaked out and grabbed them. "Yes, they are. Thank you very much, officer." It was Amaray. He casually handed them to Onge who disappeared down the hall.

"Detective!" Parker yelled. "Don't let that man take those papers. He's going to destroy them."

Quik stared at Amaray. "Where's he going with those?"

Amaray gave his best corporate smile. "He's going to make copies. You can have the originals but we must have copies. Much of our research data is on those documents and without it our work would be in chaos."

The detective swiveled back to Parker. "There. Does that make you happy? Now, what do you have to tell me?"

"Forget it." Parker hung his head. *Whatever Onge returns with, it won't be what he's carrying now.*

There was a shout to Parker's left. "Detective Quik!"

Quik glanced over at an officer shouldering his way through the milling crowd. "Over here, Becket," Quik responded.

Becket was short and thick, with a beer gut peeking out below his bulletproof vest. "Well, we found the two security guards. One just has a few bruises. The other one wasn't as lucky."

"Becket, how many times have I told you to just give me the facts?" Quik shook his head in disgust. "What does 'wasn't as lucky' translate into?"

"He looks dead, sir."

"What do you mean 'looks dead'? Didn't you examine him?"

It was Becket's turn to shake his head. "Not with a Doberman the size of a small horse standing over him."

Quik gestured to one of the nearby officers. "Watch this guy. I'll be right back." He left in Becket's wake.

Parker asked and received permission to sit down. After collapsing into one of the couches, he stretched back and closed his eyes, marveling at how comfortable he was becoming with his hands cuffed behind him.

He felt a sharp kick to his feet. Parker stared up into the outraged face of Detective Quik. "Is that your work back there?" He motioned over his shoulder with his thumb.

"Why don't you ask Amaray about it? It's his dog, not mine."

Quik spoke over his shoulder, never taking his eyes off Parker's. "Get Amaray, now. Then call the animal control people and an ambulance." He paused. "Also call the coroner."

His stare made Parker feel defensive. "It's what they had originally slated for me, Detective. I merely altered their plans."

Quik took in Parker's ravished face, his blood-stained clothes, and his obvious exhaustion. "What the hell is this all about? I want some answers now and no bullshit."

"I'll give you answers, officer." It was Amaray.

Quik shifted his attention to Amaray.

"That man is Dr. Parker McGraw, recently accused of murder and drug dealing, if my memory of the newspaper article is accurate."

Quik swung back to Parker. "Is that correct? You're that Dr. McGraw?"

Parker nodded wearily.

Amaray continued. "The doctor broke into the premises, setting off a silent alarm installed in my house. I informed my head of security and he drove over, with one of his assistants, and met me here."

"Why didn't you call us, instead?" Quik asked.

Amaray shrugged his shoulders. "We've had several false alarms in the past so I didn't want to call until I knew the score."

"Always call us, Mr. Amaray, and let us determine the score. Okay?"

"You're right, of course, detective," Amaray replied. "If I'd called you instead, Carlos would still be alive."

Amaray paused, bowing his head. Parker wouldn't have been surprised to see tears fall. Nothing Amaray did anymore could surprise him.

"Please continue, Mr. Amaray." Quik's voice was flat, dispassionate.

Clearing his throat, Amaray went on. "Bernard and Carlos, our security officers, accompanied me into the building to my office. We found my safe room door open and papers scattered all about. I called Dr. Onge and asked him to come over immediately. As head of our research division, Onge would be the most cognizant of what might be missing."

"Safe room?"

"It's actually a modified closet where I keep our most important experimental data. There is information in there, which given to another pharmaceutical company, could be worth millions."

"Where those the papers that the doctor was carrying?" Quik asked.

"Yes, they were."

Quik glanced at Parker, then back at Amaray. "What happened next?"

Onge reappeared at Amaray's side and handed him a sheaf of papers. Amaray passed them to Quik. "These are the papers we were discussing. They are the formulation of our new antihypertensive drug, Normopressor."

Quik leafed through the papers and then passed them to one of his junior officers. "We'll keep a close watch on these, Mr. Amaray. Go on with your story."

"I called the police and waited in my office for Dr. Onge to get here. Soon after he arrived, Dr. McGraw suddenly appeared in my office, waving a gun, even firing into one of the office machines to scare us."

"Why would he come back to your office after he had already burglarized it?" Quik was fast on the uptake.

Removing a handkerchief from his back pocket, Amaray dabbed his lips, wiped his nose, folded it and put it back. "It shocked me that he'd returned. Apparently he hadn't found the papers he wanted. Maybe we had interrupted his search with our arrival." His shrug was very casual.

"And then?"

"He held us at bay, gathered up several documents on the desk, and fled the room."

"Why would he leave you alive to testify against him?" Quik was probing, but Amaray stood way ahead of him.

"I think the doctor underestimated the extent of his fame and figured we'd never be able to identify him. Unfortunately for him, I'd seen his picture in the paper and remembered who he was."

"And where were your security guards while all this was occurring?" Quik asked.

"They'd gone off to examine the rest of the building," Amaray replied smoothly. "Why don't you ask my security chief, Bernard Johnson? I see him standing in the corner with Dr. Onge."

You mean over in the corner being coached by Dr. Onge.

One of the officers led Bernard over and Quik proceeded to question him. "Mr. Johnson, I understand you're chief of security here. Tell me your version of what happened tonight."

Bernard appeared uneasy and glanced at Amaray. "Go ahead," Amaray said encouragingly. "He wants to know what happened after you left my office and went to check the premises."

Bernard nodded, cleared his throat several times, then spoke. "Me and Carlos Stein, my assistant, went to check the premises as Mr. Amaray says. We wanted to make sure the burglar had left. At one point, we split up and that's when they got Carlos."

"What do you mean, 'they'?" Quik interjected. "I thought this McGraw was alone."

"No, he wasn't alone. He had a female with him," Bernard answered.

Quik looked over at Becket who shook his head. "The place is clean, Sergeant. Unless she's in the room with the Doberman."

"No, I saw her leave with him." Bernard pointed at Parker.

"Describe her, Mr. Johnson."

"Long dark hair, about five foot eight, kind of thin, dressed in dark clothes. Good looking."

"Did you catch that, Becket?"

"Yes, sir."

"Take a few men and search the place again. Check around outside too." Becket moved off with several eager, gun-toting officers behind him.

Quik motioned for Bernard to continue.

"Ah, I'm not exactly sure what happened between Carlos and this guy. I overheard him and his lady friend talking. I guess he and Carlos had a fight and Carlos banged him up pretty good. Somehow, though, he and the girl captured Carlos. This guy, McGraw, was so pissed off at Carlos that he stuck him in that room and let the dog loose."

"You mean they deliberately set the dog on him?" Quik sounded shocked.

Bernard shook his head. "No, it wasn't both of them. Just him. The girl was against the idea from what I could hear."

Quik was silent for a moment, staring at Parker. "And how were you able to overhear all these comments, Mr. Johnson?"

"Well, I'm ashamed to say I got careless and they got the drop on me with Carlos' gun. They handcuffed me, then got into an argument on what to do with me. This bastard wanted to dump me in with Carlos, but the girl talked him out of it."

Quik gestured toward the officer standing next to Parker. "We've heard enough. Take this man and book him."

A muscular policeman yanked Parker to his feet and led him toward the doorway. Parker pulled loose and spun around. "Hey, Quik! What about my side of the story? Aren't you interested or is justice a foreign word in your working vocabulary?"

The officer Parker had broken from put one hand on Parker's collar and the other on the chain linking the cuffs, waiting for Quik's word to jerk him off to jail.

The room was silent with all eyes on Quik. His face was impassive. "I want you to answer me two questions, doctor. And I want yes or no answers. Nothing more. Understand?" The voice was as cold as his eyes.

"Okay." *I can see it coming but what can I do?*

Quik moved closer to Parker. "Did you break in here tonight?" He held up his hand stopping Parker's attempted explanation. "Answer yes or no. Nothing else."

The question floated in the air for a while before Parker spoke. "Yes," he said softly.

Quik's eyes narrowed and his face hardened. "Did you force that man into the room knowing that vicious dog was there?"

It was just what Parker had feared would happen if Amaray got his story in before his. He looked around at the sea of faces waiting for his answer. Thumbs up or thumbs down was the old Roman method of expressing the fate of a deposed gladiator in the Colosseum. Parker knew which way the thumbs would point with his next answer.

He sighed. "I want my lawyer."

Quik turned away from him and instantly Parker's arms were almost yanked out of their sockets as his enthusiastic captor started leading him away. Parker groaned with the pain but no one seemed to notice.

They'd only gone a few steps when a familiar voice rang out.

"What the hell are you doing? He's innocent. There's the ones you should be arresting."

Lifting his head, Parker saw Susan framed in the entranceway, her hand pointing to the left. Everyone turned in the direction she indicated and there were Amaray, Onge and Bernard standing in a group, seemingly as shocked as Parker with Susan's sudden appearance.

Amaray was the first to regain his composure. Parker saw him nudge Bernard who then cried out, "That's her. That's the woman who was with McGraw."

Susan strode over to Quik, boldness in her stride and manner.

"Are you the officer in charge?" she demanded.

Quik looked her over, a little uncertain at the change in events. "Yeah, I'm in charge. And who are you?"

Susan glared into his eyes. "I'm the person who's trying to stop you from making one of the biggest mistakes of your career."

Quik returned her stare, giving no ground. Finally, he shook his head. "Let's hear what you have to say."

Susan nodded. "In the meantime, tell your subordinate over there to lay off the gestapo techniques with the doctor."

Quik shot a menacing glance at Parker's guard and instantly the pressure on his arms disappeared, replaced by a gentle restraint on his forearm. Parker straightened up and rolled his shoulders around, trying to ease their discomfort.

"Hold on here!" Amaray shouldered his way up to Quik. "Do you mean to tell me that the ramblings of this drug-dealing killer and his mistress hold any weight against my word and those of two reputable employees of this company?"

There stood Amaray, a picture of respectability with his pristine appearance and commanding ways matched against Susan, her clothes tattered, dried blood on her face, and her hair a bramble bush.

Amarary sensed Quik's indecision and pressed on. "These two burglarized my company and were involved in the brutal death of one of my employees. Who would listen to what they have to say?"

"I might," said a deep voice from the entrance.

The entire group swiveled in unison, like a trained drill team, to view the owner of this new voice.

It was Detective Ivan Hall.

"What the hell are you doing here, Ivan?" Quik asked. "You're not on duty tonight."

Hall smiled but without humor. "But it seems that my case is."

He walked over to Parker. "Looks like you've been busy tonight, doctor."

It was Parker's turn to smile. "Thanks for coming, Detective."

Hall glanced from Parker to Quick. "What's going on?"

Amaray lightly touched Quik's jacket. "Who is this man, Detective Quik?"

Quik looked at Hall and raised his eyebrows. "Ivan, introduce yourself."

"Detective Ivan Hall of the Monterey Police Department." He bent his head toward Amaray but didn't offer his hand. "I've been investigating a murder case that involves Dr. McGraw." He paused. "And who are you?"

There was no attempt at cordiality by Amaray. "Randall Amaray, president of this company. And I don't intend to stand idly by, while these lowlifes make insulting innuendoes against my employees and myself."

"So what gives, Ivan?" Quik asked.

Hall replied, "The doc here said he'd found some papers that would answer all the questions in the murder case I'm investigating." Hall gestured to Parker. "So where are they?"

"Maybe this is what you're looking for?" Quik took a stack of papers from one of the nearby policemen and handed it to Hall. "He had these stuffed in his shirt when we apprehended him."

Hall removed a pair of bifocals from his pocket, put them on, and moved to a nearby lamp. He was bending to inspect the documents when Parker's comment brought him up short.

"I wouldn't waste your time with those, Detective Hall. They aren`t the papers I had in my shirt when I came out of Amaray's office. Isn't that right, Onge?"

With the attention suddenly on him, Onge squirmed like a worm on a hot brick. He straightened up and smoothed back his hair before he spoke. "I have no idea what you're talking about."

Parker snickered. "It doesn't matter anyway, Onge. The papers I had in my shirt, the ones you no doubt destroyed, and then substituted with these others, were not the ones you and Amaray were trying to shred."

Onge developed a furtive cast and Amaray lost some of his smugness.

Squirm, you bastards.

"I was afraid the original papers," Parker continued, "might get taken from me and disappear during the confusion of my arrest. So I hid them in Amaray's office and stuffed some other papers in my shirt before surrendering."

Hall held up the papers in his hands. "So these are worthless?"

Parker nodded. "Yes. But if we go down to Amaray's office, I'll show you some papers that are pure gold."

Hall gestured to Amaray. "Why don't you lead the way, Mr. Amaray?"

Amaray stepped in front of Hall and raised his hands, palms out. "Stop right there, Detective. Unless you have a search warrant, you go no farther."

"I'm afraid you're wrong, Mr. Amaray," Hall said with steel in his voice. "We're already inside the building investigating a crime. During our search for other victims, evidence in plain view may be seized, especially if there is concern about it being destroyed or removed, as Dr. McGraw has insinuated." He paused, giving Amaray a hard stare. "Is that clear?"

Without waiting for a reply, Hall grabbed Parker's arm and pushed him in the direction of the main hallway. "Let's go, McGraw. We'll find our own way."

A small entourage followed them through the corridors to Amaray's door and into his office. Susan, Amaray, Bernard, and Onge were among the onlookers.

Death has a List

Parker inclined his head toward the bookcase against the far wall. "The papers are folded inside the third book from the right, top shelf."

Hall reached up and removed the book. As he did so, a number of papers fell out and fluttered to the ground. Hall bent over and began to pick them up. Amaray walked over, leaned down, and stared at one of the pages.

"Please don't touch those!" Hall growled as Amaray reached down.

Amaray halted his downward motion, but continued to peruse the paper until Hall, having collected all the other loose pages, picked that one up.

Amaray's composure was back in place as he moved away from Hall. Parker felt an icy dread. *Something's wrong. He looks too confident.*

Hall held the papers in front of Parker. "Are these the papers you were talking about, doctor?"

"Yes, they are." Parker took a quick peek at Amaray and wondered again why he looked so complacent.

"Detective Hall," Amaray said. "Before you get too involved with your reading and try to imply something from those documents, there are a few facts that you need to know."

Hall glanced up. "Such as?"

"Doctor McGraw was here several days ago posing as an FDA inspector. While here, he asked numerous questions about our research and reviewed many of our records. Ask him if that isn't true."

Turning to Parker, Hall said, "Well?"

Parker felt like a man stepping into quicksand, knowing that each step, in this case each reply, might sink him deeper. "Yes, that's true."

Amaray went on. "During his visit, he was left alone with his female friend in Dr. Onge's office for a period of time. A fact I'm sure he'll confirm."

Hall's questioning stare received a reluctant nod from Parker.

"The day after his visit, Dr. Onge reported to me that a large amount of company letterhead paper was missing. The same type of paper that you're holding." Amaray looked at Onge. "You remember I told you it would turn up." Onge nodded as Amaray proceeded on. "Only I didn't expect it to show up as the support for some fabrication created by Dr. McGraw."

Hall held the papers up. "These papers aren't from your company's files, is that what you're saying?"

"Exactly, sir. These papers are lies created by Dr. McGraw for some nefarious purpose. Notice the paper I handed you. It mentions a study entitled `Chem 18'. There was no such study performed by this lab, and our records will support that, if you would like to review them."

"No cry of search warrant this time?" Hall asked.

Amaray bowed slightly. "I'm sorry about my stubbornness earlier. This whole situation, especially Carlos's death, has upset me very much."

"Who's Carlos?" Hall asked.

Quik stepped in, eager to take charge. "He was a security guard working here. McGraw was allegedly instrumental in his death tonight."

Hall's shoulders sagged as he closed his eyes.

Parker knew what was coming. Amaray had boxed him nicely.

Dropping the papers on Amaray's desk, Hall approached Parker until his face was just inches away. "McGraw, just to demonstrate my open mindedness, I was ready to give you a break. And now this." He rubbed his hand across his weary face. "Goddammit," he bellowed.

Grabbing Parker's arm, Hall roughly spun him around, only to come face to face with Susan.

"Out of my way, miss," he snarled.

Susan didn't budge. "It you're going to arrest Dr. McGraw then you should also arrest me, since I was his accomplice in the events of tonight."

"Fine! We'll be happy to arrest you too. No problem." He glanced around. "Quik, put some cuffs on this woman." He moved to go around her, but she stepped in front of him and away from Quik.

Hall shook his head. "Now what?"

"I wouldn't want you to make a false arrest, Detective Hall, so why don't you have Mr. Amaray or one of his people confirm that I was with Dr. McGraw tonight."

Hall scanned the people in the room. "Is there anyone here who can confirm this woman's claim that she was with Dr. McGraw when he broke in here tonight?"

Bernard stepped forward, his face suffused with joyous revenge. "I can testify to that, officer."

"And you are?" Hall asked.

"Bernard Johnson, head of security," he responded proudly.

"Thank you, Mr. Johnson." Hall turned to Susan. "Satisfied now? Ready for the cuffs?"

Susan held up a finger. "Just one statement first. Okay?"

Hall shrugged his shoulders.

"Detective, I can understand why you would ignore whatever tales Dr. McGraw, a man accused of murder and drug dealing, or myself, described as a mistress by Mr. Amaray, would concoct. Dregs of society, like ourselves, are often disregarded. But if the respected president of a pharmaceutical company and his chief assistant, a Ph.D., were to speak, you'd listen, right?"

Hall got a funny look in his eyes and the hint of a smile appeared. "If it came from such higher authorities, of course I'd listen."

Susan smiled back at Hall, the two of them way ahead of everyone else. Susan proceeded to pull up her shirt and exposed a piece of electrical equipment taped to her stomach.

"During my sojourn here with Dr. McGraw, which Mr. Johnson gladly confirmed, I wore this microphone. And here is the recordings I obtained." She pulled a digital recording device from her jacket pocket and tossed it to Hall. "I think you'll find the comments of Mr. Amaray and his respected assistant, Dr. Onge, very enlightening."

Chapter Thirty-Two

Sunrise was peeking over the eastern horizon when Parker walked out of the Monterey police station. Yawning and stretching his arms, he paused to enjoy the sight. Pink-bellied clouds, suspended in a pale blue sky, were layered above the orange rimmed backlit mountains.

Smiling, he strolled from the station over to the lawn which extended down the hillside to the city streets below. From his elevated vantage point, the city and its harbor glistened in the dawn light. Monterey Bay shone like a glass-covered blue table, with a small naval destroyer as its centerpiece.

In the crisp morning air, Parker heard the harbor seals and sea lions barking their greetings over the stirrings of the city preparing for another day.

He inhaled deeply, trying to fill his lungs with the healthy taste and feel of ocean air, while ridding them of the stench of stale coffee and nervous sweat he'd been breathing all night. His deep breath was cut short by the pain in his ribs.

"Damn," he said as he winced and grabbed his side. His aches and pains had been lost in the events of the long night, but now they were returning. Standing at the top of the world, or so he felt, he played back the events of the evening.

Hall and Quik had bundled everyone over to the Monterey police station to begin a long night of questions and answers. Jeff Gilman had spent most of the evening at Parker's side, making sure Parker's answers didn't expose him to any further charges. When it was all over, the charges of murder and drug dealing against Parker were still standing, but Jeff assured him they would be dropped soon.

Amaray, Onge, and Bernard were under arrest, but all were loudly protesting their innocence. Susan's tape, although very helpful in explaining all that had gone on, was not usable in the state of California which requires the consent of both parties to record a conversation. Despite that, the Chem 18 and 19 papers, along with Jeff Gilman's list of the fate of the Chem 19 enrollees amounted to very damning evidence against their cries of blamelessness, and was going to led to a more in-depth investigation.

When Hall finally finished with Parker, Jeff offered him a ride home, but he'd declined. Yesterday, the Coast Guard had returned the *Sun Chaser* to its berth in the harbor, just a few blocks away. A walk in the early morning air, followed by a languid day dozing on his boat, had struck Parker as a nice way to celebrate his first day of innocence.

He glanced once more at the sunrise, then slowly hiked down the grassy slope onto the sidewalk. A horn blew and someone called his name. Looking around, he saw Susan getting out the passenger's side of a white van, waving to him.

As she hurried over, Parker caught a glimpse of the driver of the vehicle. He had red hair and a mustache.

When she got closer, she slowed her approach, allowing Parker time for a long appraising look. Gently, he shook his head. *How did Bogey put it? "Of all the cheap gin joints in the world..."*

"Hi."

"Hi, yourself," he said. "Thought you were long gone."

"I couldn't leave without an explanation," she said softly.

"Considerate of you." He paused. "I already know you're not Susan Beckman."

"When did you find that out?"

"Jeff told me that morning after breakfast. He'd seen a picture of the real Susan Beckman."

She nodded slightly. "That explains a lot."

"Who's the guy in the van!?"

She looked back and then at Parker. "Where are you headed?"

"My boat, down at the harbor."

"Why don't I walk with you and explain as we go."

"Sure. Whatever."

She eyed him strangely for a few seconds, turned and headed toward the van. "I'll be right back," she said over her shoulder.

Parker watched as she went up to the van and leaned in the passenger window. He couldn't hear the words but it wasn't a friendly exchange. After a bit, she returned. "Let's go," she said through clenched teeth.

They'd gone about a block when Parker noticed the van keeping a constant vigil thirty yards back.

"We seem to have a shadow."

"Ignore him." She cleared her throat. "You asked who I am. For eight years I was a cop in San Diego, four of them undercover. Now I work for a well-known company whose only function is to handle insurance investigations, both for private parties and for insurance companies."

"How did you get involved with this case?"

"The real Susan Beckman approached our firm and asked us to investigate her father's death. The story I told Warden Morris was actually true. There was a million dollar life insurance policy on Michael Beckman."

"And the clause nullifying the policy if he was killed while engaged in criminal activity?"

"Also true."

Parker smirked. "And I thought that story was your great imagination."

They walked on, Susan's gaze alternating between the sidewalk in front of her and some distant internal horizon. "In light of the insurance stipulations," she said, "Susan Beckman asked the company to investigate the charges against her father."

"Why would you bother with all the evidence against him?"

"Two reasons. I wasn't busy at the time, and Susan Beckman's my best friend." She shrugged. "I'd have done it even if she didn't ask, we're that close."

They walked in silence along the nearly deserted streets, the air crystal clear.

"Susan suspected something wasn't right about her father's death for many of the same reasons you were suspicious. Her father had a number of vices, but he was vehemently against drugs and drug dealers. He classified them one step above child molesters.

"Since I had a resemblance to Susan Beckman and no one knew her here except the investigating officers, I decided to impersonate her and see what I could find out. All I had to do was avoid anyone who knew her." She looked over at him. "Shortly after I arrived, you called."

"And if I hadn't called?" Parker asked.

"Then I would have found some pretense to meet with you since you were our only lead."

Parker didn't want to ask but he had to know. "And how far were you willing to go to pursue that lead?"

Halting, Susan turned toward him. "I don't sleep around to get information if that's your question," she said angrily.

Neither of them spoke for the next block. They arrived at the entrance to wharf number two with their silent companion, the van, still locked in thirty yards behind them.

"And the guy in the van?" Parker asked as they walked onto the wharf.

"A man I work with," she replied staring straight ahead.

"How does he figure in with the bomb on my boat?"

Susan paused next to the pier railing to watch several pelicans dive for fish. "He'd already searched your house without finding anything, so he'd gone on board to search your boat. Fortunately, he is a very careful man. He discovered the bomb and defused it. He opted to leave it in place as a warning to you about the kind of people you were dealing with." She looked over, half smiling. "After all, we couldn't afford to lose our only lead."

Parker leaned up against the wharf railing next to her, studying her face. "So where was this careful man while we were trying to stay alive in Amaray's trap?"

"He was recording our conversation with orders to stay away unless I asked for help."

"You mean with those two dogs trying to make a meal out of us, you didn't think we needed help?"

"Hey, I knew we needed assistance. If you remember, when I was lying on the floor just before the dogs were released, I was calling for help."

"What took him so long?"

"Bernard's goodbye kick broke the microphone. He never heard my calls." Susan paused. "Answer me a question. I heard a rumor that some convict had seen you and Beckman together several days before the killing. I thought you'd never met him?"

"Yeah, Hall mentioned that to me last night. For personal reasons he wouldn't elaborate, he didn't believe the guy's story. He checked out the exact time and date that I was supposed to have been with Beckman and discovered that I was giving a medical talk at a dinner one hundred and fifty miles away."

"Why would someone make up a story like that?"

"My exact question. Hall didn't offer an answer."

The cries of the gulls and the pelicans suddenly increased in volume. They both looked over and saw one of the fishing trawlers throwing fish entrails off the back.

After the noise died down, Parker spoke. "Where did you go after you left me alone with Bernard?"

"I went out to call the police, but they arrived before I had a chance. I had a feeling things might get sticky so I brought back a copy of the conversation Mark had recorded as insurance."

"Good thinking." Parker found himself mesmerized by her profile. Her long dark hair. Her full sensuous lips. Her eyes that sparkled in the morning light. "This guy, Mark. You just work with him, nothing more?"

Watching her eyes, he knew the answer before she spoke.

"I live with him, and have ever since my Sun Valley days."

"You mean those stories you told me that night at the Highlands' Inn were true?"

Her smile was a little crooked. "Except for my being an interior decorator, everything I told you that night was true."

They stood quietly for a while with Susan watching the pelicans and Parker watching her.

"Why haven't you married him after all these years?"

Her response was lost in the cries of the pelicans fighting over fishing rights

"Say again," he said.

"I love him but neither of us is ready for marriage. At least not yet."

Her announcement drained whatever energy Parker had left. The fatigue, the pains, the disappointments of the last few days were all suddenly more intense, weighting him down, sucking away any jubilant feelings he'd felt about the night's results. He sagged against the railing, shaking his head.

"I'm not sure if the people framing me were any more deceitful than the one's trying to help me." He grimaced. "I feel like a cancer patient who's gone through a long, painful, agonizing course of chemotherapy and is miraculously cured. Only on my triumphant departure from the hospital, my doctor runs me over on the way to his golf game." He looked into her eyes. "It might have been less painful to have died from the cancer."

Susan placed her hand on his arm. "I never meant to hurt you, Park. I just let myself get in too deep." She sighed. "I could blame that night on the wine, but that's a poor excuse."

"I'll have to remember that label."

They stood and stared at each other, neither saying a word, each reluctant to take the next step.

Finally, Parker took her hands in his. "I hate long goodbyes."

"I hate goodbyes of any type," she said softly.

He pulled her gently around the corner of a nearby building, out of view of the van. "A goodbye kiss, for old times' sake?"

She leaned up against him, putting her arms around his neck. Her voice was husky. "Just for old times' sake?"

From the beginning, there was never any pretense that this was a platonic smooch. It was a pedal-to-the-metal, let me climb inside your clothes, full speed ahead damn the torpedoes type of kiss, leaving them both wanting when they parted.

Susan's eyes searched his face for a long moment, then she swung around and walked toward the van.

"Hey! Lady detective!" Parker yelled.

She looked back.

"I never got your real name."

She smiled and it was all he could do not to beg her to stay. "It's Susan."

With that she turned and walked away.

Chapter Thirty-Three

The name on the door read, Max Pollock, Inc. Finding the door unlocked, Parker entered.

It had been more than a week since Susan left. The newspapers had been filled with reports of Citadel Corporation's suspected crimes and their repercussions. Mention had also been made of Parker's help in solving the case and the subsequent dropping of all charges against him.

Before the newspaper stories, Parker had been as popular as Typhoid Mary. Now the phones wouldn't stop ringing. Suddenly patients couldn't get enough of him so he was working overtime in the office and at the hospital, trying to catch up with his neglected practice. The call from Detective Hall, earlier today, had come as quite a surprise, and its message an even greater surprise. "Meet me tonight at eight in Max Pollock's waiting room."

So here Parker sat, on a rainy Thursday night, waiting for Hall to make his appearance. He checked his watch again. It was ten after eight, and still no show.

Blam!! Blam!!

The sound of gun fire shattered the quiet night. It had come from Max's inner office.

With his hands white knuckled on the armrests of his chair, Parker remained motionless, scared the nightmare was starting over. He stared at the door to the inner office for several moments before rising. Striding quickly across the room, he grabbed the doorknob and turned. It was locked. He twisted, pulled, yanked, and finally bullied the door open with his shoulder. The sight that greeted him riveted him to the spot, sending chills down his spine.

The room reeked of cordite. Two men, one on the floor and the other slumped over behind Max's desk, were covered in blood and appeared dead. Parker moved to the man nearest him, face down on the floor. As he bent to check for a pulse, he noticed a gun held

Death has a List

loosely in the man's lifeless hand. Parker was searching for a pulse when the corpse rolled over and smiled up at him. It was Detective Quik.

Parker jumped back. "What the hell?"

The man sprawled out on the desk straightened up, blood running down his face, and grinned.

"Dammit!" Parker said. "Someone tell me what's going on!"

"Good evening, doctor."

Parker spun around and saw Ivan Hall step from behind the door Parker had just forced open.

"I apologize for the dramatics, but demonstrating exactly how you were framed seemed so much more effective than just telling you."

Parker fell into one of Max's leather chairs, trying to calm his galloping heart. "For a minute there, I thought..."

"Yeah, I can imagine what you thought." Hall dropped into the other leather chair. "I wanted to give you a feeling of what Susan Beckman experienced when she heard the same shots, forced the door, and was presented with the spectacle we re-enacted for you."

An open mouth was Parker's only comment.

"Your first response was Ms. Beckman's first response. To see if either of the victims were still alive. Only in her case, she went first to check her father, slumped behind the desk."

The man who'd been behind the desk was now sitting on it, wiping blood off his face. He smiled at Parker and held up his towel. "Theatrical blood." Parker recognized Officer Becket from the night at Amaray's.

."Do you know why Ms. Beckman's first response was so important?" Hall asked.

"I have no idea." Parker said.

"It's the key to the solution of this 'locked room mystery'. Think back. You had to struggle with the door, finally it opened. It opened because I unlocked it during your attempts, but only after you had struggled enough to know it was locked. You burst the door open, stepped into the room, and were spellbound by what you saw. So much so, that you gave the room only a cursory glance as you rushed toward the fallen figures."

He's right, Parker thought. *My whole focus was on the two men with no concern for the rest of the room.*

Hall continued. "And while Ms. Beckman was hastening to check on her father, the killer, Bernard, stepped out from behind the door and slipped out of the room unseen. The result? A beautiful frame job."

"Ingenious. But why me?"

Hall snickered. "What you heard sounded very smooth and preplanned. In truth, it was a comedy of errors. First, the other victim was supposed to be Max Pollock, not you. There was apparently some miscommunication and Pollock never showed. When you walked in, Bernard slugged you thinking he was hitting Pollock. By the time he realized his mistake, the plan was in motion and it was too late to change."

"So all of this was because I was in the wrong place at the wrong time?"

Hall shrugged, smiling one of his mirthless grins. "Anyway, this was to be Amaray's opportunity to get rid of one of the Chem 19 participants and at the same time eliminate the private investigator who was getting too close for comfort. The double killing was to appear like a drug deal gone bad. Susan Beckman had been given a message to pick up her father and was to be an unwitting accomplice."

"You mentioned errors. What else went wrong?"

"What didn't?" Hall replied. "Susan Beckman showed up much earlier than expected, trapping Bernard in the room with you and her father before he used the guns. The original plan had been for her to walk in and discover the bodies, not actually be present when the shooting occurred. Forced to improvise, Bernard came up with the behind the door trick. Read it in a book somewhere."

"Bernard read a book?" Parker said with amazement.

"The next error," Hall continued, "was related to speed. The shots had to sound almost simultaneous, as if one fired and the other instantly responded. Bernard sat you in a chair, wrapped your hand around the butt of one of the guns and shot Beckman in the chest. He felt a chest wound would theoretically still allow Beckman enough time to shoot back before he died. Then racing over to Beckman, he placed Beckman's hand on the other gun and shot you. It was supposed to be a kill shot to the head, but he was rushed and so his aim was off. True to form, Bernard didn't bother to check if you were dead. He just assumed it from all the blood."

Shaking his head, Parker said, "You mean basically what saved me was a woman arriving early for an appointment?"

Hall smiled. "Yeah, that about sums it."

"How did you figure all this out?" Parker asked, still shaking his head.

Hall hesitated, and Quik's voice broke in. "Don't even think it, Ivan. Remember I was sitting in with you and Onge."

"So you were, Mike. So you were." Hall laughed.

"What's going on?" Parker asked.

"Ivan likes to dazzle people at times with his deductive abilities," Quik replied. "Unfortunately, this case is not a shining example of deductive reasoning for any of us. I could see he was tempted to try and salvage some of his pride by claiming responsibility for sorting this out."

Hall grinned. "Mike. You know me better than that." They both laughed again.

"But I can't say I wasn't tempted," Hall added. "The truth is that Onge, faced with an accomplice charge in ten murders, agreed to testify against the others for a chance at a lighter sentence."

"Ten?" Parker said. "You mean nine, don't you?"

"No, ten. The eight prisoners from the drug study, Max Pollock, and Jackson Rivers."

"Who's Jackson Rivers?"

"While you were in the hospital, Carlos came by for a visit and left a lethal dose of barbiturates in your wine."

"Oh, hell! Rivers was the kid who asked for my wine. Damn! I sentenced him to death giving him that glass."

"Not your fault, doc. It's just another example of the wrong guy in the wrong place at the wrong time."

Parker stared down at the floor, rubbing his forehead. *It's still my fault. I knew better.*

"Hey, doc," Hall said.

Parker glanced up.

"Ever remember why you came down to Pollock's office that night?"

"Yeah, I did. The Sherlock Holmes group I've been involved with needed a speaker for its next meeting. I was coming to ask Max if he'd be interested."

They talked a little longer, then Parker rose to leave. He gestured toward Beckett and Quik. "Thanks for everything." Turning, he held out his hand to Hall. "Special thanks to you, Detective, for coming to Citadel that night and seeing this through."

Hall shook his hand. "No thanks needed. I owed you one after the way I treated you earlier."

Parker was almost out the door when Quik's question stopped him.

"Still looking for a speaker for your Holmes group?"

Parker turned back and saw Quik, standing behind Hall, pointing at him exaggeratedly with his index finger. Parker got the hint.

"Not if Detective Hall's free that night."

Epilogue

It was three months before Parker finally surfaced from the deluge of work that had backed up in his practice. By then, he'd paid back everyone who'd covered for him, and he'd gotten his office back on an even keel. Since it had been eight months since his last vacation, he decided that a prolonged respite from work was definitely indicated.

Determining where to go posed no problem - Mexico via a long, slow sail.

Planning the vacation required a bit more work. Wheeling and dealing, crawling and begging, he finally managed to set up coverage for his practice for when he'd be gone. Even harder, though, was finding a crew. He called everyone he knew but no luck. As the time for departure grew closer, he got desperate, putting advertisements everywhere.

There had been only three responses in two weeks and not one of them would he consider spending an evening with, much less several weeks, in the cramped quarters of a sailboat. He resolved to take the next applicant, no matter how undesirable, sail to Los Angeles, and try again there.

Two days later, the next applicant called.

"Hi! I am, how you say, interesting in your sailing ad?" The voice was French and feminine.

"And I am interested in meeting you," Parker replied, mentally crossing his fingers. *Lord, let this person be at least halfway decent.*

"We can meet, no?"

"We can meet, yes! How about my boat tomorrow morning?"

"It would be my pleasure."

It had been raining fairly heavily most of the morning, and Parker began to think she might be a no-show. *Too bad. I enjoyed the French accent.*

Taking one last look out the porthole, he went back to working on the galley sink. He'd been hunched under the countertop most of the morning trying to repair a leak in the drainage pipe and he was almost done.

The job clearly qualified for the category of backbreaking work, for his back ached from crouching under the sink, and his arms felt like lead from holding them up all day, screwing and unscrewing various items under the counter.

"Ahoy, zee *Sun Chaser*!"

Parker climbed wearily to his feet and looked out the starboard porthole. Through the driving rain, he viewed a soaked figure in foul weather gear.

"Come aboard," Parker shouted.

He groaned as he knelt back down under the countertop.

"Two more bolts and this damn thing is done," he muttered.

After getting the first bolt in place, he began screwing in the second one, when he heard the new applicant come down the companion way.

"Bonjour. Hello," she said.

"Grab a seat," Parker yelled, his head still under the sink.

Suddenly, he felt a hand on his buttock and then a firm squeeze. He was so shocked, he rose straight up, bashing his head on the countertop, then falling to his knees. Through the pain, he heard his new companion laughing.

"What the hell are you doing," he said pulling his head out from under the sink.

"You said grab zee seat. Yours looked zee most inviting."

His head still throbbing, Parker turned to give his new French friend a piece of his mind, and there stood Susan.

"I'd like to apply for the job of sailing companion," she said, putting her arms around his neck. "I think you know my qualifications."

Made in the USA
Las Vegas, NV
25 October 2023

79554426R10162